W9-BSF-386

SHIRLEY ANN GRAU

Roadwalkers

ALFRED A. KNOPF

NEW YORK

1994

 *THIS IS A BORZOI BOOK*
PUBLISHED BY ALFRED A. KNOPF, INC.

Copyright © 1994 by Shirley Ann Grau

All rights reserved under International and Pan-American Copyright Conventions.
Published in the United States by Alfred A. Knopf, Inc., New York,
and simultaneously in Canada by Random House of Canada Limited, Toronto.
Distributed by Random House, Inc., New York.

A portion of this novel was originally published by Alfred A. Knopf, Inc., as the short story
"The Beginning" from Nine Women, *copyright © 1985 by Shirley Ann Grau.*

Library of Congress Cataloging-in-Publication Data
Grau, Shirley Ann.
Roadwalkers : a novel / by Shirley Ann Grau.
p.   cm.
ISBN 0-679-43233-7
1. Mothers and daughters—Southern States—Fiction.
2. Afro-American women—Southern States—Fiction.
3. Homeless persons—Southern States—Fiction.   I. Title.
PS3557.R283R63   1994
813'.54—dc20   93-37262
                CIP

Manufactured in the United States of America

First Edition

Contents

~~~~~~~

Stand now with thine enchantments,

and with the multitude of thy sorceries,

wherein thou hast labored from thy youth;

if so be thou shalt be able to profit,

if so be thou mayest prevail.

ISAIAH 47:12

ROADWALKERS

IN 1934 this is the way it was.

Homeless people were moving in a steady flow across the southern part of the country, back and forth across the surface of the earth, seaweed on a tide that ebbed and rose according to the seasons, following rumors and hopes, propelled from place to place by police and sheriffs and farmers with shotguns, and closed doors and locked gates.

They weren't the usual tramps and hobos. Some were farm families, walking away from a life of chicken-foot soup, gullied fields, trace-galled mules, and creeping wire grass. They drove trucks, packed tight with furniture and litters of children, had a little gasoline money in their pockets and a look of far-off places in their eyes.

But most were mill-town poor, with nothing more than a

sack and a bedroll and a piece of oilcloth against the rain. These were people used to streets and the closeness of houses, and they shivered with fear every time they had to cross a stretch of open country, as if the trees might lift their roots and drag them down into the dark ground and consume their bodies for future green leaves.

They were called roadwalkers. Each night they closed their eyes on a day of nothing and opened them in the morning to the exact same thing. There was nothing behind them and nothing ahead of them; they didn't have a past and they didn't have a future. Floating, drifting, they clustered together for comfort and safety.

Sometimes the groups were children. Just children. Sorted into groups according to color, black or white, they were all ages, from boys whose beards were beginning to grow to babies carried on the backs and hips of the girls.

These groups stayed off the roads and out of sight, though sometimes in the shadows of evening, two or three children would appear at a kitchen door, not knocking, not speaking, letting their silent presence demand food. But mostly they were invisible, only leaving their sign in hay barns where they spent the night, and with cows milked dry as proof of their passing.

Some of them were truly orphans without parents or relatives. Some, with the constant moving, had lost their families and couldn't find them again. And some had been abandoned, dropped off along the way, like extra unwanted baggage. Occasionally townspeople, mostly preachers' wives, spoke out their pity and tried to help, but there were so many, and times were hard.

Frog spawn, people called them, as if they had germinated from the surfaces of creeks and streams and rivers.

Wild devil, heathen, limb of Satan, people said when they came upon one of them at night. When a flashlight showed the dirt-streaked face, the eyes half closed with white sticky pus, and the scrawny body, poised like an animal's, before it vanished in the dark.

Her name was Baby. And she was one of those children. She, her brother, and her sister. Roadwalkers, frog spawn. And black.

~~~~~~

BABY

~~~~~~

T H I S is what she knew.

Light and dark. Long nights and short ones. Long days and short. Rain, soft and fine, brushing your cheek like fog. Rain, hard, riding the wind, running you down with its weight. Round hot summer suns and thin yellow winter ones. Sweat and shiver and the mildew-smelling insides of haystacks, warmed by decay.

The pitch of the land beneath her feet, steep or flat, up or down. Stretching, reaching. Slopes and gullies. Always. Endless.

She knew the surface of the earth. Head down, hour after hour, she studied it as she walked. She knew all its forms: dry and blowing with each of her steps; wet and oozing through her toes with a sucking sound. And the grains of the earth: sand fine as sugar; soil black and oily. And rocks, all kinds of rocks, some small as mockingbirds' eggs, some speckled like thrush eggs, others with tiny flecks of mica shining in the sun. Rounded edge and knife edge.

Also she knew in passing: dry wispy tufts of animal fur. Scattered bones of rabbits. The small white shape of a squirrel's skull. Dead birds, feathers flattened and smeared by rain. Clumps of brown grass, with stumpy stiff seed heads, rooted in stiff red clay. Clumps of green grass on the bottom of streams, current streaked across the gravel beds. Low creeping meadow grasses with flowers of pink and white and bright red berries.

She knew fear in the snapping of branches and the thudding of boots on leaf mold. She knew how to run in darting zigzag rushes, how to find cover in thin flickering shadows. How to go to ground like a fox, frozen, immobile, not even eyes moving. She knew the unbelievable joy of escape when her whole body shivered with spasms of delight.

But especially she knew wonders.

She had seen them, all of them. The signs and ghosts and marvels.

A jacaquaré, an alligator, crawled out of the scum-coated swamp and stood upright on the bank—tall as a man, straight up, balanced by its tail, scales shiny and dripping— and fixed bright yellow eyes on her. At full moon a hoop snake held tail in mouth and rolled down a white shell road, singing loudly—a special song, high and shrill, like wind around fence posts and barbed wire. A rooster, ash gray and ten feet tall, perched on the very top of a white oak tree and crowed like thunder. Round green formless lights chittered like squirrels as they played tag across the sky. She had seen them, all of them.

She knew the ways of a campfire at night, how it grew and gained strength, baby into man, as it moved from dry grass to twigs to kindling sticks to logs. She heard fire's voice and she saw into its world, into the heart of the burning.

She knew that safety was with others, around a fire, packed close together, partly for warmth, partly for the comfort that huddling and the feel of another body gave.

These were things that she herself knew, the fruits of her few years on the earth.

She knew other things also, things beyond the short reach of her memory. Things that her sister Sylvie told her.

"We call you Baby," Sylvie said, "but Mama gave you a true name, a secret name, she whispered it in your ear the day you was born."

Baby nodded seriously. She liked Sylvie's stories, which were always about the family they had once been.

They were six children and a mother and a father and they all lived in a house with their grandparents. The house had four pecan trees in the yard, and every fall they gathered the nuts and shelled them, all the children together, evenings, sitting on the floor, in a circle around the kerosene lamp. Their grandfather worked as a porter at the feed store until he was run over and killed one night by a bootlegger's car that was driving fast without lights. The very next day that bootlegger sent their grandmother a hundred dollars and four bottles of likker so that their grandfather had a proper funeral. A year or so after that their father, whose name was Joshua, took up with another woman. When she cheated on him, he strangled her in her bed and then ran off, leaving behind his wife, whose name was Lannie, and his six children. He promised to send back for them all, but they only heard from him once—a postcard from Mobile, without an address. Baby was born just about then. Lannie named her secret name into her ear, nursed her for six months, and then one day she packed all her things in a croaker sack, walked out, and disappeared. Sometime after that, they all caught the summer fever and the grandmother died.

The six children were left in the house with the yard and the pecan trees. They sold the pig and the chickens, they sold the beds and the chests and the chairs and the enamel-topped table and the washtubs and scalding tubs and the jelly pan and the woodstove and the kerosene lamp. They sold the doors and the glazed windows to Amos Hartley, who lived just down the road. He needed a woman too, so the oldest girl, whose name was Corey, decided to move in with him.

The five of them started out: two boys, Buster and Joseph. And three girls: Sylvie, Della, and Baby. They went first to their father's brother, who sharecropped near Johnson Springs. They stayed there for over a year, keeping out of the way, quiet, shy, eating whatever was left. Buster took up with the old woman who owned the sweet shop. Della fell into a rain barrel and drowned. No one heard her—she didn't make a sound, didn't cry out, she was that afraid.

Sylvie and Joseph and Baby left without saying goodbye to their kin. They had decided to go to their Aunt Rosie in Greenville. It was two long days walking. They took turns carrying Baby on their shoulders.

Greenville was the biggest town they'd ever seen, and they were bewildered and lost for almost a whole day in the unfamiliar crowded streets. Sylvie remembered the address, and they just kept asking until they found the house.

Rosie recognized them the minute they turned the corner—they seemed to be wading through the heat which shimmered and danced in the air like a living thing. She was sitting on the front steps; her husband was sleeping in a rocking chair on the porch; her two children were playing jacks in the shade by the side of the house. She waved them to come on.

Rosie and her husband, whose name was Vernon, lived in a house with two bedrooms and an inside bath, the first the children had seen. The kitchen stove was kerosene, and an iceman came twice a week to slide a chunk of ice into the top of the icebox. Vernon was a stevedore on the river docks and made good money when he wasn't on strike. Rosie cooked for an Italian family across town. She worked six days a week and always came home with her shopping bag filled with food for their supper. She said, "This is Italian food and it is too good to waste." But her husband never even tasted it. He ate meat and potatoes and potgreens and most evenings he sent the children to buy ice cream for everybody. He wore a truss and his belly gurgled when he poked at it. Each evening he stretched out flat on his bed and pushed the lump back inside his body while the children stood around watching.

One day two policemen came looking for him. Rosie told them the truth, that he had gone to work that morning and she hadn't seen him since.

"He ain't coming back here," one policeman said to the other.

Rosie screamed and kicked and cried facedown in her bed, but then she got up and went to work, leaving the five children to watch her go in silence.

At the end of that month they didn't have the rent money, so they moved across town to live with the Italian family, in a small house at the back of their property. Sylvie and Joseph and Rosie's two children went to school. Because the black grade school was a long way off, and because there wasn't any money for carfare, they left very early in the morning. After school they played on the swings until the custodian ran them off, so they never got home until long after dark. Baby, who was too young for school, stayed by herself, digging small holes in the soft ground next to the steps (splintery and rotten wood), singing quiet wordless songs to herself.

So Sylvie said. And her stories went on. . . .

It was a fine happy time, the two years they spent with the Italian family. The best they'd ever had. The house was crowded, there was only one bed, they made pallets on the floor, but there was plenty to eat and they liked school and the company of other children, they were doing well at their books and their numbers.

The Italian man died, tumbled from his chair one night at dinner. His widow moved away to her family in Chicago.

Aunt Rosie said they were all going to Atlanta. She had a cousin there who worked as a Pullman porter, and he would take them in.

It was farther than she thought. Her money ran out and she had a hard time feeding the six of them, but they kept going, heading toward Atlanta. She was a pretty woman, and she had no trouble hitchhiking, even with five children along. On one of those rides, Joseph and Sylvie had to go into the woods. They'd been chewing peppergrass, and it gave them the trots. When they came out, they saw that Rosie and her children hadn't waited for them. The truck was gone. They could see it in the distance, appearing and reappearing, up and down the rolling road, getting smaller and smaller until it finally vanished into the black heat haze at the horizon. Their bundles were at the side of the road. Baby was standing next to them.

The three of them sat on the ground, silently. The white shell dust stirred by the truck's passing sifted gently back down through the still air. Finally they picked up the bundles and began walking. They weren't following their Aunt

Rosie; they only walked that way because they could think of no other direction to go.

So the three of them lived, and travelled, according to the season. Baby grew older and became aware that she breathed and was alive on the earth.

She learned to count time: by intervals of light and dark; by intervals of movement along roads, across plowed fields; by intervals of weather, of rain and wind and thunder, of frost and cold.

That was the way she reckoned. Not by days, nor hours. Time did not lead one day to the next. Her days were like a hoard of bright-colored beads, their connecting thread broken, lying loose, single, jumbled.

She grew still older. And she learned how to live.

She learned to stand at the edge of the road and beg passing cars for a lift. They didn't get picked up very often, though people often slowed down to look at them carefully. Once they got a ride in a surveyor's van. "You all stink something awful," the white man said. "Get way off in the back and keep that door open." He took a long gulp from the quart jar on the seat next to him, coughed, screwed the cover back on. "You hear me. Hold that door open." The gears caught and grated every time he shifted, but he did not seem to notice. He drove with his elbows and played the Jew's harp and every now and then sang at the top of his voice: "Hang down your head, you're bound to die." And tears ran down his cheeks.

He finally fell asleep, head on the wheel. The car slowed, lurched, stalled, and finally drifted off the road to stop with a gentle thump against a small pine tree. Sylvie ran her thin fingers through his pockets: money, four dollars, neatly folded in a square; a pocket knife, a plug of tobacco, a pair of glasses in a snap case. (They each tried on the glasses, then left them lying on the seat.) Joseph found an ivory-handled knife in a leather sheath. Baby pulled a monkey wrench and a tire iron from under the seat. In the back of the van there were two pairs of rubber boots, a green raincoat, a jar of strawberry jam, a loaf of bread, two screwdrivers, and a chisel. They took everything, including the jar of whiskey and the Jew's harp. They ate the bread and jam, found the boots too big to walk in, tasted the whiskey, grew tired of carrying the heavy tools, and left everything in a heap.

Now and then they'd see a sign that said MOBILE, and they would remember that their father once sent a postcard from there, and they would follow whatever direction the arrow pointed. For a while.

One early spring day, air fresh and bright with green new growth, they walked through a little wood of oak and hickory; they were looking for a honey tree and turning over fallen logs for the fun of seeing what was under them. When they came to a wagon road—two tracks through the grass, deep rutted—they followed it over a little rise of ground to a gate and a pasture. There was a coat hanging on the gatepost, below it a tin lunch box and a thermos jug. Sylvie picked up Baby and hurried back the way they had come. Joseph waited, listening, his head twisting side to side like a bird's. Nothing. He put on the coat, grabbed the lunch box and thermos, and ran back into the cover of the woods. They ate the sandwiches, one was fried egg and one bacon dripping, and drank the sweet milky coffee. They threw the empty lunch box and the coat into a brushy ravine. Joseph kept the thermos, for a few days, until the liner shattered. He shook out the wedge-shaped pieces of silver glass, and the three of them pushed them about with their fingers, making patterns in the gravelly red dust.

Food did not often come so easily. Some days they saw nothing to steal. Baby learned to make rabbit snares, the braided grass loops curled around her fingers so delicately. Joseph laughed at her skill. He hunted with his knife, struck as silently as any owl. He'd wait, endlessly patient, unmoving, hardly blinking, until a rabbit edged into the open, twitched its ears and nose, and lowered its head to the grass. With a motion so small that the air barely stirred, Joseph threw his knife, and the rabbit was dead.

He had half a dozen other knives in the baggy pockets of his clothes, he'd stolen them one place or the other—clasp knives and switchblades, pig-sticking knives and sheath knives—but that throwing knife was his favorite. He kept it wrapped in a piece of cloth inside his shirt and practiced with it hour after hour, every single day.

He whittled too. He'd take out his clasp knife, test the blade against his thumb, then curl up his legs and lean back, whistling. He whittled faces and animals, sometimes from small pieces of wood, sometimes from peach and plum pits, and traded them as charms to the children they met at the summer gatherings.

Baby remembered those times—no need for Sylvie to tell her stories. She remembered the short summer nights, a dozen, two dozen children sitting in silent circles, firelight washing their faces like a yellow river as they rocked back and forth, slightly, lightly, half dozing like cats watching each other.

Fire was the world. Its yellow light burned through Baby's days shaping and forming them. Children came and went constantly, appearing, vanishing. The center fire stayed the same, the large dancing fire of summer, fed with branches and bushes and fence posts.

Fire was their keeper and their enemy. Their life and their destroyer. Sometimes Baby picked up a little burning twig and sang to the nubs of fire gathered along its length, a wordless humming song of praise and love.

Fire pushed away the darkness and left them safe within the round cave of light. Fire showed faces, companions for as long as the glow lasted. When a fire went out, when a sudden burst of rain turned it into sizzling small plumes of gray smoke, they were all frightened, and they scrambled into their shelters of brush and canvas. The night smothered them, sucked their breath, as a black cat would. Times like this Baby hid behind her eyelids like drawn curtains, envisioning fire, tremendous fire, so that the inside of her head blazed with light and she was safe within its sphere.

As soon as the rain stopped, they hurried to build the fire again, to make it even brighter.

During the large gatherings, there were often shouts and curses and shoving and fighting and sudden blood on rock or knife.

And there was sickness: red crusty spots of measles and chicken pox, coughing and retching and gasping for breath. Bones grown crooked after a fall. Sores on elbows and lips that would not heal.

Like darkness, sickness frightened them all. There'd been one boy, ten or twelve: thin face, heavy lips, and hooded sleepy eyes. Dirt-stiffened overalls stood out around him like a barrel. His black skin had a shiny polished quality, as if there were a greasy stuffing inside it. When the group moved, he could never keep up but straggled along behind, coming in long after everyone else had settled down in their places. He had a friend, a bigger boy, who brought him food, but he took very little except water. He was always thirsty. Once he drank so long at a creek that he lost his balance and pitched in headfirst. He seemed not to remember how to get up but lay facedown, creek water running across the back of his neck. His friend pulled him out and shook him until he sputtered and strangled and began breathing again.

One night, late, that boy began moaning. At first the sound was so soft that it seemed to come from nowhere, might almost have been a sudden night wind that set the pines to soughing. It grew into a wail, like a distant train whistle, shrill and shivering. The boy began to move, rolling on the ground, flipping over and over, coming to rest at last on his back, surrounded by the stiff casing of his overalls. His arms stuck straight up, fingers curled like the claws of a bird. He shivered. Then, slowly, the way an inchworm moves, he lifted his back. A flattened patch of wire grass and a small pink flower appeared beneath him. His clenched toes scrabbled against the ground. His chest rose higher and higher; his body became a perfect arc, touching ground only at head and heels. His arms still reached straight up, fingers hooked in empty air.

They all scattered in fear. Sylvie grabbed Baby's arm and dragged her stumbling across the night-shrouded ground. Joseph was right behind them. He had his largest knife held ready, as if he were expecting an attack.

After a bit, their courage returned; they went back to gather their things silently, swiftly. By dawn the entire camp was empty, except for the boy, who now seemed to be sleeping, curled on his side, and his friend who sat with him.

As the days shortened, groups drifted away by twos and threes. Sylvie and Joseph always stayed until the last, hating to leave the wide yellow circle. Winter fires were different. They were blue like frost, and small like the winter days. No longer in the open, winter fires were built against the face of a bluff, so that their heat reflected out. Summer fires were for joy. Winter fires were for survival.

. . .

One year they were especially late starting south, and the cold followed hard on their heels. They travelled slowly and cautiously, avoiding the sight of people. They'd been fired at twice, pellets pattering like rain into the deep dust at their feet, so Sylvie and Baby stayed hidden, leaving Joseph to forage by himself. He moved like a shadow, even in daylight, stealing pork from pickling barrels and pitchers of cream from unlocked springhouses, taking apples and small late tomatoes, pulling handfuls of green onions from garden rows. Occasionally, too, he'd find a house where company was expected, where Sunday dinner waited in the kitchen and everybody gathered on the front porch. In less than a minute he'd fill the flour sack he carried with him. Later, safely hidden, the three of them bolted the warm salty food in silent delight.

Mostly, though, he foraged by night. On one of those trips, he noticed a sign: OYSTER OPENERS WANTED. APPLY SOUTH PLANT. (He'd gone to school enough to read that, though it took him a while to spell out the letters.)

Sylvie knew how to shuck oysters—Aunt Rosie had taught her—so she scrubbed her hands and face and put a handkerchief on her hair and went to the South Plant to show them how good and quick she was. She got the job, and all that winter, six days a week, she and a dozen other women, wearing white aprons and heavy gloves, stood at a long table, prying open oysters and dropping them into chipped enamel bowls. She was paid at the end of every day. The first thing she bought was a pair of heavy rubber boots, the concrete floors were that cold.

While she worked, Joseph and Baby searched for a place to make their camp.

It was a small settlement, too small to have a name: seven or eight houses, a cluster of sheds and a dock where the oyster boats unloaded All the houses were tin-roofed and whitewashed, with screened front porches and cisterns at the side. They were all set far back from the road with twin paths leading to front porch and kitchen door, deep rutted paths filled with oyster shells. Under the winter sun swarms of flies swept back and forth across the warm reeking surface.

In the empty scrub country a mile or so beyond the settlement Joseph and Baby found a small stream, not deep but fast and clear, that skirted an old Indian mound. Against its sloping side, in a shallow depression, they built their fire pit. They would winter here; real cold hung in the damp air.

One night Sylvie and Joseph stole three large tin 666 signs from the wall of the seafood plant. The same night they pried off four Coca-Cola signs that were patching the walls of a barn. Joseph stole a new wood door from the back of a carpenter's truck. It was so heavy he hid it in a clump of wax myrtle and came back for it later, with Sylvie to help him.

Baby waited for them. She was too little for running and climbing and hiding from dogs. What she could do was this: she could wriggle through the least crack in a fence or window and open it wide for them to come back to later. They stole all they dared. An almost new tarpaulin and a coil of rope from an oysterman's shed. Two shiny new cooking pots from a general store. Armloads of old license plates from a junkyard.

License plates were the walls that held back the sandy crumbling soil of their fireplace. Coca-Cola and 666 signs made walls and ceiling, with the tarpaulin fastened over them. On top of it all they piled brush, the way people made mule breaks, until the whole thing seemed to disappear entirely. The new wood door was the floor, placed carefully on a mat of pine branches. They'd cut those branches from trees half a mile away and dragged them along the rocky creek bed, leaving no human mark behind.

Every day Joseph left with first light and returned long after dark. He was looking around, he said. Alone, Baby stayed close to the shelter. She kept a fire burning, feeding it one stick at a time so that there was always a small red eye gleaming in the depth of the dark sandy hole. Sometimes, even, she sprinkled a few pine needles on it. She liked the way they smelled, burning.

Once in a while some curious woman tried to follow Sylvie home. Then, whistling loudly, Sylvie led her a couple of miles in the wrong direction before disappearing in a silent double back to the camp. No matter how late she was, or how tired, Sylvie always took out her money and counted it carefully. Then counted it a second time to be sure. The bills and coins were increasing steadily. They did not need to buy food. There were plenty of squirrels and rabbits; Joseph took them almost every day with his throwing knife. And once a week Sylvie brought home a sack of groceries, a present from her friend Milo. Sometimes there'd be a crumpled dollar bill in the bag; that was from her friend too, she said.

Milo was the white man who delivered ice to the plant, a short thick man with a beard so heavy his jaws looked bruised. Twice a week he backed his truck up to the locker doors and kicked the hundred-pound blocks down the chute into the cooler. When he finished, he reached for the bottle of corn likker he kept under the driver's seat. He made a great show of it, shaking the bottle to study the bead as it rose in the clear liquid, testing the proof. Satisfied, he'd shout: "Johnny Allen, you black son of a bitch, where are you?" Johnny Allen, the plant's manager, came out of his office, which was only a boarded-off corner of the packing

floor. If the weather was fine and sunny, they sat on the
dock and watched the women work. If it was cold or
raining, they sat by the stove in the cramped office. They got
drunk quickly in the stifling warmth.

Milo sometimes invited Sylvie to sit with them. She ate
handfuls of the peanuts that were parching on the stove top,
and she even had a small taste of the whiskey. But most of
all she was glad of a few minutes' warmth before she went
back to work.

Everyone knew that Milo would drink with a black man
and would sleep with a black woman if she was young and
pretty and the price was right. What he wouldn't do was
use a black man's outhouse. When he left the plant, a little
unsteady with liquor, he always parked just past the big
swamp maple and went into the woods.

One day Joseph waited for him, slashed two tires, and
slipped away unseen. Milo put on his one spare, then walked
back to the plant to find a second. Sylvie said they could
hear him coming—he was cursing so loud.

That was a winter for sickness. Some mornings there'd be
only a half-dozen women in the plant, and Johnny Allen
had to double their pay. People were dying from congestion
of the lungs, Sylvie said, and children coughed so hard that
blood ran out of their mouths. Those children, Sylvie said,
repeating what she'd heard, made sounds like somebody
drowning, and their arms made swimming movements in
the air.

Sylvie herself was never sick, nor was Joseph or Baby.
They even began to put on weight from regular eating.

Even when the weather was very bad, they stayed warm
and dry. The fire burned steadily and the greasy smell of
food hung on the unmoving air. They played cards, teaching
Baby as they went. They sang songs, softly. Joseph told stories, long stories of devils and ghosts. And Sylvie told stories

of what their life would be like when they got to Mobile and found their father. He would have a house like Aunt Rosie's, only bigger, so they each would have a room of their own. There'd be plenty of hot water; they could take three baths a day. Their father's woman would be so happy to see them, she'd kiss them on both cheeks. That's what Mobile would be like, Sylvie said; she saw it clear because she had the second sight.

Sylvie also told fortunes—cards or toss of stones or, her special favorite, the shoulder blade of a rabbit. She'd turn the bone around and around in her fingers, looking at the depth of the socket, counting the spots of mottling. That's your house, she would say, and that's your goods and there's your children, those dents there all in a row, one's born dead and one soon to die and the others fine healthy boys.

Through all the long nights and the rainy days when the sides of the little stream froze and the hollows and ruts of the woods were skimmed with a gray glaze, when the morning hoarfrost was thick as snow on the ground, they never stirred from their shelter. Like the little animals they lived among, they dozed and waited, black noses and black eyes withdrawn from the world beyond their burrow.

Winter ended. They grew restless. They shook themselves like puppies, packed their bundles. Joseph and Sylvie pulled down their shelter so that it lay against the Indian mound, a jumble of wood and tin and cloth and branches.

On the road a truck passed them, fast, bouncing, spraying water from ruts and puddles. It was Milo returning from his ice delivery, friendly with liquor. He stopped, skidding side-wise, backed up to them.

"You want a lift?" he said to Sylvie.

"I'm with them," she said.

"All you niggers get in. I'm going to town."

He drove strangely, sometimes fast and sometimes slow, sometimes down the center of the road and sometimes along the gravel shoulder.

"End of the ride." He stopped and waved them off.

They were in the center of a town, stores and buildings on four sides of a small park—its grass just beginning to turn a bright spring green—with a flagpole and benches and a statue of a man holding a gun.

"You ain't allowed in this part of town," Milo said. "So you'd best just go right straight through."

On the far side of the park, there was a two-story brick building, a line of rocking chairs across its porch and half a dozen cars parked at the curb. A smell of cooking came from the open windows.

Carefully, explorers in unknown country, Sylvie and Joseph and Baby circled the building, slipped through a narrow brick alley to a back courtyard. Behind a torn screen door four black women worked in a crowded kitchen.

Sylvie walked straight up to the door, knocked. The women stopped, turned their heads. One, who had been scraping plates into a wide flat pan, said, "Wait."

She pushed open the door, a thin black woman whose apron was so large it wrapped twice around her narrow hips. She put the pan of plate scrapings on the edge of the steps, the way she'd feed a dog. Sylvie carried it across the courtyard to Baby and Joseph. The pan was almost full, the food covered with stiffening grease.

They ate quickly, silently. Sylvie returned the empty pan.

"Give it here." The same woman reached through the tear in the screen. "Clear off now," she said. "We got people of our own to look after."

They walked the roads again, days flowing one into the other. They collected things as they passed, discarding them a day or an hour later: shotgun-shell cases, shreds of old tires, bits of metal. Once they found a box of handkerchiefs, a small flat cardboard box, rain streaked. There was only one handkerchief inside, white with a green border, flowers and a windmill embroidered in the corner.

Sylvie left them for a man she'd met at one of the WPA road projects. She didn't tell Baby goodbye; she just disappeared one day. "Gone off to Mobile," Joseph said.

They never spoke of her again. The space where she had been filled up with time and vanished.

In the warm lengthening days the two of them, Joseph and Baby, felt themselves grow large with courage and boldness. The winter spent hiding in a burrow was over; their feet thudded on the solid surface of the earth; their lungs grew like flowers in the freshening air; their blood bubbled through their veins like Coca-Cola. They walked, openly and unasked, into any yard that didn't have a dog, and drank from the well, laughing when people screamed threats at them and sent shotgun blasts over their heads. They entered henhouses in broad daylight, choosing the sleepy time of afternoon. Joseph killed a chicken with a single motion of his hands while Baby filled her pockets with eggs, cramming them in so hard that some shells broke and the yellow-and-white liquid ran down her body. The eggs they did not eat they threw against stones to watch them spatter. They stole milk from cows in far pasture corners. Joseph always cut a cross on the animal's flank when they were done; he'd rub his finger along the track of the oozing blood while flies circled eagerly. Once they stole a mule, a big ambling cotton-field mule, and rode for a day and a half until the hungry animal turned mean and surly and bit Joseph on the hip. While the wound healed, Joseph and Baby ate duck potatoes and berries and the rabbits Baby caught in her grass snares.

Then they were moving again, through country where

cotton fields stretched for miles, green and tall with just the
first bit of white showing in the brown boles. There were always dozens of people working up and down the rows,
chopping. They sang and shouted back and forth. Baby and
Joseph stopped to listen to the faint far echoes.

The sound made them restless, as did the sight of so
many people. (They no longer went to the summer gatherings; they travelled alone.) They left the bottomlands for the
ridges, where even the midsummer breeze was cool and
light, and pine needles made soft sleeping, and the ground
was covered with brightly colored mushrooms.

Early one morning, while the air was still filled with
night damp and mosquitoes' wings had not yet dried, they
made their way along a slow descending sweep of ridge to
a small valley. There were two farmhouses, tin-roofed, with
narrow porches all around, and fenced dooryards of clean-
swept dirt. Between them a raggedy line of barns and
smokehouses, lean-tos, and stock pens strung out along a
rocky fast-running creek. Beyond, up the valley, were alfalfa
pastures and fields of corn, heavy tassels drooping in the unmoving air. A white woman in a yellow dress fed chickens
in the yard. Her voice floated out, faint and rasping, like
one of her birds. A black woman hung out washing. A black
man harnessed a team of mules to a wagon, whistling.

Joseph nodded toward the house and began to scramble
down the long slopes. Baby followed slowly, stumbling. She
was sleepy, her head ached, and daylight burned her eyes
so that she couldn't look up. She followed by sound alone,
seeing only the small blue and yellow flowers that passed
beneath her feet.

At their approach the chickens scattered in a bobbing run;
their toes had been smashed to keep them at home. The
woman in the yellow dress walked to the gate and looked at
them.

"Where'd you two drop from?" Her gray hair was pulled to a tight knot, and a red sunbonnet was tied to her belt, its long ties flapping down her thigh.

Joseph shifted slowly from one foot to the other, silently.

Baby scratched at the sore on her leg, pulling up the scab to look at the pulpy yellow skin beneath. Her head hurt more when she bent over.

"You want something to eat?"

"Yes," Baby said.

Joseph swung at her with the stick he always carried against snakes. She jumped away.

The woman chuckled. "Going at each other like feists, and no doubt about it. Maybe we got something left. Come over by the porch."

There was a square dark patch of shade at the side of the house, close to the foundation stones. Baby dropped her bundle and stretched out there, feeling the cool air from underneath, smelling the soft sweet breath of mud. The pain in her head fanned out, like a sunset, shot out bright colors, flashes and periods of black.

"That one's sick," the woman said.

"She's little," Joseph said, "and she's tired is all."

A second woman came to the porch. She had thin yellow hair and round blue eyes, and she was heavy with child. "We got this and some milk." She held out a pan of cornbread to Joseph, who took it with a snatch. Baby didn't move.

"That little one looks sick to me." She rested hands on her belly, absentmindedly feeling for movement.

The older woman said, "All those woods and this gotta come to my front door."

"Well, she can't just stay under the house, all curled up like a doodlebug."

Joseph ate the cornbread, held out his cup for the milk. He held it out a second time, and a third, but by then the pitcher was empty.

"Get her out of here, boy."

"You wouldn't turn out a sick dog like that," the pregnant woman said.

"I'd shoot it, is what I'd do."

As if she'd not heard, the yellow-haired woman said, "Listen to me now, boy. Down the bottom of that far lot, there's a lean-to. The roof's good and there's hay to make it easy. You could shelter there."

Wordlessly, Joseph picked up the two bundles.

"Down the road, across that fenced pasture, past that rise," the woman repeated. "A couple of pines on the left. Right there."

Joseph nodded. He picked up Baby, holding her in the crook of his arm. He had to walk very slowly, his heels striking the ground hard with each step.

It had been a mule lot once. You could see where the fences had been, and the tree trunks were still galled by the animals' constant rubbing. The shed was small, no more than ten feet long, and half filled with hay. The side shutters sagged open, and a few boards were missing across the back, but the slab roof looked solid and new. They settled there to wait out the term of Baby's sickness.

She did not remember much, only the sweet smell of the hay, the noise of the birds, the whistling of the black man as he drove the mule team to work in the mornings. She followed his song as it thinned and faded, until all that was left were bits and pieces, torn apart by the intervening air, drifting down across the ridges like leaves from a tree.

She shook with fever; her teeth chattered with chill; her knees and elbows puffed and stiffened.

Joseph stayed with her, sitting just outside, sometimes whittling and sometimes practicing with his throwing knife. And twice a day he went to the farm for food.

The older woman asked, "Boy, is that baby still alive?"

Joseph nodded, eyes on the plate in her hand. He held out his own empty pan.

"What about that sore on her leg?" She transferred the food in one sliding motion.

He shook his head, eyes sliding up to her face, slyly, betraying nothing.

"You think I didn't see? Don't be a fool, boy. You got to put carrot scrapings on it. Like these."

He nodded. She handed him a heap of yellow-brown carrot shreds in a piece of thin old cloth.

"Don't eat it, you ain't that hungry. Put them parings right on the sore and tie them on with that cloth. You don't touch it until tomorrow, then you come back and get some more."

"Her knees is swelled." His voice sounded harsh and rusty. He was surprised to hear himself speak. "She don't never rest."

"Breakbone fever," the woman said shortly, turning away. "If there's a God of niggers, you better be praying to him."

In the shelter Baby lay curled in a ball, a tiny black spot on the surface of the earth. She drank whatever Joseph held to her mouth; she whimpered with pain whenever he touched her swollen arms and legs. The black man from the farm left his team one morning to bring her a cup of slippery-elm tea sweetened with honey. She screamed at the sight of his unfamiliar face and clenched her teeth when he put the tin cup to her lips. Joseph fed it to her later.

In the cooling days of fall, Baby's fever ended. She crawled on hands and knees from the matted straw to sit in the bright yellow fading sun. She discovered a small hollow between two large boulders. The sun reached there early; the rocks held its heat all day long and far into the night. She lay there day after day, dozing and waiting, drinking from the cup of water Joseph left for her.

Joseph now worked at the farm. He picked cucumbers and tomatoes and green beans and brought the filled baskets to the kitchen porch. He dug potatoes, gathered pumpkins from the field, pulled sweet corn for eating, and stacked field-corn sheaves. He was slow and sullen and clumsy. The women shouted instructions and screamed complaints at him. He did not learn. He did not remember what he had been taught.

One morning Baby stirred and opened her eyes and knew that Joseph was gone. Not to the farm for food, not to the fields to work. He had tired of waiting and had gone on without her.

As usual he'd left her a cup of water. Four or five gnats floated on its surface; she felt them tickle her throat as she drank. The black man came, but she covered her face and would not talk to him. He left food for her, and filled the cup with water. She waited for him to leave before touching it.

He came again on the second day, again with food. On the third morning, Joseph was back, bringing her a dish of mush and syrup before he went to the fields.

Baby grew stronger; she could walk to the edge of the cornfield; she could climb the steep pine slopes, though she moved slowly, panting.

Joseph was restless. Each night, though she never once saw him leave, he was gone. She banked their small fire, had a final drink of water (the fever had left her always thirsty), and walked across the pastures to the farmhouse where the two white women lived. She sat quietly, on the far side of the stream, in the shadow of a scrub apple tree, and watched. At first dark, the gray-haired woman lit a lamp. The yellow light ran out the window, crossing the sill like flowing water, to empty itself into the dark. The two women faced each other across the kitchen table, hands busy, heads nodding. When they went to bed, when the window was only a flat empty square, Baby walked back by starlight. In the clear fall nights the earth cooled quickly, and she shivered occasionally.

One night she stayed long after the house was dark. With the gray glittering galaxies to light her way, she crossed the little river, low this dry time of year, hopping from rock to rock. The yard dogs noticed her and came to the fence to watch. She circled past the house, the kitchen garden, the well house, the chicken yard, dogs shadowing her inside the fence. Past the two smokehouses, new-roofed. Mule pens. A big hay shed. The cow barn, lower door closed, small high window left open. She stopped, the dogs in front of her. Saw the white oak, growing just outside the fence, slender arching branches reaching over the barn. Slowly, because she was still weak, she climbed the tree, inched along a high branch. It bent gently, lowering her to the roof. The dogs watched, curious and unalarmed, as she slipped down the roof and wiggled through the small window.

Inside was rank and warm and dark. The still close air was heavy with the sweet moist breaths of six cows. They stirred restlessly at her presence, grumbling, shifting. She backed into a corner under the feeding trough and fell asleep at once.

Something nudged her side, lifted her slightly. She opened her eyes slowly, saw heavy laced boots, coated with straw and dung.

"You." She recognized the voice of the black man.

She was still sleepy and in no hurry to leave the darkness under the feeding trough. She didn't move.

"How come the dogs let you get in here? You put a charm on them?" A cow wheezed and stamped. "Get over, Bess." A slap of hand on rump, the thump of a wooden stool. Then the noisy rattle of milk into a pail.

She saw his black hands moving, saw the empty foolish face of the cow, its silent gratification.

"Come here now, girl."

She crawled out. Beyond the open barn door the day was bright and clear; its chilly air cut into the warm layers of barn odors.

"Come round over this side where I can see you." He went on with his milking. "By rights you ought to be dead of fever, not sneaking into barns."

Through the door, a shape floating against the radiant morning, a gray-and-white cat, tail held high, picked her way delicately across the floor to sit at the man's side. Perfectly still. Waiting. Expecting.

"You ready?" he said to the cat and shot a short spurt of milk toward her. Her mouth opened, caught. Ever so carefully, she licked the rest from her whiskers, her paws, her chest.

Baby moved closer to him, her eyes on his hands. Next to the cat she stopped. Asking.

The jet of milk hit her face with such force that she choked swallowing it.

One morning, Baby woke early, before clear light. During the night a spider had spun a web across the corner of the door; in it a captured deerfly buzzed and thrashed. She heard a single pinecone rattle down, bouncing end over end. A small wind made a ragged uneven hiss in the needles and branches overhead. Crows called, their voices rising and falling as they swung in wide circles. Baby sat up—and there it was, gurgling in her veins, like a stream over rocks: the knowledge that it was time to move, that the roof was too tight atop her head, that the world was too small. Again.

Joseph packed their bedrolls, their cup and pan, the extra food. Then, methodically, he pulled the sagging shutters from the windows, smashed them into kindling against a rock. He whittled a pile of tinder. Deliberately, carefully, he began setting the shelter afire. It was difficult, the hay was damp, but he kept at it patiently, until little wisps of smoke appeared in a dozen places. A small rat ran out and disappeared into the brush.

Day after day Baby followed Joseph. Sometimes his figure seemed wrapped in shining fog and sometimes she saw him as the distant end of a long black tunnel. Once when it rained, a hard thunder-filled downpour, they took shelter in an abandoned mill. The big stones were still in place, but the gears were blocked by rust, the belts decayed into tattered flapping strips. Most of the roof had collapsed in a tangle of beams, leaving only one small dry area. They spent the rest of the day and the night there, while rain poured down the walls all around them, and Baby watched the millstones appear and disappear, blue-white in the lightning.

Once they managed to climb into an empty railroad car and spent a whole day rolling effortlessly over the surface of the earth, the steady beat of the rails counting time for them. So many fields and trees and towns drifted past the open door they grew tired of watching, and Joseph began a game of solitaire. At a switching stop a white man swung into their car, a young man, with blond hair and a thin face and a bundle in his hand. Like theirs.

He gave them a long silent look and moved to the far end of the car. Joseph stopped playing cards and held a knife in

each hand; the shadowy daylight outlined the blades. The
three watched each other, hour after hour. When they pulled
into another siding—when a fast passenger train overtook
them—the blond man swung off and disappeared.

Another time, a state trooper stopped them. "You from
around here?" he asked.

Joseph shook his head.

"Where you going?"

"Mobile," Joseph said, as he always did.

"Ain't he kind of little for roadwalking?"

"That's my sister and we are going to our people in
Mobile."

"Get in," the policeman said. "I'll give you a lift."

The motion of the car made Baby sleepy, so that she
heard the white man's voice from far off. "Beats walking,
kid." And then, "This is as far as I go."

They got out obediently. "Hey, you," the policeman said to
Baby, "take this." He put a nickel in her palm, closed her
fingers on it.

She held her hand tightly shut, feeling the metal press
into her flesh. She wanted to look at it, study it, turn it over
in the light, but Joseph was already moving and she had to
keep up with him. She put the coin in her mouth for safe-
keeping.

Now the earth beneath their feet was dark red and deep
black by turns. The fields were gone to weeds and half the
houses stood empty, windows blank, doors missing from
their hinges. They slept inside every night now, dry and
warm by a fire in a proper fireplace. Every morning Joseph
took the coals, blew them into life, and tossed them up on
the roof. Sometimes they even waited awhile to see if the
house would burn.

They travelled through new pine forests, young trees in
endless neat rows, through wide pastures, carefully wire

fenced, green with rye, speckled with shade trees, dotted with herds. An airplane flew overhead and they stopped to watch its shadow run across the grass. They heard the far-off sound of a sawmill before the wind changed and the thin wisp of sound blew away. Two horses nuzzled their hands, then galloped away at a sudden movement. Everywhere in the woods were scuppernong vines, heavy with fruit; they left them for the raccoons and the birds.

They crossed a railroad bridge over a small river that ran deep and fast between high banks to follow a gravelled road into a wide valley. After a couple of hours they came to an iron gate. On the high overhead arch was a name. Joseph could not puzzle out the letters; he had forgotten most of his reading. Beyond the gate, half a mile of green lawns sloped up from the river to a large white house with columns all around. Peacocks strutted and fanned. A black woman in a stiff white apron was sweeping the porch. She stopped to stare at them, shading her eyes.

They moved on at their usual slow pace between the lines of neat white fences, passing other buildings: barns and men working in them; stables, where two colts played in the near field; row on row of smokehouses; a garage where a man worked on a tractor; lines of greenhouses, thousands of glass panes winking in the light; flower gardens pruned and trimmed and waiting for the winter; vegetable gardens, bare and hilled against the frost; orchards, leafless now.

A truck overtook them, stopped. The driver, tall, thin, black, a wad of chewing tobacco in his cheek, said, "Get in back and I'll give you a ride off the place."

They did, dangling their feet over the tailgate, watching gravel spin up under the wheels. Past endless pastures, woods, a second house, small copy of the first, with its own small stable and barn and garage.

The truck jolted to a stop, throwing them on their backs.

The driver stuck his head out the window. "That there's the public road." He pointed to the two lanes of blacktop. "Choose your direction and keep going."

He watched them for a while, then turned back, clouds of yellow dust marking his passage.

For an hour or so they followed the road, then moved into the shelter of the trees, climbing (as Joseph always did) to the highest ridges. The following day they found a place for their camp—a steep gullied slope, dense with fallen trees and heavy underbrush, studded with granite boulders that glowed green in the moonlight. From the top of the biggest boulder, they could see the length of the entire valley, could see cattle grazing in pastures and hogs turned into cornfields to fatten before slaughter, and white specks of sheep on one far slope. They could hear the flat metallic clank of bells as the dairy herd moved back and forth twice a day. Now and then they heard shouts and whistles. They heard hammering and sawing, the sputtering backfires of truck engines, and the deep rough rumbling of tractors at work. An unfamiliar sound—they listened carefully.

In a narrow space between two boulders they made a frame of fallen tree limbs, spread their tarpaulin, added more brush on top. The ground was soft, inches deep in leaf mold, smelling dank and sweet and secret. Nearby a small spring ran from a crack in the rock face into a shallow basin, slippery with algae.

Baby stayed here, never moving more than a few hundred feet in any direction. She played all day, building toy houses of rocks and sticks and weaving small twigs into roofs. With her own knife she whittled furniture for them—tables and chairs and beds with rabbit-fur covers. As soon as she finished one house she immediately began another. She did not make any people to live in them; her houses were always empty.

Joseph, restless, angry, came and went, bringing her food every day, but not speaking, not even looking directly at her. Baby kept her distance and her silence so that he would not fall into one of his rages. Once she stood too close to him, and he knocked her backward into the fire. The burns on her legs still hurt.

Their daytime cooking fire burned down to a tiny red speck under its gray ash. Each cooling night was completely empty except for animal sounds and the muffled beating of owls' wings. Baby wrapped herself in her blanket (and Joseph's too for extra warmth) and stared up through the branches at the stars. She sang a silent song that was her own, making circles all around herself, secure and strong as steel, protective as a knife. She felt the magic rings rise around her like the walls of a house, enclosing her completely. Then she fell asleep.

At first she thought they were dream sounds without meaning or sense to them. Then she thought that the wind had come up suddenly and was blowing down the slopes the way it did before a rain, and she pulled the blanket over her head. Then she heard stones rattling down the slope and thought a large animal like a deer or maybe a bear must be moving. She settled all these sounds into her dream, wrapped them all around by soft black breathing into the blanket folds.

She woke to a bird's cry. Or a man's whistle. She recognized the sounds now. Human sounds, four or five men, shouting to each other on the slope above her, coming down. She wondered where Joseph was. And what she should do. She saw brief stabs of light overhead, like flickering summer lightning. She wanted Joseph. She called to him silently, asking which way to run. When no answer came, she curled up tightly inside the shelter, pressing hard against the earth, hiding behind her own closed eyes.

Then she was being crushed. She screamed aloud, a small whine like a cat. The earth surged upward, she hurtled into the air, dangling in a large black fist. She kicked and squirmed, then froze and stiffened. A voice was roaring: *Here, here.* Pinned in the beam of a torch, she stopped breathing, stopped moving, only her heart pounded against her ribs, saying, *Run, run.* The hand holding her shuddered, relaxed. She fell, then a heavy body fell across her. She pulled free, crouched, paralyzed, whimpering. She smelled the prickly sweet smell of blood. A torch was caught in the brush, still burning. In its dim glow she saw the man next to her. He was on hands and knees, heaving, retching, struggling. There was a knife in his back, high on his shoulder. She saw the handle clearly, recognized it. Joseph had carved that design, that twining twisting vine with its small round leaves. It was his throwing knife. Now it stuck in a plaid wool jacket.

So Joseph had been out there after all. Close by. But he was lost now, lost forever in the tightening circle of shouts and crashing boots.

It was his favorite knife, she thought dully. His favorite. How would he get along without it.

THAT cold November, on the back slopes of Aikens Grove Plantation, Baby ended her wandering days. Shaken, tumbled, cursed, she entered the world of houses and jobs, of lives lived in one place. A world of order, of continuity, a world whose people knew what tomorrow would be like.

She was a stranger in a strange place, drifting, drowning. Stiff as a possum with fear. Not knowing where she was. Nor who.

A pair of tired, bloodshot blue eyes stared at her. Charles Tucker, like a midwife, dragged her into the world of humans, his world. He knew exactly who he was: Charles Tucker, son of Hiram, grandson of Onslow. From Clark County.

THE PEOPLE
OF CLARK COUNTY

O N S L O W   T U C K E R came to Clark County the first spring after the war, in early April 1866. A time of poverty and fear and uncertainty, when sensible people minded their own business and asked no questions.

Before the war, Clark County was a prosperous place. There was one large plantation, called Aikens Grove—thousands of acres and hundreds of slaves. There were a dozen large farms, twenty or so slaves on each. (And there were three times that many sand-trap farms, poor land, poorly kept, where hunger always hid in the shadows of the washed-out gulleys.) In late summer the wide fields were white with cotton; in fall the gins roared and clanked all day and half the night while barges waited for loading at half a dozen river landings.

In those days Clarksville was a thriving town, with a three-story county courthouse and a town square of green grass with a white painted bandstand in the very center. There were two banks, a hotel and dining room, a dry-goods store with a very large selection of ladies' dress goods—the county had a lively social life. There were two churches on Main Street and a Second Baptist Church around the corner near the schoolhouse. There were three law offices, a feed store, two general stores, three livery stables. There was a doctor's office and a pharmacy with a jar of leeches in the window. Off Main Street there was an area called Newtown, a settlement of free blacks—Redbones and Freejacks, people of mixed black and white and Indian blood—who did the fine blacksmithing and bricklaying and carpentering and cabinetmaking and elaborate coffin building. Their wives were the fancy dressmakers and milliners and confectioners who had their own small shops with their own small signs over the doorways.

(By 1866 Newtown was gone, only three or four houses and a few old people who whispered of the wonderful life their children had found in Cincinnati and Pittsburgh and New York.)

The owners of Aikens Grove left for England soon after war began: master and mistress, sons and daughters and in-laws, unmarried aunts and feeble old cousins. Twenty or so of them and almost that many personal servants. Parasols open against the June sun, the ladies stepped into carriages drawn by teams of matched grays. The men, all heavily armed, pulled their wide-brimmed hats over their eyes and mounted their horses. The Irish valet and his wife the seamstress drove a cart with crates of family silver. The black nurses and the white babies and the white governess and the younger children crowded into two small carriages. The servants settled themselves carefully, stiffly (not to crease their new travelling clothes) in the remaining baggage wagons. Behind them in the house, workmen were busy hammering and sawing, crating everything—furniture, rugs, china, paintings—for shipment. The house would be left closed and empty.

For a year nothing changed. The overseer, Silas Fortier, ran the plantation just as he had done before. He and his wife and four children still had Sunday dinner at the hotel dining room. Crops were still good, but by the second year of the war there was no way to get them to market. Silas Fortier built temporary warehouses by the river and filled them with the gray-brown cotton bales. That same year he took his family, all five of them, to Arcadia Landing and saw them on the packet boat for New Orleans. They would have to pass through the lines of two different armies, but the travelling was safe enough. He himself stayed another year, still having his Sunday dinner at the hotel dining room. There was little he could do. Slaves ran away in groups of tens and twenties. Stock disappeared every night, all the poultry and hogs, the cattle and the mules and the horses—excepting for the two teams of matched grays, which he drove, one dark night, to the Reasor farm, twenty miles away, a marshy place dotted with secret sheltering islands; they would be safe and well cared for there. At night he stabled his own mount in his dining room while he slept on the floor with two guns at his side. Finally he too left— for New Orleans, where he took the Union Oath of Allegiance and went to work for a drayage company.

Before he left, following orders the owner had given him nearly three years before, he set fire to the full warehouses by the river, then to the empty barns and the stables, and finally to the houses, one by one, and watched them burn into heaps of black timbers and matchstick chimneys, shelter only for small animals and nesting birds.

All through the county, fields went back to weeds that rustled together like dry bones in the winter ice. Hogs, run wild, thin, and scrawny, rooted along rain-washed gullies. The houses—those that were still occupied—and the smaller farms seemed shrunken and drawn tight in on themselves. All the young men were gone, both slave and free, leaving only the women and children, the old and the sick and the war crippled, those who had managed to find their way back home. They raised hogs and chickens on carefully fenced small plots, newly cut out of the pine forest, hidden from the Jayhawkers who roamed the roads. Kitchen gardens could be grown in dooryards, in plain sight. Jayhawkers didn't have a taste for vegetables, never stole them, though they sometimes rode their horses through them, trampling out of pure meanness.

The war itself passed by Clark County. There were no battles, no skirmishes. Once scouts from Sherman's army appeared on the high ridge overlooking Clarksville, but that was all. The two main armies, shadowing each other, passed to the east and to the west, not stopping, leaving a trail of dysentery and graves behind.

In March—the last month of the war—the courthouse burned to the ground. Some people, hearing trotting hooves and jangling tack and harness, peered though their curtains. They saw a dozen men, torches in hand, hats pulled low, and clothes of butternut color, riding horses smeared with mud to make them unrecognizable.

The men released two prisoners (the jail was the back wing of the courthouse), smashed chairs and desks into kindling, broke a few lower windows for a good draft, and set their torches to the varnished wood. They watched, hunkered down on the new spring grass of the town square, passing a jug back and forth between them. When the fire grew large enough to explode windowpanes on the second floor and run long red fingers up the edges of the roof, the men gave a cheer—small against the voice of the fire— mounted up, and cantered away into the dark.

The people who had watched all this stayed in their locked houses until long past daylight, happy that there was no wind to spread the glowing cinders over the roofs of the town.

In early spring of 1866 Onslow Tucker was a young man, tall and blond and pale blue eyed. Not handsome but not ugly either, strong looking and enduring. He drove a mule and wagon. The mule was young too, a lively pretty cottonfield red. The wagon was a small light rig, more like a city toy than a farm wagon. It was painted blue, new painted so carelessly that the original varnished wood showed clearly. Onslow Tucker was in his shirtsleeves, because the day was warm, but his clothes were new, and all civilian, not one piece of government issue from either side. His boots were solid and only just a little bit dusty. He had a Sharps on the seat next to him, and a revolver at his belt and a derringer in his boot. The roads were dangerous. A traveller had best be prepared.

Onslow Tucker drove his fine young mule and his silly light wagon into Clarksville one April afternoon, clucking and talking to his animal as he eased down the grass-clogged street. He passed the line of empty shops: the cabinetmaker's, shutters hanging lopsided on their hinges; the livery stable, doors standing wide to the empty courtyard and the ruined stalls beyond. He passed the burned-out courthouse without turning his head, and pulled to a halt at Wharton's General Store.

Young Tom Wharton was sitting on the front railing,

swinging the stump of his left leg back and forth. "Morning," he said politely.

Onslow Tucker lifted his hat. "I was wondering," he said, "if you could maybe give me some directions."

Tom Wharton shifted his seat on the railing. "I might could." He saw Onslow's eyes reach to his missing leg and hang there for a second. "Shiloh," he said.

"Grass grows green on blood at Shiloh," Onslow said, "with the Lord's mercy."

"You were there?"

"Yes," Onslow said. "I am looking for the Widow Andrews. Her husband was Seth Andrews and he was a miller here. I have heard she takes in boarders."

"And glad to have them." Tom Wharton hopped down the steps to point out the way.

Onslow Tucker and the Widow Andrews, whose name was Selena, stood talking at her front gate for such a long time that her four cats left their hiding places and came to rub about her skirt. Finally she nodded; they shook hands, and Onslow Tucker carried his rifle and his two bags into the house and led the mule to the small barn in back, where there hadn't been an animal since Seth Andrews went off to war.

He didn't have to go. His wife, Selena, wept and argued and told him he was an old fool, but he went off with the other men from town, marching away down Main Street, straggling columns with a young boy banging a drum at the front. He didn't write—he was never very good at writing—but he did send her a picture of himself in his sergeant's uniform. She kept it in the drawer of the parlor table.

In the third year of the war, Seth Andrews died and was buried somewhere in Tennessee. She never could remember the name of the place—she never looked at the letter again, not after that first time when she read it in her parlor, sitting up straight and formal in her usual chair. When she finished, she let it drop from her fingers to the floor. Her neighbors, who came as soon as they heard the news, folded the single sheet of paper and put it in the nearest drawer, which was the one that held the picture of him in his sergeant's uniform. So in a way the news was buried where it fell, just like the man it concerned.

Selena Andrews had no one to comfort her, neither children nor family in Clark County. She'd come from South Carolina to work as governess at Aikens Grove Plantation.

Even in those days she'd been a churchgoing woman, faithful in attendance whatever the weather. (On rainy days she wore a brown-hooded cape, for all the world like a monk's.) She came to Sunday-morning services, and she taught evening classes in Christian Endeavor. Her employers at Aikens Grove didn't go to church in town—they were Episcopalian—but they saw to it that Selena had her Sundays to herself, and they provided her with transportation, a buggy and a slave to drive her. The slave, an old man named Josephus, spent his waiting time in the back of the livery stable, playing cards and drinking. Often, going home, Josephus fell fast asleep and Selena took the reins herself. She had always liked to drive.

Seth Andrews, a bachelor in his late thirties, saw her one rainy day in her brown monk's cape, courted her at fellowship meetings and choir practices, and married her within the year. She moved into his house in town and walked to church every Sunday, as regular and faithful as before.

Beginning with his first Sunday as a boarder, Onslow Tucker walked to church with her. He looked, everybody said, very nice. His high stiff collar gleamed blue-white, his dark suit was brushed carefully and pressed. His hat was square on his head, and his boots were carefully polished.

Some people whispered that Selena Andrews had given him her dead husband's Sunday suit. But other people pointed out that Seth Andrews had been a good six inches shorter than Onslow Tucker. And, they said, not even the cleverest seamstress could make a suit stretch that far. So, the churchgoing part of the town decided, Onslow Tucker, whoever he was and wherever he came from, had brought with him his own good dark Sunday suit and fine Sunday boots.

For three succeeding Sundays he and the Widow Andrews walked to church together through the warming spring air. They joined the crowd on the lawn after service, where all the talk was of weather and planting. (The farmers checked their fields every day, pressing their hands to the ground to see if the earth gave heat or took it away.) It was a perfect spring; the rains were gentle and windless. Moisture hung like smoke in the air. Mr. Patterson, the minister, mentioned the fine soft rain in his sermons. "The earth is grieving, healing our wounds with her tears, striving to assuage the pain and tragedy of these past years. God has given us an end to the war. God's will be done."

And Onslow Tucker's voice was loudest in the amens.

Soldiers were still coming home, those who had been sick or hurt or had a long way to travel. With them came news of others, sometimes of death and graves, sometimes of new lives begun by men who had chosen not to come back, men who had seen the world and were no longer content with their home fields. At every Sunday service Mr. Patterson reported the latest news, beginning always with the same words: "Greetings from our brothers who have chosen to adventure across the vastness of God's earth." Josh Bledsoe, cousin of Adam Sillitoe, had found a farm in Victoria,

Texas. Thomas Davis was now a blacksmith in Eureka Springs, Arkansas. Andrew Patterson, the minister's own son, had sailed from New Orleans for California; with him were three other Clark County men: James Provo and Edward Reasor and Joab Fowler. Ned Martin had been sick with fever in Atlanta, had recovered and found work as a carpenter there. . . . Mr. Patterson ended his roll call with the same prayer: "And for those of whom no word is heard, may God protect and restore them with his everlasting mercy."

In that soft spring of 1866, the town and the county began to come back to life. Horses and mules and cattle and chickens, so long hidden in woods and hollows, began to appear in dooryards and stock pens. Some farmers even began building shoat houses for the sows and their twice-yearly litters.

One month after his arrival in Clark County, Onslow Tucker bought a farm, a good farm, of middle size, part of what had been Aikens Grove Plantation. The cultivated fields had lain fallow for years, but they were still rich and not too resistant to the plow. There was good timber in the woodlots and smooth well-watered pasture—needing only a little work—sloping down to the Providence River. (For most of the year that stream flowed gently and quietly between its reddish-yellow sandy banks; at spring flood it grew deep and swift enough to float crops and timber to market.)

Onslow Tucker built his house, helped by two men he'd hired in town. When he finished, he married Selena Andrews. The ceremony was performed by Mr. Patterson and recorded in the new *Book of Records*, which the church kept until the county got around to building a new courthouse.

Selena sold her house in town and moved her furniture to the empty rooms of the new farmhouse. There, a year to the day after their marriage, she bore a son, a healthy screaming boy who shrieked for food day and night. Selena, her calm middle-aged face creased by pain and exhaustion, sent for a wet nurse. Then she sat contentedly and proudly in her rocking chair and watched her son suck at the black breast of the other woman.

He was called Hiram, and he was her only child.

Hiram grew to a man, tall and angular like his father, and married a preacher's daughter from Webster County. He saw her one day by the bridge over Black Dog Creek. He and three other young men had been to a Jubilee, and they were walking home, weary and sick from moonshine. Hiram stopped to drink at the creek, asked to use her cup. She handed it to him with a shy small smile.

"This water here sure makes a funny sound, don't it?" he said when he'd finished drinking.

"Hollow rocks," she said. "It's lonesome water here."

Hiram's friends shouted for him, and he left with a smile and a wave to the girl by the creek. But the spell worked, just as everybody said it would, the spell of lonesome water calling him back. Hiram couldn't rest. Not through sorghum-grinding time, not noticing, not caring that the syrup turned out full and sweet. Not through slaughtering time while the smokehouses filled with fine pieces of pork, and the pantry shelves lined with jars of sweet white lard.

"I drunk lonesome water from under hollow rocks," he finally told his parents. "And I got to go back and get her. I don't know her name, but I know where she is." He took a mule and cart, figuring that a woman would have household stuff she'd want to bring along.

Her name was Lucy Crawford, and she smiled at him in her careful lopsided way so that her broken tooth didn't show. He so much wanted to be relieved of the spell of the lonesome water that he asked her to marry him at once, just where he found her, pulling the last of the turnips in the garden. She said yes just as quick, because she'd been dreaming about him too, the young stranger who'd passed on the road and taken a drink of water from her. And she wanted to leave her father's house—the grandmothers and the eight younger children. She wanted a bed just for herself and her husband, and a garden where she could grow anything she wanted, and a flock of chickens to raise.

They had their picture taken on the day of their wedding, him standing, hand in coat, her sitting next to a tall vase with ostrich feathers in it. They put the picture in the new Bible her father gave them and wrapped it tightly in oilcloth against the damp and put it in the wagon with her other things: an empty birdcage; her Sunday bonnet in its round box; an iron pot and its cover; a wash boiler; two hens and a rooster; a black trunk from her grandmother—in it were her clothes, a quilt her mother had made, a feather bolster, and a white linen case she'd embroidered against this very day.

Lucy Crawford was happy in her marriage. She thought the house was fine and comfortable. Her flower garden filled with color every spring and summer. She got on well with her mother-in-law, Selena, who admired the way she quilted. Onslow and Hiram liked her cooking and her quiet smile, and the way she worked steadily all day long, never seeming to hurry, but never stopping either.

Lucy Crawford Tucker's first child was a daughter, Mattie. Her last child was a daughter, Nancy. In between were four boys: Caleb, Buck, Samuel, and Charles.

Charles was born in his parents' bed in the house his grandfather built, on November 2, 1902. His sister Mattie washed him and wrapped him in a blanket because the weather had a touch of early chill to it. His grandmother poured a cup of scuppernong wine for his mother—the sweet red alcohol would strengthen her blood. His brother Samuel, who was five, put on his cap and trotted off to give the news to the men out in the fields. And that evening, his grandmother Selena, who still kept her beautiful governess's handwriting, entered the name Charles in the family Bible.

Charles remembered his mother—close-set blue eyes and thin blond hair pulled to a knot at her neck. He remembered her hands, long and strong with big knuckles and thick nails, always chapped, always moving, always doing something in kitchen or garden or barn. Pushing wood into the stove for more boiling water, scrubbing and scalding and cleaning. She had them all take baths on Saturday, whether they were going to church or not. (She herself didn't go very often. A childhood spent listening to her father's sermons had lessened her liking for services.) She brought her husband his strop and razor and held the mirror for him while he sat in the tub in the middle of the kitchen floor.

Charles was his mother's favorite. She kept him with her, even after Nancy, the last child, was born, holding his hand, singing to him, having him follow her step by step through all the chores. Onslow grumbled that a boy's place was in the fields with his father and his brothers. She paid no attention. "I need him here," she said, "now that Mattie is gone."

Mattie, the oldest, was living with Mr. and Mrs. Eli Smith in Logansport. Lucy had arranged it, wanting something more for her daughter than a repetition of her own childhood. Mr. Smith owned the feed store and was a deacon of the church. Mrs. Smith had taught school before she married. Mattie, the granddaughter of a minister and a governess, was happy with them. She helped in the house (they had no children), ran errands, brought Mr. Smith his dinner each noon, swept out the store twice a day, and went to school regularly. (Logansport even had a high school.) Mrs.

Smith saw that she did her homework every evening on the dining room table under the big kerosene lamp.

"Now that Mattie is gone," Lucy repeated to Hiram, "Charles must help me. I have your parents to care for."

By this time Selena's mind was so confused that she talked and laughed with invisible people and called her son, Hiram, by the name of her long-dead first husband, Seth Andrews. Onslow could still walk across the earth with the long set strides of a farmer, but he seemed not to want to. He spent good days in the shade of the apple tree in the yard, rainy ones in the corner of the kitchen, hunched inside the straps of his overalls, so thin that his shoulder blades stuck out like wings behind.

Charles helped his mother day after day, season after season. Scald the pans, strain the milk, make the butter and the cheese, clean the springhouse. Plant the kitchen garden, water it during droughts, bucket by bucket from the well. Climb trees for apples and peaches, pick tomatoes and beans, collards and mustard, onions and turnips and potatoes. Sort them and store them. Potatoes and turnips into the root cellar. Apples to the attic, spreading them in a single layer on a floor cloth. String the field peas, still in their husks, on long threads and hang them from the rafters over the apples. "I feel much relieved," his mother said, "to have another year put by."

After that, in the free and easy weeks of late fall, they picked the wild persimmons that grew in the woodlot on the far side of the pasture—small bright orange balls, pulpy flesh sweet as honey on the tongue. They never ventured very far, never beyond that woodlot. His mother wasn't happy away from her house. Like a yo-yo on an invisible string she was pulled back to the enclosing fences and tin-roofed shelter.

. . .

In the early mornings she had him shake up the coals in the range so she could set the breakfast pies to bake. (As they worked they chewed bits of raw fatback, the oily saltiness comforting to the tongue.) He peeled the potatoes and chopped the onions for the thick heavy stews (squirrel, or deer, or rabbit, or quail, or dove) they ate every night for supper. He made the biscuits and the cornbread. "I think you do that best," she said to him.

His father and the older boys came home long after dark. They washed at the pump on the back porch, combed their hair with their fingers, kicked off their mucky boots. Sometimes they were too tired to be hungry, and eating was just a chore for them, like any other chore, something that had to be done in preparation for the coming day. Afterward, they sat hunched in their chairs at the table, resting but not sleeping, eyes wide open, breathing softly and slowly, empty of motion and sound, solid and enduring and earth tired.

Charles and his mother washed the dishes and scoured the pans, scrubbed off the top of the table, emptied the dishwater into the yard, and banked the fire for the night.

The next day it was all to do again.

Every spring they made soap. "I like to do this," Charles said. "I like this." All around the earth was beginning to stir, birds in the trees, seeds underground. He could almost hear the rustle of leaves as they unfolded themselves from the winter-bare branches.

He got the soap boiler and set it up in the yard. He filled the ash barrel with good hardwood ash and poured buckets of fresh water into the top, collecting the lye water that dripped from the bottom drain. All winter long they had saved every bit of grease, and now his mother put it to boil with the lye water, stirring carefully and steadily with a heavy stick that had been whittled clean of bark, watching the heavy plopping bubbles rise sluggishly to the surface.

She made bar soap first. "Just a little batch or it don't harden," she said, carefully pouring it into a shallow pan of chipped white-and-blue enamel. With an old bread knife, Charles cut it into square pieces.

Now and then she stopped work to rub the back of his neck, just the way she would have rubbed a cat or a puppy.

They made only two pans of bar soap. All the rest was liquid. They poured the thick brown stuff, still hot and smelling sharp and harsh and clean, into a hollowed-out log set on a low trestle under the shelter of the porch roof. They fitted a plank across the top, to keep out prying varmints. Whenever his mother needed soap, she dipped it up in a dried calabash gourd.

Every winter, he went to school. After most of the year's work was done, after slaughtering time, when the smoke-houses dribbled their slow thin smell into the cold air, when field work was over and his father and his brothers spent all day in the barn seeing to the cattle and repairing a season's worth of broken tack and harness and rigging, his mother sent him to school.

School was in Winslow Junction, three miles away. His mother wanted him to ride one of the mules, but his father refused. Winter was a time of rest for the animals, a time for them to grow fat and lazy in barn and feedlot, scratching rounded sides and flanks against trees and fences, snorting in bad-tempered contentment.

So Charles walked. Across his father's fields, through a scrubby woodlot, cut over years before and gone to scraggly bird-sown bushes and small trees. Past the Widow Ratcliff's house—she watched for him and waved—and the Mount Olive Baptist Church. Along a razorback ridge with granite boulders higher than his head. Down one last slope to the school building. It took him more than an hour, because the ground was hard with frost and slippery with ice. Once he saw a dead dog in the baptistry behind the church. It had fallen through the ice, got caught in a tangle of myrtle and willow, and drowned.

Winter was also the time for weddings. His sister Mattie married George Varnado, a railroad conductor from Bakersfield, an older man, a childless widower. They were married at the Smith house, where Mattie had lived for nearly five years. All the family went, dressed in their best clothes. Charles scarcely recognized his sister in her dark green silk dress and small veiled hat. The front parlor was cold with the damp of January; he shivered and couldn't seem to stop. His shoes were much too small; he tried curling his toes under, then he tried standing back on his heels. His brother Caleb gave him a slap on the ear and told him to stand straight. After the ceremony, after the coffee and the cookies, they all walked in a solemn serious group to the railroad station—Mr. and Mrs. George Varnado were going to Atlanta for their honeymoon. Charles's feet hurt so badly that tears streamed down his face, and people thought he was sad to see his sister leave.

The family drove home, all together in the big wagon with two mules between the shafts. The animals were surly and restless; all mules hated cold. When the early winter dark closed in around them, his brother Caleb lit the lantern and hung it out. The yellow spot jolted and swung against the empty night. Like a star, Charles thought, a star they had made themselves. His father and his grandfather and Caleb sat on the box, shoulders jammed together, faint kerosene light outlining the edges of their hats. His grandmother, mumbling and singsonging to herself, and his mother, with the baby Nancy close under her shawl, and all the other children rode in the bed of the wagon, huddled out of the wind, wrapped in blankets. The deep ruts of the road held a dull film of ice. Charles could hear the iron wheels crunch through it. In the warmth of his blanket he noticed a faint spicy summer odor: his mother always put sweet shrub blossoms between the layers of good clothes when she stored them away in the big chest in her bedroom. He fixed his eyes on the swinging lantern, their star, sniffed the sweet leftover smells of summer, and listened to the sounds all around him: the small continuous rubbing of the planks of the wagons's bed, the creaking of the axles shifting and shuddering over uneven ground, occasional deep loud groans from the mules, his father's steady cheerful whistling, and his mother's wordless singing to the baby.

Lucy Crawford Tucker died one August morning in her flower garden, among the tall blooming cosmos. Charles found her stretched full length on the sandy red earth. She seemed asleep, the bright flowers and feathery stalks for her pillow, but her eyes were open, dulling and filming with the no color of death. The baby Nancy sat next to her, legs stuck straight out, crying silently, steadily. The tears left shiny traces across her fat cheeks, silvery like snails' tracks.

Lucy Tucker was buried in the cemetery of Elliott's Ridge, with a granite marker that said LOVING WIFE AND MOTHER. All her family came from Webster County. Her father, the preacher, led the prayers and the mourning.

Charles went on, doing all the things his mother had taught him, Nancy always with him. (At the funeral she'd shoved her hand into his, forcefully, like a kitten butting its mother.) They kept the vegetable garden, tended the cows and chickens. Nancy hunted for eggs and carried them in her basket, not cracking a single shell. The Widow Ratcliff came to do the canning; the pantry shelves filled against the winter. Caleb took a load of corn to the mill for grinding

into meal. The hogs fattened. The calves took almost all of
the milk now and thrived.

He did not touch his mother's flower garden. It shrivelled
and browned, seeds falling to the ground, ungathered.

One morning, a year later, he woke very early, long before
anyone else, heart racing with fear, feet twitching. The walls
of the house seemed to bend over him, pressing on him. He
snatched Nancy from her pallet, ran out, through the yard,
around the vegetable garden, past the corncribs, into the
woodlots. He felt better there, so he put Nancy down, panting. When they had rested, the two of them went for a long
walk up into the ridges and watched the sky turn light with
morning. For the first time he did not fix breakfast for his
father and his brothers.

After that morning he was afraid to fall asleep, knowing
what could happen in his dreams. He was afraid of the
house, of the cheerful kitchen. He and Nancy stayed outside
all day long, wandering, catnapping in corners of fields and
woods. He still fed the chickens and turned out the cows,
but he no longer tended the garden; vegetables wilted in
their rows. Sometimes he forgot the milking, and the animals howled their misery. He stopped cooking altogether.
His father and his brothers cursed and shouted, so he and
Nancy waited in hiding until the men fixed supper for
themselves and were too tired to do more than grumble.

Mattie came. She bustled through the house, talking
loudly, angrily, the small feather on her veiled hat shaking
furiously. Her father and her brothers nodded silent agree-
ment, looking embarrassed and relieved. "You are coming to
live with me," she told Nancy and Charles. "Starting right
this very minute, we are going to Bakersfield."

George Varnado met them at the train station, still wearing his conductor's dark uniform and cap. He shook hands

with Charles and kissed Mattie and Nancy. And he smiled at the peaceful contentment in his young wife's face. She had been lonely, with him away so much and no baby of her own to care for.

George Varnado's house was larger than any Charles had ever seen: two stories tall, tin-roofed porches all around, ferns hanging at the corners, geraniums lining the railings. They sat down to supper on the porch, where the evening breeze was cool with the threat of changing seasons but still smelled of honeysuckle and rose. Nancy fell asleep on the porch swing. Mattie and her husband spoke quietly together, long comfortable silences between their words. Charles ate hungrily; he'd had nothing all day. The soft white cheese in his bowl tasted exactly like his mother's. So did the bread and butter.

He thought of his mother now with puzzled wonderment. He remembered her lying dead, remembered the streak of red clay on her outstretched hand, the greenish tinge of her skin—the colors and shapes were bright and clear but not real anymore, more like pictures in a school reader.

The moonflowers on the porch trellis shrivelled and dropped to the boards with small soft thuds. Mr. Varnado took out a cigar. In the match flare Charles read the name on the box: HENRY GEORGE. His sister stacked the plates and carried them away. The screen door opened and closed quietly, a kettle whistled, and the sink pump made soft sucking stroking sounds. Mr. Varnado tipped his chair back, balanced himself against the porch rail. The tiny red point of the cigar hung in the air. In the sky over the trees two stars appeared, one pale, one glistening blue. Someone walked whistling down the street. In a nearby house a baby cried, sound high and clear, as if filtered through crystal.

. . .

In the morning, Charles stood at the window of his room
(small room, he could almost touch both walls with his outstretched arms), the first he had ever had all to himself. He
saw a kitchen garden where a black man hoed the neat
straight rows, a washhouse and a brick-surfaced drying yard
crisscrossed by clotheslines, a tall shingled cistern raised off
the ground on stilts, a poultry yard, and a small barn, doors
standing open. Beyond, the land sloped away to a swampy
stretch of tangled brush and willow, and a small pigpen.

Charles listened to the unfamiliar noises all around him:
barking howling whining dogs, the steady unhurried clop of
hooves on the street, the creak of traces and wagon wheels,
the shouted games of children. Mattie called him downstairs
to breakfast. She kept on calling until he found his way
through the unfamiliar halls and rooms.

Mattie took him and Nancy into the washhouse. She had
fired up the copper boiler. "I usually only do this on wash
day," she explained, "but it is going to take a lot of hot water
to get you two clean." She cut their hair very short, fine-
tooth combed it, and then rubbed coal tar into their scalps.
She soaked them one by one in the tin washtub and
scrubbed at them with a bar of yellow-brown soap. "Now
you can get dressed."

He had never seen these clothes before.

Mattie chuckled at his astonishment. "The people at
church, they got these things together for you, so you could
look respectable when you go to school and not be a shame
to me and Mr. Varnado."

So he began his new life—in a strange house, in a strange
town, dressed in other people's clothes. Some of them, the
jacket, the corduroy shirt, the wool knickers, still smelled of
other people's bodies. Charles Tucker walked into an unfamiliar world, enclosed in other people's wrappings.

. . .

For the first few weeks, he did not go to school. "You look just too pitiful," Mattie said to him, "thin little twitching thing that you are. People'll be saying Mr. Varnado can't feed his family. . . . Anyway, the school won't take you with Indian Fire sores all over your face. You got to stay home till they dry up."

Every morning after milking—Mattie did that herself, singing, her voice muffled by the animal's flank—they strained the milk and put it away to settle and separate. (When there was enough cream, she would churn.) Then they drove the three beasts to the pasture lot Mr. Varnado owned on the lower slopes of Tower Hill. There would be plenty of grass there well into the winter.

The first time they went, he and Mattie, and Nancy tagging behind, they climbed to the very top of the hill. "That's where you live," Mattie said. Bakersfield was spread out below them, a jumble of houses and yards and brick buildings and steepled churches, streets crowded with wagons and people, railroad lines running in all directions like snarls of wool. "Look at it now," Mattie said. "But don't you dare come back here and stand gawking when you bring the cows out by yourself. There won't be any time for wasting like that. You'll have to hurry to get to school."

World of rules and chores, of time and appointments that must be kept. . . . Charles forgot the farm, his dead mother and his live father, his brothers, his grandfather, the fields, the stock, the cats who lived in the barn. He started school. The weather was mild and dry; the trees were puffs of yellow leaves; bright purple dahlias bloomed by front-porch steps. For a month Mattie walked with him mornings and met him afternoons at the school gate.

Then she said, "Go by yourself today, you know the way."

That very first morning, he got lost. He was watching the

sky—it was a shimmering gray, color of a bream's belly—
when the biggest crow he had ever seen flew overhead. He
ran after it, following as it skimmed trees and roofs and
chimneys until at last it rose straight up and disappeared.
Charles looked around. The tree-lined street, the houses
with their low picket fences and neat gardens, were completely unfamiliar. He had never been here before.

He began walking, curious, interested, exploring. The
streets were empty, house doors closed and curtains drawn.
Dogs barked at him from the yards. He stuck out his tongue
and made yapping sounds back at them.

He kept on walking, book bag slung over his shoulder.
The streets grew narrower; the yards were unkempt, leaves
piled against the fences. There were small white signs
in front windows: ROOMS. (He had always been clever at
reading.)

He passed a livery stable where the familiar thick sweet
smell of horses hung in the chill air. Four men sat outside
playing cards on a box top; they did not look up. He peered
into the windows of small shops: Reiss the Hat Man. Peer-
less Bakery. (The smell made him hungry. He took a small
apple from his lunch box and ate it as he walked.) Harold's
Upholstery. Milton Cabinetmaking.

He came to a wide avenue, brick paved; streetcars ran
down the middle, bells jangling. The sidewalks were made
of wooden blocks; a faint odor of creosote clung to them.

Crossing the street, he tripped over the rise of a storm
drain and fell flat. For a long moment he lay on his stomach
and stared at the drain—a ring of concrete with an iron grid
on top. He'd never seen one before. Then he got up, brushed
off his knickers carefully, and picked up his schoolbag.

Two men were unloading crates and barrels from a dray.
Charles ducked between the horses, rubbing his hand across
their steamy sides as they shifted and snorted, muscles mov-

ing under his touch. He hoisted himself to the loading platform and stared through the open door into a dark jumble
of crates and sacks and barrels.

A loud voice behind him said: "I hadn't heard anything
about today being a school holiday."

A hand grabbed his shoulder. He tried to shout, but only
a small hissing sound came from his mouth.

"I have caught a truant," the voice said. "Now let me
have a look at you."

The hand dragged him across a board sidewalk, past an
expanse of window, through a door. "I am fixing to call the
police to put you in jail for playing hookey."

"Mr. Carswell," a woman's voice said, "you are frightening that child."

The hand left his shoulder. Charles looked around. He
stood at the end of a long room with display cases and
counters on both sides and barrels in a line across the back:
pickles and coffee and the faint dusty smell of flour.

"Boy!" The woman was old; wrinkles ran along her
cheeks and down her neck, disappearing into white lace ruf-
fles. She was half leaning, half sitting on a stool at the
counter nearest the window. "You go to school?"

He nodded.

"They did not teach you to take off your cap inside?"

His voice came back. "They did, but I forgot."

"Where do you go to school?"

"Grammar school." The words were coming easier now.

"I can see that. You look to be about six."

"I'm eight, going on nine."

"You are small. Do you have a name?"

"Charles Tucker."

She turned away to study the row of cans on the shelves
behind the counter. "Are you named for King Charles?"

"No, ma'am."

"Good, you don't look very much like a king. Mr. Carswell, the last butter you sent me was very poor. I wish you would taste what you sell. The animals must have eaten wild onions or some such thing."

Charles said, "My sister makes butter and it's very good."

She turned, light catching the frizzled wisps of gray hair under her large hat. "Are you trying to sell me something?"

His mouth opened and closed silently.

"You are. And right in the middle of Mr. Carswell's grocery store."

Charles looked toward the man, saw only an expanse of striped apron, black trousers, and black shoes.

The woman was laughing, deep coughing chuckles. "Mr. Carswell, you have a competitor. An audacious young man. King Charles, what is your sister's name?"

For a moment he could not remember. Then with a snap and a click the confusion in his mind cleared and he said distinctly, "Mattie Varnado."

"Do you know her, Mr. Carswell?"

"No, ma'am," he said, "she doesn't come in here."

"It would be too expensive for her, I think," Charles said, turning to look at the stacked shelves and the counters filled with tall glass jars.

The woman coughed out her laugh again. "King Charles, you are absolutely right. It is too expensive in here for anyone. Homer, call for the car."

A small elderly black man in a tight black suit shuffled out the door. At the edge of the sidewalk he lifted one arm in a kind of Indian salute. Close by, an engine started, sputtered, died, sputtered again.

"King Charles, I will take you to school. Have you ever ridden in a motorcar?"

He could only shake his head. He had not even ridden on

the new electric streetcars, though his sister had promised to take him one day.

The old woman stood up, slowly, painfully, using a cane, a man's cane with a curved silver handle. "As usual there is trouble starting that machine. It sounds like it has hiccoughs. The buggy would have been quieter and more reliable."

"Ma'am," Charles said as politely as he knew, "would you like to try some of my sister's butter? I could tell her to save some the next time she churns."

She nodded, abruptly, as if the movement hurt her.

The car stopped at the curb. Homer held open the door; two clerks carried packages; Mr. Carswell bowed gravely.

She paused, cane firmly planted. "My bones tell me we will have rain. Mr. Carswell, a bag of peppermint Zanzibars for King Charles. Run back and get them, boy, quick. You've missed enough school."

Charles scurried back, feet thudding on the boards, snatched up the small white bag. Mr. Carswell said softly but clearly, to no one in particular, "Wool hat bastard. Worse than niggers, that lot. White niggers."

Charles raced back to the wonderful car. The door stood open; her hand beckoned him inside; the door slammed.

The motion made him faintly sick, and he didn't remember the roads having so many holes and rough spots. He hung his head out the window, air rippling over his face like water, and he thought that this must be like galloping along on a fast horse, a big strong horse whose hooves tore up the miles like dust, whose shoes left a shower of sparks like stars behind.

They stopped in front of his school, and a surge of regret like pain made him sigh. Homer opened the door for him. Carrying his lunch box and his books, he got out slowly, still feeling wind singing in his ears.

"King Charles!"

He stopped, dropped his lunch box, picked it up. "Yes ma'am."

"How am I to buy your sister's good butter if I don't know where she lives."

Another panic-filled blank, then the relief of memory. He said firmly, "You take Old County Road. All the way to the river. There's a road going east, a wide good road. My sister lives in the last house on the river side of the road. The front gate is painted pink."

Her wrinkled mouth smiled faintly. "Homer should be able to find it. Now, another thing. You have forgotten to ask me who I am."

He held his breath, dismayed. He hadn't forgotten; he hadn't dared.

Again the wrinkled smile. "I am Mrs. Harrison. My husband is Judge Terrence Harrison. I am also known as the crazy woman from New Orleans." A single chuckle. "Homer, close your mouth, you look like a fish. You know perfectly well that's what people call me behind my back."

"That grocery man," Charles said, "he called me a nigger."

"Did he?" Her pale blue eyes opened wide. "Well, people will call names. You are not a nigger, Homer is. The Lord put many colors in the world the better to confuse us. . . . Here, don't forget the Zanzibars. I liked them when I was a child. Of course they don't come from Zanzibar. I believe they are made in St. Louis."

The door closed; the car moved off, springs creaking over the ruts. The neighborhood dogs barked long after it was gone.

He pushed open the door, and the warm school air, smelling of peanuts and dirt and urine and children's sweat, flowed out to meet him. He went to the office. The principal was there alone, a short heavy woman wearing a thick red wig over her own thinning hair. She dipped a pen in the inkwell. "Name. And excuse."

His throat ached with remembered excitement. "I've been riding with Mrs. Judge Harrison. In her car. I was helping her find some butter."

The hand holding the pen stopped in midair. "Yes, I did hear that noisy car. Now, your name. And it is not polite to say Mrs. Judge Harrison. It is simply Mrs. Harrison."

Flooded with new confidence, he nodded. He would have to remember things like that.

He was in the hall again, staring into classrooms, all alike. Desks in rows, dark blotches of ink on their surface and on the floor beneath. Crossed flags beneath pictures of George Washington. Tall windows with tattered shades carefully and precisely aligned. All the familiar things. But different now.

He thought fuzzily: I have travelled a long way and seen something different, something important. I have been called a nigger when I am white. I have flown like the wind down long streets, I have ridden with a lady in a rustling silk dress.

For a few days after that, all things were very special to him.

He was careful to set his feet just so against the ground. Sometimes he walked holding the back of his thighs so he could feel the muscles that moved him across earth's surface. At curbs and ditches he took long soaring leaps, floating through space. He stared at a single dry leaf on a winter-bared tree and willed it to fall. He waited with a stalking cat in the shelter of a privet hedge. He lifted his lips in imitation of a dog's growl. All around him the air was un-breathed, unused, new. He was the first and only person in the world. In his blood, oxygen sparkled like shiny pennies as his heart tumbled them through his veins.

The shell of excitement faded so gently he was not exactly sure when it was gone, or what it had been.

. . .

Later that month—a cloudy afternoon with the feel of
winter wrapped over the town like a fog—he came home
from school, took off his muddy shoes, as he always did, and
opened the kitchen door. The gathering dusk wedged into
the room with him, chill hard at his heels.

"Close the door quick," his sister said. As she always did.

He put his books and lunch box on the cupboard in the
corner, as he always did.

She sat at the table, watching him and smiling broadly. "I
been hearing about you."

I've never seen her smile like that, he thought. And I've
never seen her sit and do nothing either.

"I hear tell you've been playing the salesman."

"Been doing what?"

"You don't remember? You told Mrs. Harrison about my
butter."

In a flash it all was back, the sense of importance and excitement. The wind and the movement and the freedom.
"Yes, ma'am," he said, though he never called his sister
ma'am.

"Oh, Charles, you should have seen them. A little black
monkey, whose name was Homer, and a tall thin woman, a
Redbone if ever I saw one, Sophie the cook she said she
was." Mattie leaned her elbows on the table. "They drove up
in the prettiest little cart and a real nice-looking roan pony."

He nodded.

"I guess they were supposed to see if the house was clean,
and that sort of thing, so I showed them the barn and the
cooler."

"She's got a car, too," Charles said wonderingly.

"She's got lots of things," Mattie said. "She's rich. Everybody in town knows they got railroad money."

He blinked.

"I read about them in the paper."

His sense of wonder grew and grew, until it seemed to him that he was again rushing through space, winds blowing past his ears, stars singing.

"They bought it all"—Mattie rocked back and forth in her chair—"except for the little I kept for Mr. Varnado's supper. And you know what? I was just turning out a batch of that soft cheese Ma used to make, so the cook Sophie tasted it and asked if she couldn't take a sample back to the lady of the house. That's what she called her: the lady of the house. Are you listening?"

Charles nodded.

"I sent along the last of my white bread, too. We'll have to eat biscuits for our supper." She giggled, a high-pitched little-girl sound. "What do you think of that, little brother?"

"I think it is very nice," Charles said carefully, solemnly. "The extra money will be good to have."

His sister kissed him.

A F T E R that the sky turned a pale winter blue and the air grew colder. The kitchen garden was empty, the last apples picked from the neat row of trees in the backyard. "Now we go looking in the other places," Mattie said.

They crossed the bridge at Silver Creek and walked out into the old farmstead country. Always rushed by the early dark, the three of them prowled along roads, across fields, searching. In weed-choked orchards near the burned-out chimneys of old houses they picked hundreds of small candy-striped red-and-white apples. They filled croaker sacks with hard green preserving pears and baskets with ripe yellow quinces from gnarled trees whose branches sagged with fruit. Mattie knew all the places where the best

hickory and pecan trees grew. Her favorite was the Confederate graveyard; the ground was thick with nuts. "No one
ever comes here," she said, "except me, and I come every
year."

At first Charles was afraid and walked sidling across the
grass.

"Don't be a baby." Mattie's windburned face flushed red-
der with anger. "These people didn't know you when they
were alive and they don't care about you now."

As they left, heavy sacks slung over their shoulders, she
noticed a single large crab-apple tree by the gate. "Look
there." And Charles scrambled along the sloping twisted
limbs, dropping the small apples into her waiting hands.

"We can't carry any more," Mattie said, regret in her
voice. "And it's getting late." A cold mist had gathered, waist
high on the lower slopes. "Let's us walk fast and get warm."

But they couldn't. The baskets and sacks were heavy,
their arms ached, and their hands were stiff with cold.
Nancy whimpered, clutching Mattie's coat.

"I got to carry her." Mattie sighed with annoyance.
"Charles, you take the sacks. One over each shoulder and
you can hook a basket on each arm."

Silently Charles obeyed. He fixed his eyes on the hem of
her skirt, on her black button shoes, and he followed. His
teeth were chattering by the time they unlocked their
kitchen door.

Nancy sat on the floor and cried softly with relief.

Mattie lit the small lamp that stood just inside the entry.
"Shake up the fire, Charles." She pulled off Nancy's coat and
hat and scarf and hung them, with her own, on the pegs by
the door. "We stayed too long, for sure, but look at what we
got." Mattie pointed chapped fingers to the baskets and
sacks. "Charles, you carry everything to the pantry. Be sure
you close the door tight. I'll put supper on to warm."

He remembered that evening. Of the thousands of evenings during the years he lived in that house, he remembered that one best. He remembered the pattern of the oilcloth on the table—red and white with black diamonds. In the center was the covered glass sugar bowl on its tall pedestal and next to it a Ball jar of forks and spoons, bunched like flowers. He remembered the blue-and-white-striped apron Mattie wore; it had a large frayed hole in the center. The big black range sent floods of heat into the room. The steamy air moved across his face, soothing the winterburned skin. Mr. Varnado was away on the Chicago run, so there were only the three of them. They ate chicken stew, thick with yellow grease—Mattie was reducing the size of her flock for the winter—and biscuits left from breakfast.

When they finished, when night made mirrors of the windows, his sister pulled the curtains closed, cleared away the dishes, and lit the big reading lamp. A whiff of kerosene drifted across the room; the mantle clouded, then cleared. "The wick wants trimming," his sister said, "but it will do for now." She set the lamp in the center of the table, got the pen and the bottle of ink from the cupboard. "Charles, do two pages before bed." She set great store on penmanship and had him practice every night, in addition to his regular homework. *Running Commercial Hand,* the cover of his copybook said.

Usually he was eager to work; he liked the feel of the pen in his fingers. But this one evening he sat still, eyes staring into the dull polish of the lamp's brass base, feeling a smug proud satisfaction. He'd carried the baskets and the sacks, heavy as they were. He could look into the pantry and say: I gathered that, that is mine. He slumped in his chair until his chin rested on the oilcloth. He breathed slowly, tasting the chicken on his breath. Humming a little, Mattie put the white enamel dishpan in the sink, poured in a kettle of boiling water, pumped in some cold, and began to wash up. Head down on the table, Nancy slept, snoring lightly.

He was conscious of the house around him, of the sturdy walls and the roof. He could feel the sun pull away to the other half of the globe, he could feel the steady shrinking of the days, the steadily lengthening nights.

And he thought about things still outside. All the dead: those people in the Confederate cemetery; his mother in her grave in Clark County. (For an instant he saw her—sitting on the porch, shelling field peas; her hands didn't stop their work as she smiled at him, a small smile that lifted one corner of her mouth.) Of course she wasn't really in the ground, he knew that, she was in heaven, she had gone to glory with the saints. The dead were not troubled by weather or anything else; they were saved or damned and that was all there was to it.

He pushed himself upright, planted his elbows, rested his chin in his hands and went on thinking about things left outside.

Snakes found cracks in rocks and walls where they slept through the winter. The remaining birds fluffed up their feathers and sheltered under roof eaves. Cattle and horses and dogs and cats had their barns; mules had at least a shelter of brush piled over a low-hanging limb. Deer had their hidden brakes, rabbits their secret holes under fallen trees. Even the panthers had their winter lairs.

And that left people.

He lifted his head and asked: "You reckon there's people out there without a place to stay tonight?"

"For sure there is. Those who don't belong anywhere."

He could feel them. People in their thousands crowding around the outside walls while he and his sisters sat safe and warm within the wooden cover, while chicken cooked in a big pot and biscuits waited in the oven.

I am here, Charles thought very slowly, I belong here and that is important. Just as he was falling asleep, he wondered why that should be so.

The last leaves fell, suddenly, all at once, filling gutters and drainage ditches. Mr. Varnado raked them into piles and set them afire, and his sister complained that the soot spoiled her drying wash.

Charles climbed to the roof and found the town newly visible without its covering of leaves—water tower, clock tower, and four church spires. He saw the peaked red roof of the railroad passenger terminal. Through the winter-cleared air he heard the high-pitched clicking of the big freight trains as they sped along the tracks past town.

He went to Sunday school. He sang in the choir at the Children's Christmas Program. He won the angel-drawing contest. His prize was a grape-flavored jawbreaker. He kept it in his pocket, saving it carefully. After a few days the lint and dust on it was so thick that he had to spit out the first few mouthfuls of sweetness.

The Saturday before Christmas Mattie and Charles rode to town on the new electric trolley. (Just Charles and Mattie. Nancy had a cold and stayed home with Mr. Varnado's sister, Aunt Anna.) As they rattled along the streets, bells clanging at each and every corner, Mattie pointed out the sights: the waterworks, the gasworks, Tilton's Lumberyard, McClellan's Department Store, County National Bank, the Ford Motor showroom, the Elite Café, the General Jackson Hotel, the Armory, the Winchester Arms Hotel, Delmonico's Restaurant, the Methodist church, the Presbyterian church, the First Baptist church, all in a row.

They got off at the town square—where a bronze soldier waved his sword over a pyramid of cannonballs—to tour the county courthouse. Boards creaked noisily under their feet as they went from floor to floor staring at portraits of judges and governors and a long gold-framed list of men who had died in the Civil War.

Were these in the cemetery where they had picked the crab apples? "Maybe," his sister said, "but maybe not. Sometimes they just bury soldiers where they die, wherever it is."

So, he thought, the dead were scattered all across the earth, not just in the places they'd lived. They were sprinkled like seed puffs blown in the wind. Only, he corrected himself, seed puffs carried life.

At dusk electric lights came on in the square, clusters of five bulbs suspended from black iron poles, like giant grapes. "It is just beautiful," Mattie said. "I love to watch them come on."

"You've seen it before?" Charles's breath made Indian smoke signals in the air.

"Of course I have." His sister laughed. "Mr. Varnado and I ride down almost every month just to see them." She scrubbed at her red nose. "Now it's time to go. We'll take a different streetcar this time."

Sparks from the trolley's overhead power line showered like fireworks as they rode past redbrick buildings, stores, and warehouses, all of them glittering with electric lights inside. They crossed a weedy trash-littered river, faintly yellow tinged. "Would you believe," his sister said, "in the spring the water here rises almost to the bridge. Look, Charles, the railroad yards."

He stared at a maze of tracks, twisting in and out of each other, writhing without ever moving, the color of water snakes. Engines wrapped in clouds of steam, thudding and whistling. Lines of freight cars, rolling, coupling, crashing. One huge building, glowing with orange light. "The roundhouse," his sister said. "They repair the engines in there. Have you ever seen anything like it?"

Yes, he thought, yes he had. In a Sunday-school book, a picture of hell.

His sister nudged his shoulder. "Lean out and have a good look. That freight's going to cross right in front of us."

Black-and-white-striped gates, tipped with lanterns, dropped down to block the road. The train moved slowly across, big driver wheels turning ponderously, thudding the air with blows of steam. His face grew wet, then icy cold. He drew back, pulled up his collar, wiped his face on it.

Now his sister was leaning out to wave to the engineer; her red mittens flashed back and forth in the light. (Like she was washing a window, Charles thought.) The engineer smiled and raised his cap to her, half bowing. "That is a friend of Mr. Varnado's," she said. She settled back in her seat, comfortable on the hard wood.

Awed, Charles thought: How wonderful that must be, to have people wave to you in the easy way of old friends.

The signalman swung aboard. The brakeman came to stand in the door of the caboose. The train became a set of fading lights, and their trolley creaked and swayed into motion. Up a small hill, past a big park, and down a wide street with big houses on each side. At each corner electric lights threw down a yellow glow.

His sister nodded with satisfaction. "There'll be lights on all the streets in a few years, that's what the newspaper said."

The trolley was moving faster now; there were no stops here; no one to get on or off. The houses all seemed to be painted white. They all seemed to have iron fences, black spears pointing straight up at the night sky. Glass ovals glittered in every front door, and all the rooms were bright with electric light. Motorcars turned into gravelled drives.

"There are lots of cars here," Charles said.

"Mr. Varnado says that someday we will have a car. Look there, that is where Mrs. Harrison lives."

Charles had only a confused impression of towers and porches and frost-burned lawns where iron stags stood guard, antlers defiant against the dark.

"I've been inside there," his sister said proudly. "Just last week she sent and asked me to come talk to her." She smoothed her skirts across her knees. "She ordered all the butter I can make and three white loaves twice a week. If I do any preserving, she will take some of that too, she especially wants fig. And she has promised to tell all her friends about me."

There was a firm crisp resonant tone to her voice, one that wasn't usually there. The sound of money, Charles thought, that's what that is.

All at once Charles was very tired of seeing and thinking unfamiliar things. He closed his eyes.

"Don't go to sleep now. This here is our stop."

He stumbled off the trolley into overwhelming darkness. "Mattie," he shouted.

Close by her voice said, "Whatever's the matter with you?"

Then he saw that the night wasn't all dark, that there was a dim glow from the houses all around him, cracks of light through drawn curtains.

"Come on now." She walked briskly down the street, bent forward, hands folded under arms for warmth, heels thudding and skirts swishing. A dog barked, sound muffled by house walls. Stars glittered through bare branches overhead. On each side, slate-lined drainage ditches reflected the small light, dull and flat and frozen.

The moon, just beginning to come up, shone on the windows of their house, blind as old men's eyes. In the kitchen Nancy slept in the rocking chair, wrapped in a quilt. Aunt Anna dozed, head down on the kitchen table, her breath whistling and gurgling softly. In the silent seconds before his sister's cheery voice echoed through the room, Charles felt a soft cocoon of comfort in the old kitchen—worn linoleum, greasy sooty black range, scrubbed warped-wood counters with chipped white enamel basins hanging beneath them, rusty red pump by the sink.

At the end of school in June, his father sent for him.

"Foolishness," his sister complained to her husband. "Charles is better off here."

Mr. Varnado said quietly, "Might be he's needed."

Mattie sniffed. "There's too many people in that house right now." And then she set herself to making bread— though it wasn't her regular baking day—banging bowls and pans and talking all the time.

Mr. Varnado sighed, put on his hat, and went to play checkers with his brother Ralph at the drugstore. (They were partners there; they had taken over after their father's death.) People who came in for a soda or a headache powder would often stay just to watch them, they were such good players.

Not much had changed at the farm, Charles thought. The hinge on the front gate was still broken; you had to lift up the whole thing to get by, which was why none of them ever came in that way. The henhouse wall was still patched with a piece of roofing tin. By the vegetable garden, the small stirrup hoe was still leaning on the fence, still had a split handle mended by twisted wire. In the garden itself (who had planted it, Charles wondered) the potatoes, tomatoes, peas, pole beans, sweet corn for table eating, onions, cabbage were thriving, needing only some weeding.

But things seemed older, their edges more frayed. The piled stones that held up the corner of the porch (as they had for as long as Charles could remember) now shifted and

shook a lot more when anybody walked carelessly across
that corner. In the kitchen there never seemed to be enough
cups and plates, and only a few forks and spoons. The curtains hung limp and heavy with dust and grease—his
mother had made those curtains, had stitched them out of
odd bits of dress material into a kind of patchwork. Charles
felt a sudden turn in his stomach, which he'd learned to recognize as sorrow. He faced it, battled it, and forced it to go
away. Then he took down the curtains, washed them carefully, starched them, found the flatiron under the big bed,
and spent an hour ironing them.

His grandmother had died during the winter. His grandfather sat in the shady corner of the porch, pale blue eyes
staring at nothing, hands folded, cane between his knees. No
matter how hot the day, he never sweated. His skin had a
fine white powdery look, like dust. Sometimes, like a turtle,
he would draw down his head between the wide straps of
his overalls, so that his large hairy ears rested on his shoulders. He'd sit there by the hour, crouched inside the bones
of his body. One late August day the old man left his
chair and walked slowly to his bed. He took out his false
teeth and put them under the pillow. He lay down, face
to the wall, pulled up the quilt as if he were cold, and
would neither move nor eat. He breathed slowly through
four days, then died. His passing was so quiet and so gentle no one was ever quite sure exactly when he was
gone.

That left Hiram and his sons, Caleb and Buck and Samuel and Charles.

Caleb was planning to marry Odell Jackson soon as the
cotton was in. He was building a room just for them, adding it next to the kitchen. During the quiet period in late
summer, when the cotton was making and there was little
else to do, he finished it. Every evening he went courting.

He'd come back late, fast asleep, letting the horse find its way. It was an old animal, slow and reliable, and Caleb slept soundly, stretched along its neck, hands clenched in the scrawny mane.

Hiram was courting too: Barbara Wells, Preacher Evans's widowed daughter. She was childless, near forty, an energetic woman and a fine housekeeper. He went to church with her every Sunday (though he had never gone before), listened to her father's sermon, and had Sunday dinner at her house. He took Samuel, who was fourteen, with him. Every Sunday, early in the morning, the small wagon, drawn by the youngest and prettiest of the six mules in the yard, rolled sedately down the road, bouncing and swaying through the ruts, Hiram driving, Samuel hunched beside him on the seat, miserable.

Buck and Charles were left with the Sunday chores. They finished the work quickly and carelessly and then went swimming in the little river beyond the pasture lots. There was a pool there, a horseshoe of boulders and gravel below a small waterfall. Ferns, like a sparse beard, grew along the sides. Cedars put down their long stubborn roots into cracks of rock. The hot afternoon sun drew a strong smell of tar from their shiny blue-green foliage. The water was deep and cold and the color of dead leaves. Bees droned past, invisible in the glare. From the pasture, half a mile away, they heard the flat clank of a cowbell as the herd grazed.

Buck lowered himself into the water, swam a quick circle, shook himself dry. He was the tallest of the brothers, the whitest-skinned and the fairest-haired. In the brilliant glare he seemed to be shining from inside.

"How do you like old Pa taking up Jesus." Buck grinned at the sky.

Charles said nothing. Buck often talked to himself out loud and didn't require an answer.

"Another preacher's daughter. Just like Ma. You want to know something else?"

"What?" Charles said hesitantly.

"Little brother, you don't say a word about this, swear you won't."

"I don't carry tales," Charles said. "You know I don't."

"I joined the army. Sneaked off to Sellers Crossing and joined up."

"You did what?"

"Pa'll be madder than hell, but I got to get out of here. I got to do something before I go plain crazy. And that's the way it is."

The way it is: but Charles hadn't known. For all they'd lived in the same house and slept not a foot apart, he hadn't even guessed. And Buck hadn't said ... There were secrets in Buck, hidden places, shadows and mysteries. It was like that game at school—blind man's bluff—where he went blundering around in the dark, trying to find people who hid from him.

That was the last summer Charles spent on his father's farm.

Buck went off to the army. Caleb brought home his bride, and three months later their son was born. Hiram married Mrs. Barbara Wells who, despite her age, was soon expecting a child. The house was so crowded that Samuel, who was sixteen, slept in the barn all that winter. In the spring he ran off with Martha Thompson (daughter of Alvin Thompson, foreman at the cotton gin at Sellers Crossing) to the secret shelter they'd built along Wilcox Branch.

After a week or so their food and their money ran out and they came back. They went first to the Tucker farm, but Barbara Tucker, infant drooling on her shoulder, told them to go away, while the other Mrs. Tucker, two babies at her skirts, watched big-eyed and openmouthed. After that the couple went to the Thompson house. Martha's mother sent a message to her husband to come home quick.

The young people sat in the porch swing and waited for Mr. Thompson. He came at a run, grabbed Samuel away from his daughter, and punched him so hard that he crashed through the porch railing into the flower beds. Mr. Thompson sucked the blood from his split knuckles and jumped through the broken railing after him. Samuel crawled under the house. Mr. Thompson, who was too fat to follow, grabbed his ankle. Samuel squirmed and curled around and bit the already bloody hand. Mr. Thompson roared with anger and went for his shotgun while Samuel scrambled out the far side and disappeared. Mr. Thompson fired both barrels under the house, blowing holes in a couple of water pipes. That night he locked Martha in her room and nailed the window shut from outside, leaving only a small crack for air. As soon as he fell asleep, she broke the glass, climbed out, and joined Samuel. She came back in the morning— alone this time. Samuel's face was swollen and a couple of his teeth were loose, and he wasn't taking any more chances with her father. She walked into the house while her parents were having breakfast. "I'm hungry," she said, "and so's Samuel. I'll eat here and then I'll bring him his."

Her mother shrieked; her father said testily, "For God's sake, woman, be quiet."

And Martha, pieces of grass and straw stuck in the eyelet trim of her dress, her face smeared with dirt and her hair all uncombed, smiled and sat down at their white enamel table and began buttering herself a piece of bread. Right there and then Mr. Thompson realized that there was nothing he could do, except repair the broken window, find a preacher who was broad-minded about such things, and have a wedding in his front parlor.

Samuel found a job at the livery stable, and Mr. Thompson built a house for the young couple in the corner of his own property. Every evening the kitchen lights of the two houses shone each into the other.

Sometimes Charles dreamed about the farm, the way it had been when his mother was alive, when there'd been flowers all around the front porch, bright colors in the summer sun.

He told his sister.

"Why do you want to go and dream about that hardscrabble farm."

Charles was surprised at the anger in her voice. "It wasn't bad. I kind of liked it," he said to Mr. Varnado.

"Of course," Mr. Varnado said diplomatically, with all the experience of his years as a train conductor. "It's a good farm."

Mattie snorted. "The trouble with you, George, is that you're city-born."

"I am, my dear," he said placidly, "I am indeed. But Charles is not. And he may have very different ideas."

"He doesn't."

Mr. Varnado lit his Sunday cigar.

Charles went to school, played baseball, did his homework, worked summers at the Varnado Drugstore. In the seventh grade he began a feud with a tall red-haired boy named Earl Borders. After school each day, at the very edge of the playground, they pushed and shoved, swung their book bags and rolled on the ground, locked together, punching and biting. In the mornings they lay in ambush behind fences and houses and sheds, throwing rocks and nails and broken bits of flowerpots. Once they hit Mrs. McCrory's dog as it slept on her porch. Its howls brought her out with a broom and a poker.

Charles tripped Earl on the school stairs and sent him tumbling head over heels through the neatly marching ranks of children. Earl began carrying a pocketknife, secretly. Charles kept a short piece of pipe in his lunch box.

He was suspended for a week. Mattie put him to work housecleaning. He scrubbed floors, washed windows, shook out curtains, polished the furniture with beeswax and the kitchen range with blacking. In the evenings he did his homework and read out loud from *Pilgrim's Progress.*

Mattie grumbled and complained. Mr. Varnado smiled reminiscently. "Boys look for trouble, my dear. I remember one Saturday night we put John Price's wagon on the very top of the old town hall."

"You did?"

"We did. Took it apart, carried it up the steps, and put it back together on the roof. Price was so mad he couldn't hardly talk."

Charles shook his head with silent admiration.

"Well," Mr. Varnado said, "there were four of us and it was a small wagon."

Months and years passed smoothly in a jumble of things.

Buck wrote now and then, short letters that Mattie propped up on the table for them all to read. He was fine, he said, he liked army life. He liked travelling and seeing all different places. Right now he was in Mexico. It was a terrible country, where people were poorer than niggers at home.

Charles got a slingshot, large and perfectly balanced, leather-wrapped fork and handle; Mr. Varnado taught him to use it. . . . Nancy, now tall as he, walked to school with him every day. . . . His father, Hiram, had another son, and his stepmother, Barbara, died of childbed fever. Caleb's wife nursed that baby with her own; they were only a month apart.

Charles finished grammar school and went on to Boys' High School. . . . A war began and Courthouse Square blossomed in flags and platforms and speakers and parades. The governor came to town and gave a speech about patriotic duty.

Buck, now a sergeant of artillery, wrote from France. The people are friendly, he said, especially the girls; the farms are pretty but it rains a lot.

Mattie opened a business of her own—on Laurel Street, just around the corner from the big Methodist church. It had been Schulman's Bakery, but the German owners moved away with the outbreak of war. Mattie rented the building, its ovens and equipment still in place. She made the front a tearoom, bright and cheerful, with small iron tables and plants hanging in the windows and flower pictures on the walls. At the bakery counters she sold bread and rolls and cakes and cookies and jams and jellies and, by special order, tea sandwiches cut in fancy shapes. Nancy helped every day after school and all day Saturday. The place was that crowded.

The war ended, banners and flags disappeared, uniforms vanished. . . . Buck moved to Fort Benning, in Georgia. The President himself had come to watch them parade, he wrote.

Hiram Tucker died, sat down in his barn one evening and never got up again.

Charles and Nancy and Mattie and Mr. Varnado went to the funeral. Buck was there, stiff and straight in his uniform. "I got special emergency leave," he said.

Samuel and his wife, Martha, came too. "Tough old bastard." Samuel took a long drink from the bottle he had brought. "I come to be sure he really is going underground."

Charles noticed that his mother's grave had sunk over the years, though his grandfather's hadn't. It must, he thought, be different kinds of earth.

As they were getting ready to leave, Caleb touched Charles's arm. "I'm fixing to keep Pa's boys; Odell wants them like her own. You don't have to worry none."

Charles nodded. That would make ten children for Caleb. Luckily eight were boys and could work on the farm. For a while anyway.

"There's something else you got to know," Caleb said in his plodding serious way. "Pa left the farm to me. It's free and clear and no debts. I sure hope that don't upset you none."

"No." Charles hunted for the right words. "I got no claim here." He looked at the crowd of people in the churchyard, all of them related to him, all of them strangers. "Blood just ain't enough."

Charles finished Boys' High School and went to work as a bookkeeper at McClellan's Department Store on Main Street. . . . Buck was transferred to Camp Martin in New Orleans. . . . Mr. Varnado retired from the railroad and spent his days at the drugstore with his brother. They bought a car. Mattie learned to drive and made her own deliveries. She hung small painted signs on both doors: DELUXE CATER-ERS. (She boasted that she did all the fancy tea parties in town.) On sunny Sundays Charles and Mr. Varnado loaded the car with their fishing rods and gear and drove the new paved road to Clear Lake. They'd spend the whole day there—no reason to hurry back; Mattie and Nancy would go to Sunday school, then church, then Christian Endeavor.

"I never cared much for church," Charles said.

"Too much noise," Mr. Varnado said.

"Churches are real noisy places."

Mr. Varnado watched his cork bob gently as a fish nibbled and swam away. "After all those years on the trains, you wouldn't think noise would bother me."

"No, you wouldn't," Charles agreed.

"But I just plain don't like noise now," Mr. Varnado said, "and I don't much like people anymore. After I dealt with people all my life on the trains—it makes you wonder."

Mr. Varnado handed his rod to Charles while he took a small metal flask from his inside coat pocket, the flask that had comforted him on so many long cold rides while the noisy rails sang in his ears. He took a swallow, passed it to Charles, who had a sip just to be companionable.

On winter Sundays when the fishing ponds were frozen, Charles and Mr. Varnado sat in the parlor and listened to records on the gramophone. Sometimes Mr. Varnado played the piano and they sang together. Mr. Varnado had a pleasant light tenor, Charles a solid baritone.

There was another letter from Buck—the longest one he'd ever written. He'd caught the flu at Camp Martin and almost died, but he didn't. He'd left the army and become a policeman. He'd gotten married too: her name was Stella Arnaud. They were living with her family and looking for a place of their own. And, he said, they must all visit him anytime they came to New Orleans.

Mattie laughed at that, but Mr. Varnado said that New Orleans wasn't really so far, not with his lifetime pass on the railroads. He'd been to New Orleans a few times and wouldn't mind seeing it again. Charles said that he would go with him.

Charles was promoted to assistant head bookkeeper the same June Nancy graduated from high school and married Russell Grayson, who was assistant cashier at the County National Bank. The wedding was in the front parlor: Mr. Varnado gave the bride away. Mattie made hundreds of sandwiches and a tall white wedding cake and gallons of iced tea and strawberry punch with sliced berries in it. There was a record player on the front porch and extra chairs (borrowed from the church) placed carefully on the new-cut grass of the yard. The women sat there, talking and laughing while children in their Sunday clothes played careful games. All the men crowded around the washhouse, where half a dozen bottles of good bootleg were hidden in the tubs. Mr. Varnado had proofed each bottle himself— carefully shaking, then watching the bead rise.

Mattie said, "Charles, there is somebody here I want you to meet. She's a lovely girl. She and her parents come to church almost every week."

"Sure," Charles said. He'd learned not to argue with his sister.

"Her father's manager of Aikens Grove."

Charles whistled. "Well how about that."

"He says it's a beautiful place."

"It sure ought to be," Charles said, "considering the amount of money gone into it these last ten years."

The money belonged to Mr. William Howell Wilson, and he'd decided to use it to restore Aikens Grove. His architects and researchers fanned out across the county, searching the memories of old people, trying to reconstruct the burned-out shell exactly as it had been. The house he finally built stood on the exact same spot, used the exact same foundations.

People knew little about him, only that he was from Chicago, kept to himself, and lived quietly except for two large parties—at Christmas and at Midsummer's Night. For these occasions, Chicago caterers brought their own staff to prepare and serve their own food. The bands came from New Orleans. Special trains brought in the guests.

Mattie said, "Living way out there she doesn't get to meet many young people. Come on now. I'll introduce you."

Cora Stanford was sitting on the swing between the mulberry trees. The ripe fruits were falling all around her, spraying purple juice.

"You're sitting in a bad spot," Charles said. "Mulberry stain won't ever come out."

"Let's go have a cup of punch then. Will you put some whiskey in mine? I'm not supposed to go near the wash-house."

Charles began a second job, a night job. Four or five times a week he drove bootleg. He'd gotten the job through his brother Samuel, now a mechanic at the garage in Sellers Crossing. They rebuilt cars for liquor runners, enlarging trunks, making compartments under seats, adding heavy springs so that the cars wouldn't sag and bottom when they were loaded. They also installed big new engines. Samuel bragged that their cars could outrun anything.

Charles was always afraid—of the empty roads, of the dark turns and tree cover where police could hide—but the job paid well, ten times his bookkeeper's salary. He kept the cash in small Mason jars carefully fitted with new rubber rings and buried in the rows of tomatoes in the garden.

Mr. Varnado said, "I don't think I'll weed the garden this year, Charles. Will you take care of it?"

Charles smiled at the tall stooped old man who knew exactly what was growing in his tomatoes. "I'll do it evenings after work. Yes, sir."

And he thought: I'm a midnight gardener. With secret out-of-sight midnight crops. Or a miner. With underground lodes and veins of gold.

He was sleepy all the time, bone tired, but he was never late for work, nodding and smiling and lifting his hat as he walked through the store. Two or three times a day he rested his chin on his hand, pretended to be studying his ledger, and took a quick nap, eyes wide open.

At the six o'clock bell, he filed away invoices, cleared his desk. Mr. Adams, the head bookkeeper, held up one finger, nodding at him.

"Yes, sir," Charles said.

They got the last of the day's receipts from the registers, totalled and bundled them. Mr. Adams took a long-barrelled revolver from his desk drawer, handed it to Charles, who slipped it into his coat. It had no hammer, so it went in smoothly. Mr. Adams picked up the bag and, shoulder to shoulder, they crossed the street to the side door of the County National Bank.

Charles handed the gun back to Mr. Adams, "Good night, sir."

And he was off to his second job; his midnight garden grew.

He thought occasionally of Cora Stanford. When he could, he borrowed the car on Sunday and drove to the manager's house at Aikens Grove to see her. They sat under the deep shade of the big fig trees, in the musty-smelling air under the wide leaves, and drank lemonade and iced tea and ate small sugar-dusted cookies that sifted white across the front of his coat and his tie. When the weather turned cold, they sat inside by the fire and ate fruitcake and chicken sandwiches and cherry bounce. He sent her a lacy handkerchief for Christmas. And a lacy pink-and-white valentine.

He bought a book, white leather and gilt-edged— *Thoughts for Each Lovely Day*—and gave it to her on her birthday with a note inside: Will you marry me?

"I thought you'd never ask," she said.

. . .

They were married two months later. He took his money from the Mason jars, counted it—just over five thousand dollars. He bought a car and a honeymoon trip to Niagara Falls; the rest he put in the bank.

Cora's father offered him the job of assistant manager at Aikens Grove Plantation. "You know bookkeeping and you know farming. You'll be making twice the money. And Cora will love it."

Charles shook his head. "I can keep accounts all right, and I was raised on a farm. But not a farm like this one."

Mr. Stanford grinned. "This ain't a farm, this is an enterprise. Or an experiment. Or whatever Mr. Wilson wants it to be."

"I never even seen him in town," Charles said.

"He never goes. He was gassed in the war, so his lungs are bad. And he's worried about infections. But you'll see him out here. He really keeps his eye on the place."

"I'd have to learn a lot of things all over again," Charles said slowly.

"He was real pleased when I told him your grandma worked as a governess on the old place."

"Why would he care about that? It wasn't even his family owned it then."

"Continuity, he said. He likes continuity."

"He likes what?"

"It don't matter. He's got peculiar ways, that's all. Like the cotton. For the past two, three years we been planting way too much cotton and losing money on it. But he won't hear of cutting back. He says cotton gives work to the people around here and it's his duty to do that."

Charles asked, startled, "His duty?"

"Sometimes," Mr. Stanford said quietly, "I think he's back in slave days. He's the master looking out for his people. But don't let that put you off. He's a good man to work for."

The familiar smells of new-broken land, of animals and fodder and miles of green leaves, brought a small aching longing to Charles. "I almost forgot what this was like," he said truthfully. "Makes me feel like I'm eight years old again."

"You coming to work?"

"I am," Charles said.

T E N years later, in 1934, Charles Tucker was manager of Aikens Grove. (Cora's parents were dead, killed in a collision with a logging truck one foggy morning three years past.)

The plantation had grown larger, its operations more varied. Mr. William Howell Wilson was turning Aikens Grove into a spectacular farm, something from a picture book or a dream, a world of perfection and wonder and delight.

There was still cotton; the summer fields still turned white, and the roads leading to the gin still were edged by a thick rim of cotton frost. There were wide fields of corn and peanuts and soybeans and sorghum. And timberlands where fast-growing pulp pines stood in neat precisely straight rows, black matchsticks stretching for a mile over needle-strewn grass-bare ground. There were pastures of fescue and clover and rye, neatly fenced, dotted with feeding stations and water troughs, crisscrossed by redirected streams, sprinkled with trees for shade on a hot day. There were beef cattle, Angus and Hereford, and a dairy herd (cheeses marketed under the plantation's own label), and a model pig farm (country ham and bacon sold through specialty groceries across the country).

And the horses, all the horses. The pair of Percherons—useless young monsters, the farm was entirely mechanized—

who paraded once a year in the town's Fourth of July parade. Nine Arabians in their brand-new barn, four mares in foal with shining rounded bellies. Six sleek dark Tennessee Walking horses, whose gait was so smooth the rider never tired. The Shetland ponies, matched strawberry roans, bad tempered and lovely.

There were acres of side-by-side greenhouses of orange and grapefruit and kumquats. There was an experimental nursery for camellias, each new hybrid named for a famous battle in France. There were apple orchards and peach orchards. And, close to the main house, a special walled garden where an Italian gardener from New Jersey espaliered pears to the bricks and grafted different varieties of fruit on a single tree.

Mr. Wilson had grown thinner over the years; his blond hair was completely gray. His cheeks burned with high flushed color; his blue eyes still seemed to be staring into the far distance. And he still coughed—a quiet hacking he scarcely seemed to notice, it had become so much a part of him—and every morning he folded half a dozen clean handkerchiefs into his pockets. He'd built a large screened sleeping porch across the front of the main house, at roof level, reached by a spiraling ship's ladder. He had a feather bed and layers of blankets, and he slept there, no matter the temperature. He spent his mornings on horseback—he never seemed to cough while he rode—inspecting every corner of his property, picking his way across razorback ridges, jumping pasture fences, walking along the gravelly bottoms of shallow creeks. As he went, he wrote his observations in a small notebook, filing them neatly by subject as soon as he got home. He spent late afternoons on the telephone. (He talked to people all around the world, Bakersfield telephone operators said.) Evenings he read in the library or played the piano or listened to the gramophone. His collection of record albums filled one whole wall. (The maids were not allowed to touch them; the butler himself dusted them every week.) Sometimes he'd spend hours peering at the stars through a telescope, and sometimes he worked at his desk. He was writing an analysis of the military tactics of the American Expeditionary Force in France. He wrote by hand, carefully, slowly. In the morning his secretary typed what he had done and gave it back to him. She also took dictation, typed letters, ordered books from London and records from New York. (She was Myrtle Tucker, Caleb's oldest daughter, who'd finished secretarial school in Bakersfield.)

Mr. Wilson lived alone with few visitors. His wife came every December and stayed until the new year; his sister and her husband came in May for a few weeks. Every year the governor—whoever he was, whatever party he represented—had lunch alone with Mr. Wilson at the long mahogany dining table. Every few months Senator Smithers, who'd been in Washington for twenty years, came for cocktails. Once, even, during a campaign, he brought the Vice President with him. (Their staffs waited at the cars. Mr. Wilson would not allow so many strangers inside his house.) There was an Episcopal bishop from Charleston who came for tea the first week of Advent. A Catholic monsignor in red-piped cassock always came the week after Easter.

And once, too, the Klan sent word that they were coming to call, as they did with all the farmers in the county, expecting whiskey and a contribution. Mr. Wilson took two shotguns from his gun cabinet, filled his pockets with shells, and positioned himself on a dark little rise of ground by the entrance gates. He waited patiently for the riders to pass and then laid a neat metronomic series of blasts down the length of the road. He misjudged the range, but it had been a long time since he'd used a shotgun.

At first Charles Tucker thought nothing of the vandalism the field supervisors reported to him. On a place as large as Aikens Grove there was always a certain amount of damage and thievery by passing tramps: of food from work crews in the fields; of a hen from a chicken yard; of clothes from a drying line; of tools left out overnight.

But not like this. Every day now, somewhere in the expanse of Aikens Grove, in the miles of isolated pastures and pine lots, of houses and barns and storage buildings and smokehouses, something happened.

The night fires. They began as small scattered brushfires in the fall-dry slopes and scrubby hollows. Then one by one the pasture feed stations flamed and smoldered, trailing white wisps of smoke into the morning sun. The old gristmill on Singing Water Creek exploded into a ball of flame that spotted the night sky, leaving only fire-streaked millstones by morning. The field shelters burned. They were lean-tos thrown up over the years by work crews as they needed them, crude rough things, but handy in bad weather. (Not worth destroying, Charles thought.)

And one morning the whole of Baptist Ridge burned. At the first telltale squiggles of smoke, almost invisible in the gray-white of the early morning sky, Charles climbed to the barn roof and watched through field glasses. The mile-long crest fluttered into raggedy tatters of flames. Orange flowers bloomed along the slopes; the underbrush seethed with wriggling yellow snakes; pines launched exploding rockets into the air; a red tide began to flow down the corrugated sloping sides.

It was dramatic enough, Charles thought, but with the southwest wind, it would burn itself out harmlessly in a few days. Still, it had been deliberately set, at four or maybe five different spots.

He set two men to patrolling the roads at night.

At the farm garage, the tires of a tractor and the hoses at both gas pumps were slashed; the pumps themselves were safely locked.

The bell at New Hope African Methodist Church (just beyond the farm's east gate) rang out before dawn, wild jerky sounds that carried for miles in the still night air; a window was open, but no one was there. Pasture gates were ripped off their hinges and pounded to pieces with stones. (Heavy wooden gates, it must have taken most of the night to destroy them, Charles thought.) The roof panes of the largest greenhouse were broken by a barrage of rocks from a slingshot; the kumquat and the grapefruit trees inside were ruined by frost.

The county sheriff cleared the few remaining tramps from camps along the railroad tracks.

Charles posted watchmen at all the large farm buildings. He no longer trusted the dogs. They had turned useless and unpredictable. At times they remained silent, mesmerized, or whined softly in friendship; at times they roared with furious anger and pursued foolish circling trails.

Determined by the season, the farm work went on. The last of the beef cattle were shipped. The hog-slaughtering pens were busy. Smokehouses trailed their sweet wood scent through the air.

A can of paint, stolen from a work truck, splashed over prize shoats in their pen. The last of the hogs, fattening in the stubble of the cornfields, were driven out and scattered; it took two days to recover them.

Charles sent a mounted man with the dairy herd each day. Even so a broken fence in the pastures along Willow Creek let half the cows scatter into the swampy brushy lowlands. Shouting and cursing, the guard searched them out and drove them back. All but one. They found her the next day, hamstrung, X marks gashed along her flanks.

Cliff Whitney's old hound, rambling on arthritic legs to some secret night hunt of its own, was killed with a rock and its body dragged to Whitney's gate.

So they knew whose dog it was, Charles thought.

Junior Thurlow, who lived in one of the supervisors' houses in the east corner of the plantation, near the New Hope Church, woke to find pieces of burning lightwood on his roof, and his chicken coop completely in flames. He saw a shadow, got a shotgun, and gave chase, leaving his wife and sons to put out the fires. He fired both barrels, missing, but getting a clear quick look at a small figure.

Junior Thurlow went to the manager's office the next morning.

"I seen him, boss. A nigger kid." His own black face was sweating with fury. "A goddamn nigger kid not five feet tall. Killed all my hens and burnt a big hole in my roof."

"Only one?"

"One, boss."

That same night the yellow tom from the stables was killed, knife clean through the body.

Charles thought: I know this much about him. He loves fire. He is silent enough and quick enough to stalk a cat, even a wary half-wild creature like that. And he is good enough with a throwing knife to kill it.

He hung long cords of electric lights, like strings of diamonds, around all the farm buildings. Inside, the watchmen reached for their guns whenever the dogs howled or barked or just grew restless and paced.

The weather turned chill; there were heavy frosts at night. Charles, .38 at his hip, spent endless hours on horseback, searching pastures and woodlots, climbing razorback ridges, sidestepping along gravel gullies and streambeds, through canebrakes and bottomlands. He even hunted through the worn-out land along Little Lost River, where the soft moist ground was pocked with the V-shaped hooves of a herd of sheep, handsome in full winter coats.

Once he saw a thin thread of smoke hanging in the still air and rode toward it eagerly, to find a camp of surveyors for the new state road.

Sometimes he felt eyes watching him. Once he saw movement at the far side of a cotton field and sent his horse charging through the dry brown stalks. He found nothing but scrub and ground too hard to hold a print.

Day after day, he checked springs and runs and creeks. He saw many animal tracks and once a single set of footprints, small prints in the soft ground that told him nothing.

Finally, on the slopes above the old quarry—deep still cold water, almost black under the cloudy sky—he found a camp: a small low tent, brush and kindling laid for a fire, a neat tightly rolled blanket held above ground in a split stick, two unopened cans of beans, scattered bones on the ground. And a wooden mug, very carefully made with carvings all around the sides. They might be snakes, Charles thought, or maybe flames or maybe both, though he wasn't sure. He shot holes in the cans and the mug and burned the canvas and the blanket.

Two days later, as he stacked plates in his kitchen sink after dinner, a half brick smashed through the window, glancing past his cheek. Spurred by his wife's screams and the cries of his two sons, he fired his shotgun over and over again into the dark, aiming at nothing.

I must have come very close to finding him, Charles thought. And now I know that he has no gun. Or I would not be alive.

The next morning, precise to the minute for his weekly meeting with Mr. Wilson, he parked his truck under the porte cochere. The houseman swung open the door and nodded down the hall toward the study.

Mr. Wilson was waiting—as he always was—hand outstretched for the reports.

The study, the only room in the house Charles had seen, was panelled in dark wood. Even on this bright morning it was dim and filled with shadows. Mr. Wilson coughed softly as he turned the pages. "Yes," he said finally. "And now, the incidents. What of them?"

He always calls them incidents, Charles thought, even the fire that blackened an entire ridge line. "Last night it was a broken window at my house."

Mr. Wilson folded his arms and leaned forward into the yellow round of desk light. "And?"

"A couple of days ago, I found his shelter, one of the places he uses when he's hungry or needs a rest. But it wasn't his main camp. I know he's got one, a good one, the nights are cold. That's what I got to find."

"Yes." Mr. Wilson leaned back in his chair; his face floated against the dark panelling.

"I want to take three men off their regular jobs and put them to searching. And the men I want," Charles said slowly, "Johnson and Atwell and Frazier, they're all foremen. Work'll fall behind without them."

"No choice." Mr. Wilson stood up. "I can see no other possible course of action. Take the men you need for as long as you need them. Another thing. Could this fellow have worked here once? Was he discharged and now wants revenge?"

"No, sir," Charles said. "Nobody from around here."

"Why then? Why out of the entire county has he singled out this farm?"

"I don't know, sir."

But maybe it is because this house is big and white and all around it the pastures are green, even this time of year, and on them the herds are fat and sleek and when the horses run their tails fly past like visible wind. And the barns and stables are brick and new-painted and nicer and cleaner than most houses. Maybe it's because of the smell of money.

The three men, George Johnson, Goat Atwell, Harold Frazier, began searching, methodically, from the Providence River to the north ridges. Frazier found a second shelter in a shallow cave on Wolf Creek, in it a fire already laid, a cloth bag with a piece of fresh rabbit, a broken umbrella, a neatly tied bundle containing bits of things: leaves and twigs, a bird's wing and a rabbit pelt, carefully dried and stretched, head on. But no sight of him.

Each day Charles told them, "We keep on looking. He's got a camp somewhere. And he's not by himself, there's somebody with him."

"You sure are sure, boss." Atwell laughed.

"I am," Charles said flatly.

All those days of hunting, of feeling his eyes, of coming so close to him. That brick on my kitchen floor was still warm when I picked it up. I was holding him in my hand.... I know.

Atwell found the carcasses of two sheep from the Little Lost River flock. Their throats had been ripped clean through, their heads turned backward.

One morning there was a squirrel's head at the front door of the main house, fresh killed, its blood smeared across the white door. His footprints in the soft damp soil of the flower beds showed how he'd walked around the house, while neither watchman nor dogs stirred, and looked in all the windows.

The weather turned foggy. Sounds carried farther now; scents hung like flags in the unmoving air. The musky smell of snake nests, the crisp decay of dead leaves, a deer's rank scent, the sweet warm smell of beaver dams: they were all there to read.

Atwell said, "Boss, I heard something, don't know what, but I heard something back behind the burnt-out mill."

And Johnson said, "I seen something on Baptist Ridge. Could been a deer, but I don't think so."

"He's getting tired." Charles could feel the other's weariness in his own bones. "Why the hell don't he pull out?"

"What happens now, boss?"

"We keep looking," Charles said, "along the ridges. That's where I'd be."

And he is like me. If I ever see him it'll be like seeing myself in a photo negative, me white, him black. But lookalikes for all of that. Brothers.

Two days later Charles rode across Whiskey Ridge. The trail here was clean and wide, bootleggers had used it for generations. Above and beyond were the burned-out flanks of Baptist Ridge. Below, the ground fell away into sharp boulder-littered wooden ravines. A pale mist filtered the sunlight, blotched and deepened the patterns of leaf and branch, smoothed the sharp edges of granite.

Too many cedars, he thought, practically. I need to get a crew up here and grub them out.

He swung down from the saddle and walked, horse's snorting breath at his shoulder. And then he crossed it, the long thin waving trail of scent, held in the damp still air. Dirt and sweat and excrement and the licorice-like smell of black skin. He took a few steps. Stopped. The smell was gone. He turned, retraced his way: only his own scent, shaving soap, saddle leather, and horse sweat. He had blundered through a thread, and broken it. He swung back in the saddle and went on. A few hundred feet later another small puff of scent. And nothing more.

He crossed here, Charles thought. Not long ago. His camp is there below.

He rode on, carelessly, giving no sign that he had noticed anything.

Is he watching me, is he down below there, one eye, one speck in all that tangle? A wilderness, good cover.

Except for one thing. It's too small, not more than a quarter mile wide. A few men could sweep right through it.

He began whistling cheerfully.

In the last of the daylight, he rode, still whistling, into the stableyard. Atwell and Johnson and Frazier had come in earlier and were waiting.

"Boss," Johnson said, "you sound mighty happy."

Atwell said, "You found something."

Frazier, tobacco plug stretching his black cheek, grinned. "You sure as hell found something."

"Whiskey Ridge," Charles said flatly. "Off the old bootleg trail. He's there now."

Johnson grinned. "Son of a bitch."

"He's cornered himself." Charles scratched his fingernails against the stubble on his cheeks.

Atwell said, "We go looking tomorrow, boss?"

"Tonight," Charles said. "We go looking tonight. We never been out at night before. He won't be expecting us."

"Boss, we been out all day already." Atwell tipped his chair back against the wall, refusing.

"Don't be a bunch of niggers. You get paid," Charles said shortly, "just like me. Now I got to find me some more men."

By midnight there were five men on Whiskey Ridge. George Johnson, his son Bubba, Leroy Green, Mac Reily, Jimbo Howard. They spread out, shouting distance apart, lit their lightwood torches, picked up their shotguns, and began to climb down. The ground underfoot was broken and rough and spotted with boulders, but the night fog didn't reach this high, and the rising moon gave some light.

Far below, where the ridge slope ended in wide flat pastures and a stream called No Name Creek, Charles swung off his horse, stretched, and sat, Indian-style, on the ground. Here the windless bog-spotted grassland held fog like a bandage wrapped tight across its surface. He couldn't see the barbed-wire fence a couple of hundred yards ahead. He couldn't see Atwell and Frazier positioned on either side of him, though he could hear the snorting and stamping of their horses.

I didn't figure on the fog, he thought wearily. Half an army could walk across this meadow and we'd never know.

He lit a cigarette, settled himself, and waited. It would be a long cold time till morning.

The gullies ran like scratches down the side of the ridge, narrow and deep, knee-high leaf mold hiding a bottom of gravel and granite boulders. The moon was high now, and just past the full. Its mist-filtered light blotched and deepened the pattern of shadow of trunk and limb and brush. The five men worked their way down slowly, line across, shouting to keep in touch. Mac Reily stepped over a ledge, sprawled facedown, rose cursing. The whiplash of a branch slashed Leroy's cheek; he washed it at a small seep spring.

Jimbo Howard followed a gully as it twisted and right-angled downward. Until he found himself face-to-face with Mac Reily.

"Jesus," Mac Reily said. "Where'd you come from?" He was limping, his leg swelling over the top of his heavy boot.

"You hurt?"

"Feels like I busted my leg."

"You got to be real careful." Jimbo Howard, nearly fifty, sat down on a flat rock. His chest hurt and lights sparkled behind his eyes.

Mac Reily sat next to him. "Damn gun feels like it weighs a ton and a half."

"Well, it don't." Jimbo lay back and stared at the hazy patches of sky through the tangle of branches and vines overhead.

Mac Reily pulled off his cap and scrubbed at his kinky hair. He took out a flask, had a long swallow, held it out. Jimbo drank, nodded his thanks.

"Call out. Keep a line across." George Johnson shouted, voice far off and muffled by the brush.

"That's us, man." Jimbo pushed himself up, hands on thighs, and picked up his torch.

"Reily. Howard," they shouted back.

Jimbo said, "This way here don't look too bad."

The gully was slightly wider than the others, and deeper, with a firm sandy bottom. "They all look alike to me," Mac Reily said. He felt his leg carefully, wincing. He put his weight on it, then sat down again, and began to loosen the laces of his boot. "I'll be right behind you."

The flame of Jimbo's torch made a hole in the solid black of the twisting brushy slope, passed through and faded to a glow, disappeared.

Mac Reily tied his boot lacings, had another swallow of whiskey.

From the dark below, Jimbo began shouting, "Here. Here, man. I got it."

"Coming." Mac Reily broke into a trot, dodging around boulders, slipping on loose shingle, shotgun heavy and awkward in his hands.

A hundred yards down the slope, where the ravine narrowed abruptly, there was a canvas-roofed shelter and a rock fireplace whose coals still showed flecks of red under their ash gray.

Unseeing, Jimbo had walked straight into the camp. Now he stuck his torch carefully into the cleft of a pin oak and began tearing the shelter apart, tossing frame and blankets into the air. All the while shouting, roaring, "Here, here, I got it here." When he stood up, his left arm held a bundle, a lump, a shapeless nothing. Held it triumphantly, high over his head. Waved it back and forth like a flag.

'Hurrying forward, Mac Reily saw something else—another figure at the edge of the flickering light. A short thin black figure, arm drawn back, cocked, arm like a bowstring snapping. The knife was a single speck of light in the air.

Jimbo screamed and fell facedown. The coals of the fire flickered, flamed, and died.

Mac Reily's shotgun dragged across twigs and branches as he swung it up. The safety stuck and he fumbled to fire one barrel. In the following silence tinny bits of shot rattled down echoing rocks. He saw bushes move slightly, fired the second barrel. Reloaded and fired twice again.

Jimbo was moving, struggling to his knees, cursing in a hoarse whisper, "Goddamn, goddamn, goddamn." His left hand was reaching behind his back, straining to reach the knife stuck in his shoulder.

In the pastures below, Charles's horse startled and backed at the sound of the shots. "Easy," he said automatically. "Easy now."

"Hey, boss," Harold Frazier shouted.

"I heard." Charles stood up, rubbed the horse's nose.

Atwell raced out of the fog, came to a jerking halt at Charles's side. "Boss!"

"What the hell do you think you're doing?"

"You heard, boss. Shotguns."

"You could kill that horse."

Atwell slid to the ground. "Man, I don't like shooting."

"Goddamn fool." Charles hesitated, decided. "Harold," he yelled. "Come on back."

"Yeah, boss." His horse snorted as he swung into the saddle.

The three stood together, listening. Hearing small sounds that might have been voices. But mostly silence.

Charles began walking his horse in circles. He was stiff and tired and suddenly sleepy.

"We are just fixing to wait here?" Atwell asked. "There ain't no reason to wait here."

Charles said flatly, "You sneak away on me now and you sure as hell be looking for another job tomorrow."

Atwell grinned and shrugged and took a bite of his plug tobacco. Charles lit a cigarette. Frazier walked a few feet away and urinated. A bird or two stirred, fluttered, then grew quiet.

Now they could feel morning coming, the restlessness in the air, the wind from the turning globe.

Faint distant voices. Then, clearly, three shots. A pause and three more.

"Boss, you hear that?"

Charles nodded. Something was wrong.

"Hold your bridles." Charles fired a single shot in the air. Eventually a shotgun answered.

"We wait some more."

A couple of crows flapped overhead, talking.

"You figure they can find us, boss?"

"Yep," Charles said.

Methodically, every fifteen minutes, without getting up, Charles fired a single shot over his head. Frazier and Atwell, hunched over, dozing, didn't move.

The mist lightened to the color of a mourning dove.

"There they are." Frazier stood up, pointed.

A steady rattle of loose shale down the slopes. Then four men, carrying a fifth between them. All of them reeking of sweat and alcohol and blood.

Mac Reily said, "Boss, he was right there, the nigger kid, and he had a knife."

Jimbo was breathing in short snorting gasps, the whites of his eyes showed. He hiccoughed and belched bubbles of sour whiskey.

"How much you give him to drink?" Charles said.

"He was hurting," Leroy Green said.

George Johnson said, "After he couldn't walk no more, we carried him."

"That is some rough country," Bubba Johnson added. "We kept falling down. Even with the torches we couldn't see nothing."

"We all been drinking," Mac Reily said and blinked his eyes, slowly.

Charles said, "Put him down."

The knife had gone into the upper shoulder, almost the neck. Blood had soaked through shirt and sweater and heavy wool jacket but now was only an oozing trickle.

"We got to get him to a doctor." Charles straightened up. "We can put him on my horse. Atwell's the smallest and lightest, so he rides with him and holds him on."

"Boss," Atwell said, "I am plain gonna get blood all over me."

"You son of a bitch," Charles said quietly, "I will kill you."

Atwell shrugged, then nodded.

"Frazier, you go along too. I don't want Jimbo shook up. When you get to the road, you wait. Car'll be along to pick him up."

Frazier's wide black face smiled briefly. "Sure, boss."

"Bubba, you go stick your head in that creek and sober up, then you take that horse there and go on in to the office. You get yourself a car and fetch Jimbo. And send somebody to bring horses to us."

Bubba left at a fast trot, tack jingling. Frazier and Jimbo and Atwell moved away into the thinning fog.

The sun was a hazy disk, a little wind was rising; it would be a clear day. "Well," Charles said, "we might as well start walking as stand around."

They straggled after him, guns over their sagging shoulders. At the swift-running shallows of Laurel Ford, Charles, Reily, and Johnson crossed dry-shod, hopping from rock to rock. Leroy Green, off balance with a sack tied to his back like a game bag, slipped ankle deep into the cold water.

"He's gonna freeze to death before we get home." Mac Reily laughed as Leroy scrambled up the bank.

"Don't worry about him," Charles said. "He's too drunk to freeze."

Leroy Green said, "Maybe I oughta drown it and save all the carrying."

"Drown what?"

Leroy's thin ferret face grinned. "I kept one from up there. A real little one. The one Jimbo was holding when he got knifed."

"Jesus God Almighty." Charles sighed wearily. "I have got me one bunch of crazy coons."

Mac Reily shrugged. "It's dead anyway, most like."

Johnson nodded. "I ain't seen it move for a long while."

"What?" Charles said. "What the hell are you talking about?"

"One of them," Leroy said, "from the camp back there. There was two, boss. One with the knife run off when Mac started shooting. I grabbed this one and put it in a sack. They was so hard to catch, I figured I'd just keep one."

"One what?"

"A nigger kid, a real little one. I'll show you."

He unhooked the sack and reached in. Then yelled and stood, shaking his right hand. "Fucking bit me!"

Mac Reily roared with laughter, hunched over, slapping his knees. Leroy rushed at him, head down, sending him sprawling backward.

Charles grabbed Leroy, swung him around. "What the hell do you think you're doing?"

"Get out the way, white man."

Mac Reily lay on the ground, giggling drunk. "His pet play toy done bit him."

"Goddamn it, Mac, shut up"—Charles shoved a hand in Leroy's chest, pushing him back—"before I shoot one of you and it don't much matter to me which one."

A pause. A hiccough. Mac Reily said, "I done finished, boss. I'm on my way home."

Leroy rubbed his hand. "Drew blood."

"What did?"

"I told you, boss. I caught this little one." He picked up the sack and began twirling it around his head. "And I am plain finished with it."

Charles Tucker caught his arm. "You trying to kill it? Give it to me."

Leroy stopped swinging the sack. "I fetched it all the way down, carrying Jimbo too."

"I want it," Charles Tucker said. "Give it here."

Leroy stared at him, silent, weaving a little on his feet, sagging with tiredness, eyes so red they might have been bleeding, sweating sour alcohol into the cold air, the sickness of a mean hangover beginning in his stomach. "I caught it and it's mine."

"I'll give you five dollars for it," Charles said.

Leroy held out his hand for the money.

L A T E that morning—fog burned off, clear sky over-head—Charles drove to Sellers Crossing, to the garage his brother Samuel owned. It was empty, not a car, not a customer.

"Where's he at?" Charles shouted to Jaybird, the black boy who pumped gas.

Jaybird said, "Gone to eat."

Charles walked through the small office to the back storage room. The closet there was filled with odd bits of things: a shovel with a broken handle, a short length of towing chain, a Ford steering wheel, a few small cans of paint, and a stiffened brush. He dragged them out, clearing the floor, then got the sack from his truck. Carefully, warily, he loosened the fastenings, put it in the closet, and closed the door. There was no key, so he wedged a chair under the handle. Then he sat at Sam's desk, feet up, and waited.

"You look like shit." Sam hung his jacket on the wall rack. "And you got blood all over you."

"I been out hunting all night."

A pan of peanuts and crackers was parching on top the coal stove. Sam took a handful and looked around. "Where's the other chair?"

"Blocking the door," Charles said.

Sam chewed slowly, spitting peanut shells to the floor. "You want me to keep asking questions or you fixing to tell me?"

"Maybe you better come see."

Charles switched on the overhead light, moved the chair, opened the door.

Sam said, "At first I thought it was a groundhog."

"Looks kind of like it."

"It's all brown and black and the sack looks like fur and it's got those same shiny black eyes."

"It's a nigger kid, a real little one."

The child stared at them from the jumbled heap of sacking and ragged wool that circled it like ripples in a pool.

"It stinks like an animal, for sure."

"I bought it," Charles Tucker said. "So I guess it belongs to me. Only I don't know what to do with it."

"You think it's hungry?"

"I don't know. I guess so."

"We feed it then." Sam took the cat's bowl from the corner of the room, crumbled in two crackers from the pan on the stove, and added the last of the milk from a bottle on the windowsill. "Gone sour, but that don't matter none." He put it inside the closet. Charles closed the door and wedged the chair against it.

"Now what?" Sam said.

"I got to leave it here for a while." Charles scrubbed at the itching stubble of his beard. "I got to clean up and go to work. There's a big shipment of hams to go on the five o'clock train and I got to check the invoices. After that I go tell Mr. Wilson everything that happened."

Mr. Wilson, coughing lightly, delicately, stood by his study window. Behind him was the dark vastness of Aikens Grove Plantation, around him a kind of halo—silver hair, gray ascot, gray tweeds.

Charles Tucker sat in the straight-backed leather chair and waited.

"It is over then." Mr. Wilson's voice was husky and soft. "You do not think he will return?"

"He won't."

"Was he hit?"

"Maybe."

But that's not why he won't be back. He won't be back because we've won. We've taken the little one away from him. That's why he's gone.

"A boy, you said?"

"One of the men saw him close up. Yes, sir."

Mr. Wilson folded his handkerchief and repeated, "A boy."

"Yes, sir," Charles said. "There was just two of them. A boy and the young one we caught."

Mr. Wilson sat at his leather-topped desk, hands folded prayerfully, fingers touching closed eyes, as if his head had grown too heavy for his neck. "Homeless?"

"Yes, sir."

Mr. Wilson tapped his praying hands on his forehead. "The Lord seems to have given us this least of his flock, so I suppose we must take care of it. Boy or girl?"

"I don't know," Charles said. "It bites and I haven't had time to look."

Mr. Wilson coughed out his laugh. "Whatever it is, we must see that it goes on its way in life. Perhaps we could pay one of the local Negro families to raise it."

Charles shook his head. "None of them will take it. They say it's a devil child."

"Well, then, is there a county orphanage for Negroes?"

"No, sir."

Mr. Wilson stood up again, impatient. "I shall make a few telephone calls in the morning. There will be a place for it somewhere. Now, take it to a doctor immediately, it's bound to be infected. There must be a Negro doctor somewhere in the county. What do the Negroes do when they get sick?"

They mostly die, like all poor people, Charles answered silently. Aloud he said, "Yes, sir."

He left, walking carefully over polished floors, past furniture that gleamed red-brown with wax, past gold-framed portraits, and gold-framed mirrors, along halls where chandeliers tinkled slightly at his passing—where everything was hushed and muted.

Charles thought: I know how this looked to the nigger kid. A place with columns and steps and dozens of windows all shining fresh polished. When he finally sneaked a look inside and saw what I am seeing now, he hated it with a fury he never felt before in his life.

The houseman opened the door for him, and Charles stepped into the evening dark.

And went on thinking.

If times were different, or if things were different, I might just be out there with him. I might even be him.

That thought so frightened him that he broke into a sweat, drops drying in the cold, so that he shivered all over.

By eight that evening he was back in Sellers Crossing. All up and down the slopes of town the houses showed their lighted windows, and the streets were empty. Sam waited in the office doorway. "Come on in, baby brother."

The stove was out, the tin pie plate of peanuts empty.

"You smell something, baby brother?" Sam asked.

"Seems I do."

"Smells to me like your little pet shit all over the place."

"I'll clean up."

"I got this." Sam pointed to an amber-colored bottle of Clorox.

"Mr. Wilson says he'll find a place for the kid. He says he'll pay for a doctor."

Sam whistled. "You suppose he'd done that if it was some white cracker's whelp?"

"No." Charles took a swallow of whiskey from the bottle Sam offered him. The smell grew worse.

"Okay now," Sam said. "I know where the nigger doctor lives. I figure we take the kid there."

"He'll put it in the hospital, don't you think?"

"He'll sure as hell have to do something with it, baby brother. I ain't keeping it, and you ain't either."

Charles nodded. "Why'd I take it, you tell me that."

" 'Cause you are one sweet somebody?"

"Why didn't I just leave it?"

"Come on, bro." Sam lifted a wire dog cage to the table and handed Charles a piece of horse blanket. "Wrap the kid in that and put it in the cage."

They opened the closet, carefully.

The food was gone, the cat's bowl turned over and pushed against the far wall. A yellow scum of diarrhea covered the floor. Charles pushed his sleeve far up, above his elbow, before he reached for the bundle of brown and gray with the small black raisin eyes. It didn't move, didn't even blink. He picked it up by the back of the neck, like a kitten. Bits of things fell from it, knucklebones, a dried frog's leg, bone beads, a bright blue-jay feather. He put the child on the blanket, gathered the edges together, and lifted the entire bundle into the dog cage.

"Now," Sam said, "you clean up and then we go find us a doctor."

Gerttown, Niggertown most people called it, was a grid of unpaved streets on the steep slopes of the east side of town—small houses with fenced yards broom-swept to flat bare earth, small churches whose doors were flanked by young pine trees growing in old car tires. The window shades of all the houses were drawn tight, shut against the dark.

They found the house at a corner, under a streetlight. It was newly painted pale pink; there were a dozen geranium pots on the porch, pushed far back against the house for shelter against the cold. The fence had a sign: DR. WINSTON HILL.

Sam pounded on the front door, the sounds echoing like gunshots in the quiet neighborhood. "Hey, Doc!"

He opened the door, a short heavy man, light-skinned and balding, only a crinkly fringe of hair like a wreath around his ears. He wore a red sweater, its pocket ripped, and a white shirt. He'd taken off the detachable collar, leaving the button in place in the band. He'd been eating dinner; the smell of frying fat and onions swirled around him. He nodded to someone, a quick short bob of the head, and stepped out, closing the door.

"You the doctor?"

"I am the only Negro doctor in the county, yes. But I do not treat white people."

"It ain't white," Sam said, "and it ain't even ours. You just listen to what my brother's got to say."

When Charles finished, the doctor said, "I have no facilities to care for such a child."

Nearby, a rooster crowed half a call and was silent. Farther away a dog howled long thin strips of sound.

"I hate to hear a dog like that," Sam said, "makes my skin creep."

Charles said, "I told you we'd pay. You just have to clean it up and keep it until we find a permanent place."

"Today in the Negro wing of the hospital"—the doctor moved a step backward until he was leaning against his front door—"I treated four stab wounds, one of them the man who was with you last night, and two ice-pick wounds, both fatal. I delivered a dead child to a woman who had been in labor over twenty-four hours before her family called me. I amputated the lower arm of a careless sawmill worker. I set the broken leg of a drunken school janitor who fell from the second-story window he was repairing. I saw two new cases of tuberculosis, which I can do nothing for. I saw half a dozen children with scarlet fever, all from the

same house; they will probably die. Three cases of gangrene
in diabetics; they will certainly lose those limbs. I did a tra-
cheotomy on a child with diphtheria. I signed the death cer-
tificate of another child who died of complications of the
infantile paralysis she contracted last summer. I showed an
old man how to wear a truss. The living went home to their
families, excepting a very few. Those I had to admit to the
hospital, which is so crowded even the halls are filled. There
is no available bed, there is not even available floor space. I
will treat this child here, now, like any other patient. But it
must return home after."

"It don't have a home. We are looking," Charles repeated,
"but we just plain need a place right now."

The doctor shook his head. "I do not have the facilities,
you must understand that. If you have described it correctly,
the child is going to need a great deal of attention. Even if
I could find a bed, and I can't, the hospital does not have
the staff to deal with that kind of patient." A puff of wind
blew another round ball of warm onion-tinged air from his
body.

Sam said, "Keep it here."

The doctor's shoulders rose; the flesh of his neck covered
his shirt band.

"My family live here."

"That don't matter none." Sam settled himself on the
porch railing, a thin scarecrow outline against the pool of
light at the street corner. "This kid needs fixing"—his voice
grew very soft—"and we can pay you, which is a lot more
than most, I bet."

"I do not take patients into my home."

"Oh man, I am tired and I am hungry and my temper is
kind of short." Sam put one foot up on the railing. "We
don't want to be in Niggertown any more than you want us
here. We are asking you to do an act of charity, act of grace,

the preacher used to say back in the days when my daddy made me go to church. Treasure in heaven, that's what you get. Along with the pay. And Mr. Wilson ain't about to question your bill."

The doctor's hand reached for the doorknob and held it. Silent. Listening. Considering. Denying.

Sam said, "We are trying to be reasonable, man. We are just asking you to do what you went to school to learn to do."

The doctor's hand twisted the knob of the door; it made a small tinny rattle, but the door stayed closed.

Were his wife and children behind it? Charles wondered, all of them gathered closed up against the wall, listening.

"Doc," Sam said, still softly, still quietly, "you get called out at night, I bet. You feel safe riding around? You feel safe coming home?"

The doctor took his hand off the doorknob. "You are threatening me."

"Me?" Sam laughed, a happy little boy laugh. "I'm just saying that things do happen. At night. In the dark. There's one hell of a lotta dark in twenty-four hours. And you sure make one big fat target."

"I will not be threatened."

"Doc, I am only warning you against the dangers of the world. Which are manifold, the preacher used to say on Sunday."

"I know what you are doing."

"Come on, man," Sam said. "If there was another nigger doctor, we'd try him, but there ain't. You are all we got."

Sam stood up; the porch boards creaked under his weight. "Just think how happy that kid is gonna be. I reckon it's some time since it's seen the inside of a house."

The doctor said slowly, "I cannot do this." But the conviction had gone from his voice.

"Just give me a hand now"—Sam started down the steps—"and we'll have it in your office without no fuss at all."

The doctor followed him, unwillingly, as if he were pulled on a string.

Charles thought admiringly: Sam did it. I couldn't have, not any of it.

Sam was chuckling, deep rich sound. "You take good care of it, Doc. This here is a very valuable thing, it is worth five whole dollars."

Charles parked the truck at his kitchen door. It was near midnight. The house was dark and as silent as the fields surrounding it. Cora and the two boys had gone to bed hours ago. They'd be sleeping soundly, no longer worried about bricks crashing through windows.

He clamped both hands on the top of the steering wheel and rested his forehead on them. Skipping a night's sleep didn't use to bother me, he thought.

He straightened up, took a deep breath, shook himself all over like a wet dog, got out. But the one memory stayed with him: the child's eyes, empty eyes, like an animal's. Trapped. Resigned. Withdrawn. Indifferent.

What did I do, he thought, what did I do?

The night was cold and dry and perfect. The first winter night of the year.

And what about that other one, the one who'd got away, run off with pellets rattling down around him like steel rain. He couldn't be badly hurt, not with the heavy brush and the number-nine loads in the guns. He could just pop the pellets out with his fingers, if he was hit at all. He would have spent this day running and hiding and looking over his shoulder. And now it was a cold night to be without a shelter.

Charles shivered and pulled his jacket tighter. His face tingled with frost.

A boy, but what kind of boy. Alone, homeless and wandering, but carrying the child with him. Letting himself be burdened. Keeping it, protecting it, and, at the last, fighting for it.

Well, Charles Tucker thought, that boy wasn't burdened anymore. He was free. He could go anywhere his feet and his cleverness took him. Travelling light, with just himself to look out for.

Charles Tucker, hands jammed deep in his pockets, stood on the gravelled driveway outside his kitchen door and studied the stars overhead, red and blue and white, bright and dim, millions.

And couldn't stop thinking: Maybe the boy had loved that little one, whatever it was. So he'd be alone now and grieving.

But why should that bother me? There were as many poor as there were stars in the sky overhead.

Charles Tucker felt strange and excited. Afraid, as if something terrible had happened. Confused, as if he were lost.

But nothing had happened. And this was where he belonged. This was his house; his wife and his children were asleep inside, all covered against the dark.

But still, he was missing something. As if somebody inside his head was talking to him—urgently, intensely—in a language he didn't understand.

He stood outside his house, in the cold night, and listened. To the sounds of the world around him: frost-burned grasses rustling, winter-stripped trees settling their roots deeper into the soil, stiffening their hold against the cold. To the sounds of the earth whirling through space. To the stars that rattled like ice as they paraded across the sky.

THE KINDNESS OF
STRANGERS

RITA LANDRY was cleaning the entrance hall at the Sister Servants of Mary Home for Children. She began, as she always did, with the statue of the Blessed Virgin on its pedestal in the middle of the floor: a careful dusting, then a slow soap-and-water wash.

She had been told to sing the Credo or recite the Hail Mary while she did this—that it would be pleasing to the Virgin—but she hadn't yet memorized the Latin words, and this morning she couldn't seem to concentrate on the prayer. Her mind kept skipping from thing to thing: the sound of traffic in the street outside, a beam of light filled with floating swirling dust motes, thumps of plumbing in the walls, the tread of rubber-heeled shoes overhead.

She was sixteen, not yet a novice, and happy in convent

life: the quiet orderliness, the way each day was planned precisely, each hour filled with duties. She liked the way nuns' habits rustled, the way linen headdresses smelled of sun and fresh air and blueing, the way shiny starched white bands circled black faces, so that they seemed to float in air.

At times, though, content as she was, she marvelled at the events that had brought her here. She was from the country, from the Little Mirassou River country, cane and cotton and sweet potato fields, wide as an eye could reach. Until six months ago she'd never thought about becoming a nun, never once. Her mama decided for her.

"Put you on a clean dress, you," her mama said one afternoon, a hot summer afternoon with the cicadas calling a dry-bones song from all the chinaberry trees. "You and me, we go to have a talk with the priest. It is time we think about the future. You are going to be a nun."

Rita Landry jumped with surprise. She had thought, when she thought at all about her future, that she would go on day after day, living in the house where she'd been born, until she found a man.

That was the way it had been with her two older sisters. Louise married Al Abadie, who was a good man and worked in the rice mill in Menton; they lived in a nice house with his married sister and her children. Ursula, her other sister, married Jack Bourgeois; a year later she left him and took the train to Houston. She sent a postcard saying that she'd found work in a hospital and was living with a doctor's family, taking care of their children in the evenings. A few months later another card said she'd married a man named Luis Fernandez and they were moving to California. That was the last they heard from her.

But there is no man courting me, Rita Landry thought, though I am nearly sixteen years old. No one waves to me from a fishing skiff on the river, no one passes on the road and stops to lean against the fence and talk while I feed the chickens or hang out the washing. Perhaps there will never be such a one.

"We go now," her mama said.

They walked through the vegetable garden and across the road, dust ankle deep. Her mother did not hurry; her heels plopped into the dirt with steady thumping thuds. From the porch her father, tobacco plug in his cheek like a swollen tooth, watched them go. Watched them all the way down the road, and never turned his head. He could do that, rotate his eyes, like a horse almost. Once he shot a yellow stream of tobacco juice through the broken place in the porch rail.

Nothing disturbed the old man her father. A year ago, when the last baby was born, he sat on the porch and rocked while Rita tended her mama. The baby was healthy and strong, but it was a long while before her mother was able to work. She'd labored so long and bled so much the mattress soaked through to drip on the floor.

After that Rita Landry hated her father, hated him so much that her hands shook when she brought him his dinner plate. Her mother didn't seem to mind, or expect anything different. After all, Landry was already old when they married. She was his third wife and her children his third family. He spent all his days on the porch, rocking. Every month he walked down the road to the post office in Vauchon's store to pick up his pension check.

Her mother muttered to herself as they walked. Past the church to the rectory. Up the steps and through the kitchen to the parlor where Father Gautreaux waited for his supper. The radio was playing, its cord plugged into the overhead light fixture.

Her mama stood there, big and tall and heavy, hands on hips, bare legs planted on the floorboards, thick yellow nails on wide bare black feet. "We come here," she said, "account of my child. She wishes to become a nun."

Slowly, reluctantly, the priest switched off his radio. Outside, the cicadas were still sawing out their song. A cat was calling softly; her kittens must be somewhere close.

The priest began talking to her mother. His soft monotonous voice was as dry as the cicadas' song.

Father Gautreaux was a good man; some people even said he was a saint. Every Christmas, no matter what the weather, hundreds came to the church to receive his blessing. Exactly at noon, when the oldest of the altar boys rang the bell—small flat sounds like hammers on a tin roof—the crowd stopped its rustling and shoving, grew silent and fell back, opening a path. The bell stopped, the church doors opened, and the priest walked slowly through to a shell mound at the edge of the river. (People said it was an Indian holy mound.) Stiffly, helped by two altar boys, he climbed to the top. He paused for a count of fifteen—the crowd counted with nodding heads—before he lifted the hyssop and hurled holy water high in the air: to the north first, then the south, then the east, and finally the west. He did this three times, sending up showers and sprays for the winds to carry—to keep away sickness and death and bad luck, to defend fields and boats against wind and storm, to turn aside floods, to restrain rivers in their banks, to give fishermen good catches, and farmers good crops.

The priest looked very small and very old, white hair like mold on his head. The sunlight gave his black skin a dry powdery look, as if he were covered with dust.

One year the sky was dark and pocked with lightning, and the rain fell in heavy sheets, straight down. The little priest paused at the door. "Ahhhh," he said, very softly, like a breath slipping away. "Ça grimaze. It drizzles." And then his small feet began their trip through the mud to the white shell mound by the river. The altar boys hunched against the rain and flinched against the lightning, but Father Gautreaux seemed not to notice. People said later that the real miracle was that the wind did not blow him away.

"Your daughter wants to be a nun?" The little priest sounded surprised.

"I have said so."

"She has a vocation?"

"I have said so."

He nodded, rubbing his hand over the top of his head. He would look into it, he said, blinking rapidly. Yes. Someone would know. He would ask.

"Then I go to fix your supper," her mama said. "Right now. I hope you have a good appetite."

Because the old man her husband's pension wasn't much to live on—not with the bootlegger coming every week, and the old man sending down to the store for a Nehi almost every day—Mrs. Landry worked as housekeeper for Father Gautreaux. She cooked his dinner and cleaned the house— there were four rooms—and she swept out the church and put flowers on the altar when she thought about it. She didn't get paid much, but she did get food. Whatever the priest ate, she and her family ate too. And Father Gautreaux was good at finding food, begging or threatening, one way or the other.

Whenever he went into Vauchon's grocery, he reminded everybody there that he was a man like them with a stomach to feed. Every few months, regular as clockwork, he went to Buster Tebo's farm, always being careful to arrive when Mrs. Tebo was alone. After an hour spent praying with her—she was an invalid who no longer came to Mass—he gave her three or four holy cards and she gave him a bushel basket of food. The little priest smiled happily as he staggered under the weight of her gift. Despite her wheelchair, she was a fine housekeeper; the vegetables she put up were as good as fresh, her hens the busiest layers in the parish, her pigs the fattest and the tastiest. Edna Tebo smiled too, as he blessed the house and fields with a wide cross, then cranked up the old Ford and drove off, backfires shaking the pigeons from their perches under the eaves.

It was his way. The priest gathered food wherever he went. At Sunday Mass (crowded whenever a storm or a drought or a freeze threatened) he ended his sermon by reminding everyone that the rectory's pantry was empty. When people came to confession, which they didn't do very much, he always added food to the prayers of their penances. When Alcide Johnson cut on his girlfriend (so bad that the sheriff from Marysville came to investigate, only she wouldn't say anything), he had to bring a full bucket of shrimp or crabs to the rectory every week. And when Theresa Petrie went to the old woman in Marshaltown for an abortion, then had a conscience and confessed to the priest, she had to bring half a dozen eggs every week for a year.

One way or the other, food came to the priest's kitchen: sausage and ham and quail and dove, fish and shellfish, preserves and *cuite* and cane syrup, tomatoes and corn and cabbage, turnips and collards and okra for gumbo.

All sorts of food, Rita Landry remembered, drying the plaster crown of the Virgin in the front hall of the Sister Servants of Mary Home for Children. *All kinds of food.*

The little old priest, so busy from early Mass until evening, took no notice of his household and his kitchen and so never knew that Mrs. Landry took most of his food, for appearance' sake stuffing it under her clothes or hiding it in a basket of dirty laundry.

She carried off all manner of things, once even a small sack of oysters. Rita remembered her father opening them at the kitchen table, slurping them from the shells so that their juice ran down his chin and seeped across the table and dripped to the floor, oyster liquid forming puddles in the worn spots of the linoleum. That was the night, her mother told her, the old man got his last child on her.

So the busy priest stayed thin, and the Landry family managed to live. Mrs. Landry even managed to grow fat.

"We are agreed then, Mrs. Landry," the old priest said. "If your daughter has a vocation she must follow it." He switched on the radio again, and the hollow sound of a saxophone drifted across the room. He picked up his newspaper and settled himself more comfortably in his chair. And, yes, he said, he was feeling especially hungry. The eggs had been so very good yesterday. Would she fix them again tonight?

"No eggs," Mrs. Landry said.

"There were six eggs yesterday, Mrs. Landry," the priest said firmly, putting on his reading glasses. "I ate two. Which leaves four for supper tonight."

Rita held her breath. She and her mother had eaten the eggs that very morning, scrambled with olive oil and garlic—Rita could still taste the garlic on her breath.

"You see the eggs, yes," her mother said, "but you don't see inside. No yolk, none, and the chicks ready to crack the shells. All feathers and eyes and no nourishment. I put them out for your cat."

The priest sighed, and picked up his paper.

"The Bordelon boy brought you a quail, which is nice

and fat, and some cabbage from his mother's garden. It is a very small cabbage, nothing to look at, but it will make a good supper for one person."

Rita shivered with guilt. There were five fat quail—they were wrapped in newspaper in the kitchen right now. And the cabbage was very large.

They would have quail and cabbage for supper, she thought, and her mother would complain if her teeth gritted on any bits of bird shot. The old man her father and her baby sister would have quail gravy on their cabbage and some of the meat cut up specially for them.

Anyway the priest didn't really need all that much food, Rita thought. And then she almost laughed out loud because quite suddenly she knew what her mother was thinking. Her mother was wondering if there wasn't a way to give the priest only half a quail.

"Very well then, quail"—the priest turned up the radio—"if that is what you have, Mrs. Landry. And how is the other child, that last one?"

"She grows," her mother said, and turned slowly, her body filling the narrow doorway.

Rita sat on the back steps and played with the cat who had brought her kitten out of hiding. After a while her mother called to her, "Spread the cloth, *chère*. I am ready with the food."

Rita wiped her hands clean on the kitchen towel and got the tablecloth from the little dresser under the window. She gave it a snap to shake out the crumbs that had dried on it since yesterday and carried it into the living room. The priest lifted his paper with one hand, his radio with the other, and she spread the cloth on the table. He put down the radio and leaned back in his chair, reading, while she brought knife and fork and glass and napkin.

Her mother set down the filled plate, and the priest

folded away the newspaper, his nose crinkling at the smell of food. Rita got the loaf of bread and the board and bread knife and put them at his left hand. Her mother got out the bottle of wine and put it next to the bread. The priest poured a glass, drank it, then poured a second.

Her mother never took any wine, Rita noticed. Never. On the walk home, leaving the priest to wash his own dishes, she said, "Mama, you never take any wine."

"A man needs his wine," Mrs. Landry said, "even if he is a priest."

Rita Landry remembered that walk home: the soft dark, the train blowing its whistle as it passed the intersection at Belleterre, the faintly sour odor of their house, which came partly from her father and partly from her baby sister and partly from the wallpaper paste.

She could think of such things now without tears stinging her eyes like pepper. She knew she could not go back, that her mother had the old man her father to take care of, and the baby too, that there was no place for her, not anymore. But it didn't matter. She was no longer homesick. She was content. She might even have been happy.

So, on that Wednesday morning Rita Landry from Little Mirassou River, neatly dressed in brown with a white scarf covering her hair, finished cleaning the statue of the Queen of Heaven and began polishing the floor, carefully, on hands and knees. When the bell rang for morning collation, she stood up, stretched, rubbed her back and her knees. She took off her apron and rolled down her sleeves. She was hungry for milky coffee, sweet and hot, and yesterday's bread to dip in it.

"Very good work, child." Sister Agnes, hands properly tucked in her sleeves, came to the door of her office. It was a pleasant room, just off the entrance hall, with a bright patterned rug, two big chairs, and a window that looked out on a magnolia tree where squirrels played and chattered. The only telephone in the building was on the wide dark desk, and Sister Agnes was the only one to use it. She kept all records and account books and thumped her ledgers angrily when the totals did not tally. She was tall and thin, and her skin was a very light yellow, as if she had jaundice. She had been raised in a convent in Paris, people said.

Rita's stomach growled. Sister Agnes put her arm around her shoulders. "We are both hungry," she said.

That afternoon, as Rita Landry was gathering up her cloths and buckets, the front doorbell rang. She stopped, surprised and curious. No one ever used that entrance.

Sister Agnes herself opened the door to a patch of dazzling daylight, a rush of street sounds. Sister Agnes stood aside. Two men walked in, white men.

Rita Landry had never seen a white person enter the building, though she'd heard that once a year the bishop came and the children sang a song for him.

"Good day," one of the men said pleasantly. He was short and square; his hair, when he took off his wide-brimmed hat, was thin and blond.

"You are Mr. Tucker?" Sister Agnes's rosary clicked softly, bead against bead.

"We are both Mr. Tucker." The second man, who was tall and thin, carried something wrapped in a blanket. He put it on the floor; it moved slightly and was still. "There it is, Sister. You know all about it. Leastways you know all we know about it." He bent, took the end of the blanket, and jerked.

A small black child rolled out. A narrow face, small shiny eyes like a mouse's, a bald head. It wore a pair of overalls

and a green sweater, both far too large. A kind of rope harness went around its chest.

The tall man picked up the leash attached to the harness.
"You might best hang on to this," he said with a wide easy
grin. "She's mighty quick and she has led us on some wild
chases."

The shorter man said, "Her hair's shaved account of
bugs."

Sister Agnes nodded. "I understand."

"She's clean now though and she's been dosed for worms.
The doctor says she's healthy enough, though he don't exactly know how that could be possible."

"I have been told her story." The words hung in the air,
quiet, precise. "It is unusual for white people to concern
themselves with a colored child."

"Well, we didn't exactly look for her, but we got her anyway. My boss says that makes her an obligation."

"She is fortunate in her friends." An edge to the quiet
voice. "We will do what we can, but I would not expect too
much."

"Good enough for us." The tall man picked up the blanket, dropped it over the child, then picked her up. "Like
that, see. Sometimes she gets a notion to bite." He pushed
the bundle into Sister Agnes's starched wimple.

She tucked it firmly under one arm.

"Good day to you then, Sister." Their shoes clacked across
the polished boards, steel heel caps leaving tiny marks in
the fresh wax. They opened the door crisply, closed it firmly,
not quite slamming it, and clattered down the steps. A
murmur of voices, a short quick laugh, a backfire as their
car started.

"Rita, my dear," Sister Agnes said, "a bird could build a
nest in your mouth, it is so wide open. Now, take this poor
child for me."

Rita did as she was told and felt, within the blanket, something hard, a bunch of bones. "Is it dead?"

"You saw it move a minute ago. Being wrapped in a blanket won't hurt it." Sister Agnes wiped her hands down the sides of her habit, then shook them as if they'd been wet. "Since you are here, you can help me. Come along now."

Up stairs. Down corridors. Past the infirmary—six beds on one wall, empty now, two washbasins on the other. Through a small door. Along a short narrow hall. Past a storeroom lined with cluttered shelves: folded sheets, piled and toppling to one side; a roll of dark blue paper in a box marked STERILE COTTON; bedpans; scissors; five large empty glass bottles stamped HORLICKS MALTED MILK.

Sister Agnes unlocked a door at the far end of the hall. "This was once the contagion ward. Now we find it much easier to tend all sick children in the infirmary."

The room was clean and smelled of carbolic soap. Its long window, covered with heavy wire mesh, looked out on an iron fire escape. On the floor was a pallet, a folded blanket, sheet, and pillow. In a corner was a bedpan. Nothing else. No furniture, only the cracked black linoleum on the floor.

"Set her down now."

Rita put the bundle on the floor. It did not move.

"We'll leave her for a while." Sister Agnes locked the door behind them. "At suppertime, bring her food. Talk to her." Sister Agnes's rubber heels thudded, her rosary clacked. "The child seems to have no family. She has been living in the wild, like an animal." She hesitated and looked down the wide hall toward the statue of the Virgin. "But she has a soul, just as you and I do. It will be our task to return her to God. Now come to my office. I must speak to Sister Bernadette."

Sister Bernadette was tall, very black, with a thin goatee of white hairs that shivered in the light. She was in charge of the youngest girls' dormitory.

"I know that you are very busy," Sister Agnes said to her. "I know too that this new child is going to require a great deal of attention. Perhaps we should put her in Rita's charge?"

Sister Bernadette nodded. She spoke only when it was absolutely necessary.

"Rita is a capable girl. She will be able to manage perfectly well with only a little guidance from you."

Sister Bernadette nodded again.

Sister Agnes searched through the books on her desk, selected a small flat black ledger. "I must add the poor little one to our roster." She unscrewed the top of her pen, shook it, tested the nib against her black skirt. "What shall we call her, since she has no name?"

Sister Bernadette shrugged and stared out the window in silence.

"Have you a suggestion, Rita?"

Remembering the statue with the crown of stars, she said, "Mary."

"Yes." Sister Agnes wrote; the pen stuck and spattered. She wiped it on her skirt again. "And her last name will be Woods. The place where she was found. Mary Woods."

After supper, when the older girls had cleared the refectory tables and grouped the younger ones into study groups, when the room filled with the sound of sniffling and coughing, of scratching pencils and weary sighs, Sister Bernadette handed Rita a tin cup of milk and a mayonnaise sandwich wrapped in a scrap of butcher paper. "We will visit Mary Woods."

A small group of children began chanting their addition tables. "Too loud," Sister Bernadette said sharply.

The children stopped, held their breaths, and began again in a whisper.

As Rita and Sister Bernadette left the refectory, the voices increased rapidly until the chant was as loud as ever. Sister Bernadette gave a small smile, showing the tips of her yellow teeth. "I have no time for them now."

Again along empty corridors, through the infirmary. "Now"—Sister Bernadette lifted the open padlock from the hasp of the door—"we will see if our new Mary Woods is hungry."

The dim light from the hall, falling through the transom, showed them the child sitting on the folded blanket in the center of the room.

"Hello, Mary," Sister Bernadette said. "We have come to see you. Rita, switch on the overhead light."

A small face caught in the sudden glare of a bare bulb, a small, very black face. Eyes startled, wide open, luminous, with a curious bloom on them, like a ripe plum. "You are hungry," Sister Bernadette said, "aren't you, Mary?"

The eyes did not blink. Metallic eyes with a frost on them, like a knife blade left out in the cold.

"The good Lord has rescued you and given you to us."

On the shaved head new hair had begun to grow. It wrapped the small skull tightly and transparently, like a veil. Under it a network of veins showed clearly. One, just over the left ear, was throbbing steadily.

"Rita, stand by the door and keep it closed," Sister Bernadette said. "Now, Mary, here is some milk for you."

Cup in outstretched hand, she stepped slowly across the small room. With a flash and a rush of air, the child dodged past to throw herself against the door. The small body, like a tangle of wire under its clothes, thudded against Rita's legs. There was a sharp pain above her knee.

Sister Bernadette repeated calmly, "Hold the door, Rita." She picked up the child, held it squirming in the air, and slapped it twice.

"Bad," Sister Bernadette said loudly. "Bad. No. Wicked." She released her hold. The child dropped limply to the floor.

Sister Bernadette put the sandwich next to the cup of milk on the windowsill. "Rita, we must get you a new rosary."

Rita looked down. The loop of brown wooden beads which she wore, nun-like, from her belt was broken. She had not noticed.

"When she bit you," Sister Bernadette said quietly, "the rosary got in her teeth."

Rita lifted her skirts for a quick look. No blood, no broken skin.

"A bruise," Sister Bernadette said briskly, "nothing more. Come now, the child is wet. We'll take the clothes, you can wash them in the morning."

The child's eyes were closed and her head sagged on her neck. They left her naked on the pallet of blanket and sheet.

The following morning Rita went alone, carrying a cup of milk and a slice of bread with syrup. She opened the door carefully, slipped inside. Mary Woods sat on her pallet, wrapped in the blanket. She seemed to be shivering, though the room was very warm. Rita put the cup of milk and the slice of bread on the floor between them. The child's black eyes, which had lost their metallic glitter, followed her. Neither face nor body moved.

Rita sat down, leaning against the door. The room stank: there was a puddle of urine and feces in the corner. "Mary Woods, I am supposed to take care of you, but I can't even clean up that mess, because you'll run away if I leave the door."

The child waited, eyes fixed on her face. In the silence, Rita could hear pipes rattling and creaking far off in the walls. "You hear that? They have started work in the laundry. That's where I would be if I wasn't up here talking to you. I like working in the laundry."

The smell of soap so sharp it prickled your nose. The sweet smell of boiled starch and blueing. The clouds of steam that obscured everything like a warm fog. The sweat that poured off your face and ran down your body under your clothes and left you feeling washed and clean yourself.

"I like working in the laundry," Rita repeated. "And I don't like sitting here with you in a room full of shit." She crossed herself hastily, resolving to confess to the sin of bad language. And maybe the sin of unkindness too—but she hadn't been unkind, she thought, she'd only said the truth.

"Mary Woods," she said, "that is your breakfast, and you'd better eat it because there ain't going to be anything else until noontime."

The eyes continued to stare, unblinking.

"Maybe you don't like it here, but you are going to have to get used to it."

A faint movement as a hand drew the blanket tighter.

"Maybe you understand what I say and maybe you don't, but you can learn."

Rita sat in silence for a few minutes, watching the morning sky through the mesh of the window. Nothing moved out there, not even a bird or a cloud. "I have things to do now," she said finally.

At noon Sister Bernadette came with her. "This room stinks."

"I couldn't leave the door to clean it, Sister."

"I will put on a bolt, one too high for her to reach."

"Yes, Sister," Rita said.

And thought: I have seen this before. This room. The food waiting on the floor. The locked door and mesh over the window like bars. She is an animal in a cage. Like at the circus in Stevensport, in the Little Mirassou River country.

It was the week her mother won the numbers at Al Vauchon's grocery store. She shrieked and cried real tears of joy while Al counted the money into her hand. She forgot about everything, her own housework, the little priest's supper. She and her family—her daughters and the old man her husband—all crowded into the back of the grocery truck and went to the Circus Fair at Stevensport.

It was late summer. The cotton was making, fields still and white under motionless air. The fairgrounds were right on the river, their treeless expanse crowded with parked cars and wagons and booths and tents and a slow-turning Ferris wheel shimmering in the heat. Taking her mother's umbrella, Rita climbed the river levee to sit cross-legged in the thick clover grass on the top. She opened the umbrella and settled herself comfortably in the small round shade. She was dizzy with excitement, as if she balanced on an acrobat's high wire. On one side were crowds and clusters of people and the wheezing whistling panting tunes of a calliope; on the other, a batture of bright green willows and a wide fast-moving river, its surface wrinkled by currents and eddies. There was always a little breeze on the river, moving like a slow-waving flag above the surface of the water, carrying smells of mud and damp and sweet decay. People said the river was warm even in winter, because of all the decaying things in it, like a manure pile.

Jack Bourgeois was courting her sister Ursula, buying her Nehis and daring her to come with him on the Ferris wheel. She wouldn't go on any ride, not even the flying horses, but she stuck the Nehi caps to the pocket of her white blouse, one orange, one cherry.

Rita thought, I wish I had somebody to buy me drinks, I wish.

In the shade of a truck her mother fanned herself with the edge of her skirt and waved to Rita. "*Chère*, what do you do?" her mother shouted and sighed and coughed all at once. "I see you up there, like a little scarecrow, arms stuck out, turning in the breeze. You come down here to me." Her mother held out a palm of coins. "I am too old and too fat to go pirooting with the young people. This is your share, *bébé*. When it is gone, then we must go back home."

The coins grew hot inside Rita's clenched fist, grew wet from the sweat that ran down her arm. She bought an ice-cream cone and ate it quickly, from both ends at once, so that not a single drop was lost. She watched the bumper cars and saw that there was a couple in each one, boy's arm wrapped tightly around girl's waist. For a moment she thought of taking a car by herself, but the shrieking laughter of the pairs sounded threatening, and she slipped out of the waiting line. She paused at the cotton-candy booth, but her mouth was still sweet from the ice cream. She went into the circus, a tight circle of booths and wagons and tents. Her hand opened almost by itself to give up a coin to enter. The Bearded Lady, Atlas flexing his muscles, Dog Boy. And the animals. They were grouped together, sheltered from the sun by a canvas tent. There was a small elephant, leg shackled to a post, its trainer dozing in a chair alongside. Slowly, ponderously, noisily, the elephant sucked from his water bucket, raised his trunk and sprayed the crowd. Screeching and giggling they ran backward, stopped, shouted for the animal to do it again.

Rita wiped the spray from her arm. Now the elephant

squirted water on its own back; the trainer sprawled farther back in his chair and slept more soundly. The crowd grew bored and drifted off.

Rita smelled the cats even before she saw them. Three large red-and-gold cages held unmoving lumps of spots and stripes. Electric fans blew into each cage, and a man in a dark blue uniform sloshed buckets of water across each floor. The animals did not move as the water flowed around them. The pads of their feet, stretched out toward her, were big as platters.

Her second-to-last coin went for admission to the Hall of Wonders and Horrors. (The last coin, she decided, would go for an orange Nehi, so she would have a bottle cap to fasten to her blouse.) Inside this tent, the crowd thinned, people no longer pushed at her elbows, and she could move more slowly. It was hot, stinging with dust, stifling, and dark. The walls were lined floor to ceiling with black cloth. The only lights were directly over the animal cages.

A two-headed calf.

"Uugh," a woman whispered. Her man said, "It's nothing but a trick, that's all it is."

A lizard the size of a hound, its skin a shiny sparkling gold in the light.

"I bet it ain't alive," the woman said.

The lizard blinked one eye. "You lose, *tootoot*," her man laughed.

A baby in a bottle.

"A monkey," the man said knowingly.

A tank with six or eight two-headed slider turtles. Another tank with an alligator that was almost white. The largest rabbit Rita had ever seen, with floppy ears and fur that was pale pink. A snake, thick around as both her arms together, and curled into loose coils like a carelessly thrown rope.

Behind her, the couple grew silent. All Rita heard was the woman's short panting breath.

A bobcat with high towering plumes on his ear tips. A two-legged dog, forequarters resting on a small wheeled platform. A hairless cat.

The animals looked straight ahead, all staring intently at some far-off point.

They see something, Rita thought. That is for sure. And what is it that is hidden from me.

She came to the last cage. PIGMY TIGER, the sign said. She saw stripes of orange and gray. Bright orange, glowing like a fire coal. She felt a surge of disappointment. The pigmy tiger was a tomcat, an unusually large one, fur dyed orange. Nothing more. An old cat, stinking of urine and musk. She sneezed sharply, once, twice, knife slash in her nose. Stirred by the sound, the cat turned to her. Looked at her. Not past her to a distant point like the others. Not through her to an inner vision. But at her. Seeing her.

On the wide head, the stripes—so crudely brightly dyed—radiated from the slanted eyes, sun rays, power rays. Once Rita had seen a picture of a saint with such an exploding halo.

The flaming halo reversed, pointing inward, to the eyes.

Eyes round and shiny as the glass balls people put on their lawns for decoration. Eyes protruding, lidless, wakeful, unmoving, fixed on her. The pupils widened, opened like doors. Rita looked into them. And it wasn't black, it wasn't dark, it wasn't empty. It was the color of nothing and of something. It was older than time, older than rocks. The knowledge of nothing. Complete, enfolding, enveloping, swallowing. Old, beyond decay. Past hope, and without fear. Rita looked into the beginning of the world, before the universe started spinning.

She bent forward, to see more.

A hand jiggled her arm, impatiently. "I want to see," a girl's voice said, "if it's something special."

The pupils contracted in a flash, and became again only slits in the skull of an old dying tomcat, not windows on an empty universe in a time before the world was made.

That was the fair in Stevensport on the Little Mirassou River.

To the small black child wrapped tightly in the cotton blanket, Rita said: "I have seen eyes just like yours before this day. An old tomcat was wearing them, and he was in a cage too."

Rita Landry brought food twice more that day, and each time the child was huddled on the pallet, blanket wrapped.

The next day, Rita noticed that a spot on the window had been rubbed clean, a very small spot between the links of protective mesh.

On the morning of the third day Sister Bernadette again came with her.

"She is like this every morning?" Sister Bernadette pointed to the huddled figure, to the puddle of feces and urine on the linoleum.

"Yes, ma'am. I clean it up."

"This time, pick it up with your cloth and put it in the bedpan," Sister Bernadette said. "Do it very slowly and let her see."

They dressed her in clean clothes. She was limp in their hands, unresisting.

"She needs fresh air." Sister Bernadette fitted the harness, the one she had worn when she arrived, around her shoulders. "I am far too old to chase after her." She picked up the child. "When you've cleaned here, Rita, join us. We will be in the play yard."

. . .

The smallest children, the ones too young for school, were gathered at the swings in the far corner of the fenced yard; their voices jabbered like squirrels. Sister Bernadette sat on a shady bench teaching Mary Woods to stand quietly upright. Over and over again she put the child on its feet; over and over again it squirmed and pulled frantically, throwing itself to the ground, struggling, thrashing, kicking up puffs of dust. Each time, methodically, Sister Bernadette put the child across her lap, spanked her. And began again.

Such a long time, Rita thought, her arm must be getting tired.

Finally the child stood, shoulders hunched, cowering but upright, on her own feet. She had not cried, not once, nor made a single sound.

"Very good." Sister Bernadette handed the leash to Rita. "Take her to play there, in the sun. She looks pale and peckish to me."

How, Rita wondered, could you tell with a skin so black.

Sister Bernadette shook out her skirt, settled her wimple. "I leave her to you."

Rita, who never asked questions, said, "What do I do with her?" And clapped her hand to her mouth in surprise at her words.

"During the day keep her out here. See that she learns to walk holding your hand. Feed her in her room, see that she takes a nap like the other children. In the evening take her for walks up and down the halls, let her look into everything, let her see everything."

"Yes, Sister." Rita took a firm hold of the small arm.

Sister Bernadette touched Rita's cheek. Her hand was dry and hard and lumpy as a piece of kindling wood. "She will bring grace to you."

The midday bell rang. The children raced inside, passing close by them. Mary Woods closed her eyes and shivered.

In the months that followed, Rita spent every day with the tiny black child who never spoke, never made a sound, never smiled or scowled, only stared with eyes that gleamed with strangeness: knowledge, or power from some secret of her own.

One Sunday in April, right after Mass, three yellow school buses stopped at the side gate, and all the children, two by two, marched into them. They were going to a day-long picnic at Lincoln Park. Rita Landry and Mary Woods stood in the empty play yard and watched.

Rita said, "I heard a lot about Lincoln Park." Big oak trees and green smooth grass. Flower beds blooming all different colors. Fountains with water shooting high in the air. Benches where you could sit and look out over a lake, which was bright blue and so wide that you couldn't see to the other side.

"Except for you," Rita said to the child, and the black eyes swung to focus on her, "I'd be on that bus, going."

The eyes blinked once, then twice.

"Only God himself knows whether you understand a word I'm saying."

Now there was something else for her next confession: she had taken the Lord's name in vain. She hadn't meant to; it had just slipped out.

"Well," she said, "we got the whole yard to ourself, so let's try the little swings."

Mary Woods studied the swing carefully, tracing the wood slats with her finger, as if she were memorizing them. Her legs were too short to reach the ground, so she rocked her body back and forth to start. She began humming, a soft low-pitched monotone.

At noon she was still swinging. Rita pried loose the small black fingers. "Look now," she said, "we are going to get our sandwiches and eat them out here on the steps. You know what I'm telling you?"

No answer, but the small head tipped slightly to one side, for all the world like a bird.

They ate their bologna sandwiches sitting side by side, watching the empty swings move gently in the light breeze.

Mary Woods was hungry. She ate so fast that bits of the crusty bread flew out of her mouth, and the yellow mustard dripped down her chin. Rita took the newspaper that held their sandwiches, crumbled it into a ball, and wiped her face. "Let's us go in now."

The child stiffened and very slowly lifted her free arm— Rita held the other tightly—pointing to the swings.

"No." Rita said. "All little children take a nap after lunch. And you are still a little child, even though we don't exactly know how old you are. And I am pretty sure you are older than your size."

Free of Mary Woods, Rita hurried to midday meditation.

Sister Bernadette was just entering the chapel, the hem of her brown skirt twitching through the door. Rita slipped in behind her and took a seat in the last pew, behind the two novices.

She loved this time of silence, of physical rest and mental communion, though she was not sure what thoughts she should be thinking. She had a book—*On Meditation*—and she'd tried to read it, but the print was small and gave her a headache.

She studied the faces of the nuns in their side stalls, un-moving, heads bowed slightly. In the dark-wood-dimmed, stained-glass-filtered light, Sister Immaculata was no longer the fat woman, laughing and easygoing, who ran the laun-dry and the boys' dormitory. Her face was stretched taut, tense as a runner's just before the start of a race. Sister Agnes, eyes open, half smiling, cheeks flushing under their light skin, seemed years younger. Sister Bernadette's large busy hands rested one on each knee, palms up, like boats stranded by the tide; the sparse wreath of white hair around her chin shivered as she clenched and unclenched her jaw.

Rita settled herself, closed her eyes. Because the windows were never opened, the chapel held its past in layers of scents. Sunday High Masses had left smoky incense like guttering sweet candles. From the black linoleum underfoot, a dry vinegar smell. From the wooden pews, soft waxy furniture polish. From the dust motes spinning across a shaft of dim light, a tingle of sharp mold. From the folds of woolen skirts, a pepper smell of bodies.

Except for an occasional rustle of starched wimple, a small smothered cough, a creak from the organ pipes, a scratching from the mice behind the walls, thick quiet filled the room like water. The women hung suspended, fish in a tank.

A small tinkling bell signalled the end. They filed out slowly, sleepwalkers dreaming their own private dreams from that silent private time. They paused in the hall outside the chapel, struggling back to the day and its work.

Rita returned to Mary Woods.

In the isolated room, in the very same spot against the right-hand wall, there was a pile of feces in a puddle of urine. Mary Woods waited on her pallet.

Rita stamped her foot with anger. "Mother of God, did you never live in a house."

The bright eyes stared intently. Then, quick as a shadow, Mary Woods raced across the floor. In a single movement she picked up the feces in both hands and carried them to the bedpan.

Rita Landry looked at the brown trail of drops, looked at

the filthy stained hands, hanging limply down. And she began to laugh, a noisy sound that bounced from bare floor to bare wall like a rubber ball.

Mary Woods crouched on her haunches and watched.

Rita grew quiet, sighed, looked down the length of her skirt to her black shoe tips, looked up to the ceiling where a single bulb shivered in invisible air currents, looked to one side where the dirty mesh-covered window had one small rubbed peephole. "It was bad enough to begin with," she said, "but now it stinks of caca enough to offend any saint's nose." She turned to Mary Woods. "I am going to clean this for the last time. If you mess again, I am going to make you eat it."

She went for bucket and cloth, leaving the door open behind her.

I don't care if she does run away, I will not chase her, she thought angrily.

But Mary Woods did not move.

"Look now. I am going to show you how to clean." Rita picked up one rag and tossed the other toward Mary Woods. "Take that and do like me."

Clumsily, Mary Woods copied her movements. She was left-handed.

"Now," Rita said finally, "we wash the cloths and we wash you, and then we go to the swings."

They were still outside when the yellow school buses brought the children back from the picnic. Dirty and hot and tired, some crying, some fighting, they ran across the yard.

"You don't pay any attention to them," she said to Mary Woods. "I said you can swing and you are going to swing until you are dizzy."

But Mary Woods didn't get dizzy. Long after the other children were called in, she was still pumping back and forth. Eventually, in the early dark, her movements slowed, and then stopped. She had fallen asleep. Rita carried her to bed.

In the months that followed, Rita resumed her usual duties. Everywhere she went, Mary Woods followed, imitating awkwardly, silently.

Sister Bernadette smiled her thin smile. "You are doing well with her, my child."

"She pays attention," Rita said, "and she learns."

Sister Bernadette nodded. "Tomorrow at ten, make her clean and presentable and bring her to Sister Agnes's office. There will be a visitor for her. The little wild creature seems to have friends."

At precisely ten o'clock, just as the stairway bell was sounding the hour, Rita Landry and Mary Woods crossed the center hall, their feet thudding neatly together. At the office door Rita picked up the child, settling her comfortably, and knocked.

Sister Agnes sat behind the desk. A priest sat in the visitor's chair. Above his black suit the white round of his face hovered like a moon. On the desk between them was a tray with coffee and a plate of cookies.

Mary Woods shivered and stared, unblinking. Hooked, fish on a line, resisting but attached. She was so still that she seemed not to be breathing.

"And here is Mary Woods," Sister Agnes said. "That is the name we have given her."

"A good name," the priest agreed.

Rita listened, eyes downcast, as she had been taught.

"Does she always stare like that?" the priest asked.

"She is not used to people," Sister Agnes said. "She lived like a wild animal in a kind of roving pack, I've been told."

"That is quite true, Sister. Now, however, there is a man who feels a responsibility for the child. He wishes to provide her with an education, a moral upbringing, and, as far as is possible, a home."

"He is very generous."

"He can easily afford to be," the priest said calmly.

Sister Agnes bowed her head to her coffee cup.

"He himself is not Catholic, but over the years he has been a good friend of the Church."

Somewhere within the building, a child shrieked once and was silent.

The priest smiled tolerantly at the interruption. "He requests only that the child be taught to remember him by name in her daily prayers."

"He would seem to believe that the prayers of children are especially efficacious."

The slight edge in her voice made the priest pause to glance at her curiously. Her face was as bland as his.

"Who are we to say, Sister? He also wishes her to include a second name. That of the man who actually found her, retrieved her from the perils of the wilderness, as it were."

"It should not be a problem," Sister Agnes said, "even for a child like this."

"She knows her prayers then?"

"Rita, you may answer that."

Surprised, Rita stammered, "Well, in a way she does."

"Ah yes." The priest smiled at her comfortingly. "You will teach her, of course."

"She is smart," Rita said, forgetting her manners, and speaking out. "She can learn."

"Indeed she can. It will be Mr. Wilson and Mr. Tucker then."

"But, Father," Rita went on breathlessly, aware of Sister Agnes's disapproval, "couldn't she say their whole names?"

"My dear child, you are quite right. So ... Mr. William Howell Wilson and—I can't remember the other's full name—but I do think that Mr. Tucker of Clark County will be sufficient identification for the Lord to recognize him." He smiled serenely into Sister Agnes's tight-lipped annoyance. "I, or someone from my office, will visit her in a few months. We must report her progress to her benefactor."

"You are always welcome, Father," Sister Agnes said stiffly and nodded to Rita to take the child away.

The instant her feet touched the floor, Mary Woods ran—across the hall, out the door, down the steps, straight for the play yard and the swings. She stayed there for hours, body pumping, fighting against gravity. Her face was tipped back and she was scowling at the morning sky.

The months passed, flipping by like cards in a dealer's deck. Life at the Home went on. There was a grease fire in the kitchen, and firemen broke through the roof to reach the smoldering vent. Afterward all the children were allowed into the sodden room to see the damage; they marched through in orderly silent lines, awed and well behaved. . . . Two of the older girls, just finishing high school, left the home to begin nursing training. . . . Red measles appeared in the younger children. John Kimble, a small frail asthmatic boy, died choking in his sleep. . . .

Father Gautreaux, the old priest from Little Mirassou River, wrote to say that Rita Landry's father dropped dead while walking to the post office to pick up his pension check. Her mother and baby sister were fine; she could continue to devote herself to God and her vocation, which was a blessed one. As for her father, he would be remembered in the prayers at Mass.

All the faithful departed, Rita thought, the souls of all the

faithful departed. . . . So many, even in that small parish. . . .
She saw them, crowding around the little parish church, six
eight ten deep on the ground, even thicker in the air, souls
packed tight together, stretching off upwards clear to
heaven. Souls taking sustenance from prayers.

And Rita remembered: So much of the little priest's food
had gone into her father's round fat belly. Now so much
more could go to the priest. He might even grow fat himself. . . .

Mary Woods joined the other children at meals in the refectory. She went to church with them, too. Her small black
face was solemn and inquisitive, for all the world like a
monkey's. (I wonder if she is praying, Rita thought, and
what she is praying to.) At night, just before bed, when the
youngest children gathered at the piano to sing hymns, Mary
Woods sang along, confidently and loudly. When she did
not remember the words, she made up sounds to fit.

And every day she flew back and forth on the swings.
Rita saved a place for her, and the black eyes blinked their
thanks, unsmilingly. Not even rain brought her inside.

She moved into the youngest girls' dormitory and learned
to make her bed smooth and tight each morning. At recess
she played ring-around-the-rosy and hopscotch, though she
wouldn't play tag or hide-and-seek, and she didn't seem to
understand pitch-and-catch. She always tossed the ball
straight up in the air. On rainy days, when the children took
crayons and sheets of brown paper and drew pictures, Mary
Woods only scratched up and down across the sheets. Rita
drew a house for her, and a stick figure of a girl in a pink
dress; Mary Woods shook her head and tore the paper into
shreds.

When the children planted flower gardens, Mary Woods
was the most faithful and careful of all. Her hands, no

longer clumsy, brushed the seedlings gently. She watered by handfuls, dripping it carefully between her fingers. She weeded; she picked off mites and fly larvae. And when the blooms came—sweet William, cosmos, zinnias—she inspected each flower carefully, staring into them one by one, as if she were searching faces and trying to remember, as if she had known them before, as if they were friends from another time and place.

Rita, cleaning out a storage cupboard, found a large box of colored chalks and gave it to Mary Woods, who stared blankly, uncomprehending.

"Mother of God," Rita said, "but you try my patience." They found a blackboard, old and cracked, in a back room that had been a classroom once, years ago, when children were taught at the orphanage. It was a storeroom now, filled with broken tables and chairs, spare window sashes, shutters, doors, and a large broken prie-dieu.

Rita Landry cleared a way to the blackboard. "Now I will show you. This is what you do." With a green chalk, Rita drew a smiling round moon face and a daisy on its stem. "Like that."

Mary Woods stood for a long time, head crooked slightly to the side. Perfectly still. Animal still. Then very slowly, as if she were a cat approaching a bird, she stepped up to the blackboard. One hand, large at the end of its skinny arm, reached out, began rubbing at the chalk images. Slowly at first, then faster and harder, spitting on her palm, Mary Woods erased the pictures Rita had drawn.

"Fine," Rita said. "You do what you want."

All the next week, Mary Woods drew on the blackboard. She refused to go to the play yard or to story reading; weeds sprang up in her flowers. By the time the colored chalks were used up, her picture covered almost all the cracked expanse of board, a crowded tangle of colors and shapes. There was a green field with fire and flames running through the grass, exploding in the crown of a pine tree. There was yellow sun and there was rain, pouring straight down in heavy gray sheets. There was sky and moon and a ragged small cloud. The images were pressed together, so that the line of a tree trunk was also the back of a rabbit; the line of a river was the blade of a knife; the moon held a curled cat's tail.

Once the chalks were gone, Mary Woods went back to the swings and the playground. There she stole more chalk from a game of hopscotch and covered the concrete walks with huge sprawling pictures.

"Messy." Sister Bernadette sent out two girls from the laundry with buckets of hot water.

Mary Woods saw her work disappear under the suds and the brooms. One among a small crowd of children, she watched, curious but not very interested. As if it had nothing to do with her.

Rita was put in charge of the dormitory for the youngest girls, a long high-ceilinged room lined on each side with small iron cot beds. Sister Marie Augusta, who had had the job for years, moved out of her small curtained cubicle with a sigh of relief and a tight wintry smile. She took down the crucifix her sister had sent her and the rosary that had been blessed by the pope. She put crucifix and rosary in one pocket, her missal in the other, looked a last time down the twin lines of small white iron beds, nodded, and left.

Each evening Rita led the children in their bedtime prayers, then switched off the ceiling light, so that the long room was lit by a single candle high on the wall before a statue of the Virgin. In the heavy dimness she patrolled the narrow aisle, walking slowly, carefully, until the children were asleep. In winter the room grew cold and the children shivered and whimpered. Then Rita bundled them together for warmth—tight packed head to toe, three or four to a single cot, shared blankets across them. And once each night, summer or winter, at eleven o'clock, Rita waked the entire dormitory and sent them to the potty-chairs that waited in the corner.

The children fell back asleep quickly, slack mouthed, snoring lightly, mumbling in occasional dreams. (Like a chicken roost, Rita thought, all fluttering and shifting, but not waking nor leaving their perches.) Except for Mary Woods.

She lay quietly, as if she were waiting for something, eyes wide. Sometimes she lay with arms outstretched, making shadow figures with the distant light of the dim candle.

"I will tell you a story," Rita whispered to her. "Would you like that?"

She told stories from the Little Mirassou River country. Stories of oystermen who found great pearls in their catch, pearls so valuable that a single one bought a new boat. Of strange monsters caught in the nets of shrimp boats. Of beautiful naked women who appeared in the full moon and drove men mad with desire. Of obeah women who set spells like traps, for love or hate or good luck, for health and long life, for sickness and fevers. And many stories of lost princesses, like the princess Yolanda. She was stolen from her cradle by a witch and given to a cane farmer's wife who raised her and took good care of her. One day, working in her foster mother's garden, Yolanda saw a big black crow, ten times the size of other crows. Come now, the bird said to her, come now with me. She climbed on his broad feathered back and they flew off to her true and real father's castle where the crow turned into a handsome prince and married her.

When Mary Woods at last fell fast asleep, Rita sighed with weariness and went to bed herself.

Mary Woods grew tall on pipe-stem arms and legs. She was no longer content with the swings at playtime. She became as obsessed with heights as she had once been with motion. She climbed every tree with a branch low enough for her to reach. She slipped into the locked cloister gallery of the chapel—she must have scrambled twenty feet up a supporting post and crept along a narrow ridge below the line of carved-wood screens. She waited patiently while Sister Agnes found the old key and turned back the rusting lock to release her. She loosened a wall grille and slipped into the heating vents. For hours she scrambled through the maze of metal tubes, sounding for all the world like a dozen rats. She even climbed the side of the building, wedging her feet between drainpipe and wall, to reach the cupola over the main door. Once there she seemed to forget the way back. Rita, skirts hitched into her belt, climbed a clanking extension ladder, hoisted the child to her back, and brought her down. Mary Woods came willingly enough. She might even have been afraid. It was hard to tell.

Sometimes she disappeared from the line of sleeping girls in the dormitory. Then, yawning and barefoot, Rita climbed the stairs to the storage room at the back of the building, to the blackboard and the colored-chalk drawings. The nightlight in the hall, dim bulb on a high ceiling, shone through the open door and made a kind of moonlight over the jumble of things inside. On the wall the chalk images glowed, three-dimensional and alive. Before them Mary Woods crouched on the floor, staring.

When Rita Landry said, "I've come to fetch you now," the child turned her head slowly. An emotion showed in her face: relief or recognition, or even affection, as near as Mary Woods ever came to that.

She is glad to see me, Rita thought, because she wants to leave, and she can't, not until someone takes her away.

Afterwards Mary Woods fell into a heavy deep sleep, not even hearing the morning bell, until Rita, with an impatient sigh, shook her awake.

On one of her nighttime explorations Mary Woods found five or six cans of paint, each with a thin film of liquid in the bottom—blue and gray and yellow and white and tan. In the echoing silence of the sleeping orphanage Mary Woods began work again on her blackboard picture. She had no brushes; she used her fingers.

Rita scrubbed her arms and hands clean with mineral spirits and laundry soap, but the paint rimmed her nails and the creases of her knuckles. And her hair was speckled and streaked, confetti-like.

"She will just have to stay like that," Sister Agnes said, "it will serve her right to look foolish."

But Mary Woods didn't seem to mind. The very next night she sneaked back. When she found the door padlocked, she kicked and pounded it with her fists. Anyone might have thought she was angry, but her face didn't change at all.

"You are a sight," Rita scolded her, "and you've got company coming too."

The priest had been meticulous in his duty. During the intervening four years, at precisely two-month intervals, he had sent someone to visit Mary Woods. Most often it was his sister, who wore print dresses and large-brimmed flat hats and always brought a half-dozen candy canes tied together like a bunch of flowers. Occasionally it was his secretary, an old man, body bent and humped by arthritis. And once it was a stocky blond man. One of the same men, Rita thought, who brought the child in the first place.

This time it was the priest himself, who now wore the red of a monsignor. His heavy body shook with laughter when he saw the paint-speckled child.

Sister Agnes folded her hands in patient exasperation. "We would appreciate your not encouraging her, Monsignor."

"Sister, you are absolutely right." He pulled out a handkerchief and wiped his eyes. "But I was not expecting anything like this."

"Nor were we," Sister Agnes said tartly.

"I understand the difficulties." He nodded sympathy and folded away his handkerchief.

"We have tried to interest her in books and reading, but she does not respond. Rita tells me she speaks, but I have never heard her. She is in perfect health."

The priest took one of the child's thin black hands, holding it gently. "Blue and yellow and brown," he counted off the colors under the nails, "and gray too." When he smiled, his teeth were darker than his skin. Hair thin and fine as cobwebs covered the sides of his head. "You, little one, are being a nuisance. The good sisters despair of you." He turned to face Sister Agnes; his movements were quick and precise. "May we see this picture which is so important to the child?"

Sister Agnes led the way, her stiff back showing how irritated she was by the request.

"Well." The priest's eyebrows made wrinkles across his forehead. "That is quite a remarkable thing for a child her age to do." To Rita he said, "Tell us about our little wild creature. You have cared for her. You know her better than anyone else."

Rita hesitated a moment, struggling to put her thoughts

into words. "She has been very good and she has worked very hard. Harder than any of the children."

Sister Agnes cleared her throat in loud disagreement.

"Things that are easy for the others are hard for her," Rita insisted.

"How old is she?"

"Sister says she is about eight."

"Oh?" The priest looked to Sister Agnes.

"Her teeth, Monsignor. The way you would tell the age of a puppy."

He nodded. And turned back to Rita. "What else?"

"She has a hard time learning to read. But there is nothing wrong with her eyes, she can thread a needle faster than I can. She is good with numbers, I am teaching her from a fourth-grade arithmetic. What she likes most of all is painting and drawing."

"And speaking?"

"She is shy, I think. She talks to some of the other children, her friends, I guess they are. And she talks to me. She tells me all sorts of things, whatever she can remember about the places she's been, and the way she lived, and the people she lived with."

"And what was that?" the priest asked.

Sister Agnes moved forward in her chair, listening.

Rita felt her face grow hot. "She only told me because I promised I would never repeat a single thing."

Sister Agnes sucked in her breath, impatiently.

"Then keep your promise and your silence." He glanced at her intently for a moment. "Sister, your order will be well served by this young woman."

Sister Agnes inclined her head slightly. "We pray for her vocation, Monsignor."

"And in the meantime, Mary Woods." He studied the

child carefully, as if he expected to find something written on her skin, then nodded. "Little one, it is all settled. You will paint and draw and color to your heart's content and show us this fantastic world of yours."

Sister Agnes folded her arms into the sleeves of her habit; the wooden rosary at her belt clacked softly. "Indeed, Monsignor. Perhaps one day she can even send a special painting to her kind patron."

"That is a thought." The priest straightened up and smiled again, faintly.

She is mocking him, Rita thought, and he has decided to ignore it because he doesn't care at all what she thinks. . . .

More time passed, all the duty-filled days, comfortable in their monotony. Rita Landry formally declared her intention to become a novice and, following the custom of the order, returned to her family for a month to consider her decision.

Many things in the Little Mirassou River country had changed during the years she'd been gone. But not all. The cicadas still sang their quavery echoing songs in the evenings. The chinaberry trees, stunted by years of cutting for firewood, still bloomed their clusters of pale blue flowers. Roosters crowed at dawn; fat clumsy pigeons pumped on their heavy piston wings across the daylight sky; bats flew at dawn and dusk, chirping nervously to each other. There was still no word from her sister Ursula, who had gone to California. Her other sister Louise now had five children and lived in the same house in Menton with her husband, Al Abadie, who still worked at the rice mill there. And Rita's baby sister was six years old, the very image of the old man her father.

But many other things had changed. Father Gautreaux was gone, dead of a heart attack in the empty confessional box one Saturday afternoon. The church still stood by the shell mound on the river. It was even newly painted, but the rectory was empty, doors locked and windows boarded. No parish priest lived there, though descendants of the old cat still sheltered among its foundations. A priest from St. Stephen the Martyr parish came to say Mass on Sunday, returning only for special occasions, like weddings and funerals and baptisms.

There seemed to be more trains on the L&N tracks. Four or five times a night she'd wake to passing whistles from the Belleterre crossing. There were more boats on the river too. Outboards sputtered back and forth all day long. And Rita counted half a dozen new names among the big fishing luggers. One of them was the *Chère Amie*, an old boat, but well kept. It belonged to Robert Fournet, from Texas. He had come up the Little Mirassou River two years past, to wait out a stretch of stormy weather. He met the Widow Landry at Vauchon's grocery store and walked home with her. And stayed. Though he was thirty and she was nearly fifty, they seemed happy together. He'd be whistling and smiling when he came in for supper, and afterwards he never went out with the other men. He was content to sit on the dark porch and play his harmonica until he fell asleep, breathing softly in and out across the reeds. As if he'd always lived there.

Rita slept in her old room behind the kitchen. It seemed small and crowded to her now, though it was no smaller than her cubicle at the convent. Her sister shared the bed— her small hot body burned against Rita's skin—and she snored loudly.

Each night Rita walked along the riverbank, ignoring the clouds of mosquitoes. Occasionally she'd hear distant voices, a laugh or a shout, and sometimes she met people hurrying home. They greeted her respectfully, as if she were already a nun. She answered them politely and kept walking. There

was a great restlessness inside her, her legs could not keep
still, her thoughts were scattered and half formed.

And then she remembered Mary Woods.

You will come walk with me, she told her memory child.
We will keep each other company and get through the
nights. We will talk together.

The fragile image of Mary Woods settled into step beside her.

"I have walked along here hundreds and thousands of
times," Rita said aloud, softly. "If you looked you'd probably
find my footprints in the ground."

I never walked the same way twice, Mary Woods said
silently. But I am happy to walk along with you. Because I
like you. Maybe I love you. Maybe you even love me like
your own child, the one you'll never have.

"Hush," Rita said.

Those who passed Rita Landry on the shell road by the
river heard her soft muttering and paid no attention. They
thought she must be praying.

In time Rita Landry became Sister Celeste, and many
other things happened, large and small. The chapel's roof
had to be repaired, shiny new copper gleamed against the
sky. Bees got into the attic of the main building; their hollow buzzing echoed through the entire top floor. The
bishop, on his yearly visit, stumbled over a broken step and
pitched headfirst into the yard. In the space of a single week
five newborn infants were left at the home. Sister Bernadette developed cancer, grew thinner and thinner until,
nearly invisible already, she disappeared into death. Mary
Woods painted a bright flower mural on the wooden fence
of the play yard.

And in the outside world, a war began. The priest, when
he visited Mary Woods, wore the khaki of an army chaplain.

The home's custodian left for a job at a munitions plant. The maintenance man joined the merchant marine. The young gardener was drafted. The children mowed the grass and filled the flower beds with beans and corn and onions and cabbage. Along the streets army trucks rumbled past in steady streams. The city buses were jammed with plant workers; shrieking whistles from the nearby shipyard signalled the beginning and end of their shifts. Though they still lived at the home, most of the older girls left school for war work— Mary Woods worked the morning shift in the cafeteria at the shipyard.

The war ended. The priest appeared again, no longer in uniform. He went directly to Sister Agnes's office. "I have good news for Mary Woods, Sister. I know you will be pleased."

"If you say so, Monsignor."

"I have met Mr. Wilson. After all these years. He does not receive visitors as a rule, he's not in good health, but he wanted to talk to me about Mary Woods. He still concerns himself with her, and he has a plan. . . . But first I must ask: has she shown any sign of a vocation?"

Sister Agnes smiled her tight-lipped false-teeth smile. "None."

"Well then . . . Mr. Wilson wishes her to return to Clark County, to his household. What a magnificent place it is, too. She will be trained as housemaid or cook's helper, and she will live with the other staff in the servants' quarters. Furthermore, he will find a husband for her. He knows of several respectable young men just back from the army who are now working for him. . . . And that is what I have come to tell her."

"She is at work, Monsignor. She will not return until late afternoon."

"Then I shall just leave it to you," the priest said. "If only all news were so pleasant."

Sister Agnes sent for Sister Celeste. "You are her special friend. You must tell her."

"She should be very happy."

But she wasn't. Sister Celeste saw that at once. The young woman's face went totally blank and empty, like a blackboard washed with a sponge.

The next day Mary Woods collected her wages at the shipyard, emptied her savings account to the last penny, put her belongings in a pillowcase, and walked away. No one saw her go.

Sister Celeste searched through the small chest that stood behind Mary Wood's dormitory bed. It was empty except for a rosary, a steel cross on a steel chair, a daily missal. Those things the home had given her, she returned to the home.

"Mary Woods, what will happen to you?" Sister Celeste asked aloud.

Who knows? Mary Woods said, her voice a faint whisper in the creaking walls. I've gone back to travelling.

"I will pray for you."

A black shadow hovered against the glare of a window, briefly.

I don't need your prayers, said Mary Woods. I bring my gods with me. From before. You should know them. I've painted their pictures for you a hundred times. But you didn't see.

Abruptly Sister Celeste sat down on the narrow iron bed, spoiling the sheets' neat tautness. Her hands were trembling.

THE MAGIC
KINGDOM

The Beginning

~~~~~~~~~

M Y name is Nanda Woods, only daughter—indeed only child—of Mary Woods. I am now thirty-six years old and I have been, for most of my life, an inhabitant of my mother's magic kingdom.

In the beginning there was just my mother and me.

"You are," my mother would say, "the queen of the world, the jewel of the lotus, the pearl without price, my secret treasure."

She whispered words like that, singsonging them in her soft high voice that had a little tiny crackle in it like a scratched record, to comfort me when I was a baby. Her light high whisper threaded through all my days, linking them tightly together, from the day of my birth, from that

first moment when I slid from her body to lie in the softness
of her bed, the same bed she slept in now. The one we took
with us from place to place.

And there were many different places. We were wander-
ers, my mother and I, disciplined and practiced sojourners.
I even had a small wicker basket for my toys so that I could
pack and carry them myself.

It mattered little to me where we lived. I did not go outside. Wherever we were, I was too precious, too special, to
live as other children did. I did not go for walks, nor play
on park swings. Nor go to the corner grocery for a loaf of
bread or two bottles of Coke. I did not go to birthday parties
and play in sandboxes and ride merry-go-rounds. We did
not have friends, my mother and I. There were only the two
of us. On Sunday, when my mother was home, we stayed inside and worked together; all the while she sang her murmured song to me. Secret treasure, lotus flower. And in her
whispering way she told me all she knew about my father,
a Hindu from Calcutta, a salesman of Worthington electric
pumps. He had stayed with her for two weeks, never leaving her room, sending out for food and drink; when the
time came for him to leave, he cried with sadness, real tears
streaking down his cheeks. I bear a shortened version of his
name, Agehananda, shortened to fit a baby girl. Of all the
many men my mother had known, he was the only one she
had loved. She told me about his thin face and his large
eyes, black as oil, and his skin that was only slightly lighter
than her own.

"You have his eyes and his skin," she said as, after my
bath, she rubbed me with oil. (It was baby oil, its vanilla
scent soon lost in her heavier perfume.) "You have his lovely
hair," she said, combing in more oil.

And there is, to be sure, a certain look of India about me.
Even now, in the grown woman.

"You are exquisite," my mother would say, turning me around and around. "A princess of all the world, daughter of the moti mahal. You must have a lovely new dress." And so I would. She made all my clothes, made and designed. Summer dresses of handkerchief linen and soft smooth voile, winter dresses of dark rich velvets, and monk's-cloth coats so heavily smocked across the shoulders they were almost waterproof.

Of course we couldn't afford to buy fabrics like that, not in those days. My mother worked as a stock girl for Lambert Brothers Department Store. She had worked there for years, even before I was born, patient, sober, dependable, the perfect employee. Though they never knew it, Lambert Brothers provided the material for our clothes, quite a lot of it over time. It all began on a city bus when my mother met a clerk from the Perfection Cloth Shoppe. They began talking, casually at first and then with purpose. My mother arranged to exchange a bottle of perfume or a box of dusting powder or some Elizabeth Arden lipsticks from Lambert Brothers for small lengths of expensive material from the Perfection Cloth Shoppe. (My mother had to be content with blouses and skirts in contrasting colors. It was just too dangerous for her friend to steal enough material for a dress. I needed only small lengths of material, which were easy to conceal. Most of the clothes were mine.)

My mother never told me how she smuggled out the cosmetics. I suppose she'd worked at the store so long and so faithfully that they half trusted her. She did tell me how her friend robbed the Perfection Cloth Shoppe—a simple plan that worked for years.

My mother's friend collected the fabrics over a period of weeks, hiding them among the hundreds of stacked bolts. When she saw her chance, she bundled the pieces tightly and dropped them in a box of trash, making a small red check on the outside. My mother had only to pass along the service drive at the back of the building, look for the mark, and remove the package. That evening we spread out the material on our kitchen table (the only table we had) and admired it together. Only once did something go wrong. Once the trash was collected an hour earlier than usual, and my beautiful dresses went to the city incinerator. My mother and I managed to laugh about that.

"I have a nice large box of Chanel dusting powder," she said to me. "I got it only today. I will buy some velvet this time."

She never said steal or take or even remove. Not my mother. It was always the same phrase: I will buy.

During those early years, during the long dull hours checking stock in close dusty rooms, my mother began thinking about a business of her own, as dressmaker. In silence, while her body moved to its chores, she considered, elaborated, developed, until every detail was clear and perfect in her mind. Her plan was this: she would design and make clothes for the children of prosperous blacks. Unusual and expensive clothes. Unusual so that everyone would recognize their cost. Expensive so that everyone would value them.

My stolen clothes were the beginning. I was her model, the body on which her work came to life, the living sketchbook. Too small to see above the knees of adults, but perfectly quiet and perfectly composed, I displayed her clothes. My mother did not need to teach me how to walk or to act. Remember your father is an Indian prince and you are his only daughter, she would say to me.

I knew then, oh, but I knew!

And so we made our rounds, peddling our wares, much like my father and his Worthington electric pumps. It was true that he had traveled farther, half a world, but our merchandise was far more beautiful. My mother and I went to talent shows and beauty contests, to church services and choir rehearsals. Wherever ladies gathered and the admission was free, there we were. My mother sold her clothes, as it were, from off my back.

"We are selling very well in the Afro-American community," my mother would say. "Soon we will open a small showroom. The walls will be painted white, and the only thing on them will be pictures of you. On every wall, the entire way around."

Eventually she did just that. I remember it very clearly, the white room, quite bare and business-like and lined with pictures of me. They were color photographs, very expensive for a woman just starting in business, but they showed the details of the clothes beautifully. My face, I remember, was rather blurred, but the light always seemed to catch the smooth line of my long dark hair. When I modeled for the customers (seated in creaking folding chairs and reeking with conflicting perfumes), my hair was always swept forward over one shoulder. My mother ironed it carefully in the dressing room at the very last moment. I remember the glare of the naked lightbulbs around the mirror and the smell of singeing as my mother pressed my hair on her ironing board.

I don't remember saying a single word at any time. I have since noticed that people usually speak to a child, but no one spoke to me. Perhaps they did not think I was quite real. Perhaps I was not.

Twice a month, in the evenings, my mother did her books. These were my favorite times. Wearing my nightgown (always ankle length, always with a drawn-lace yoke), I sat in the corner of the sofa, its upholstery worn and prickling on the sides of my arms, and watched my mother with her checkbooks and her account books and her order books. I watched her pencil picking away at the pages, flicking, stabbing, moving. She was a very good bookkeeper. In different circumstances I suppose she would have gone to college and earned a CPA to put behind her name. But she didn't. She just remained somebody who was very quick with numbers.

There was another strange thing about her, though I didn't notice it until many years later. She was so good with figures, she spoke so very well, in soft tones as soothing as a cough lozenge—but she could hardly read at all. She wasn't illiterate, but she read street signs and phone books, newspapers and business forms and contracts all the same way: carefully, taking a very long time, sounding out the words. As a child, I thought that muttering was the way everyone read. (The nuns at school soon corrected me.) Eventually I would fall asleep on the old sofa with that comforting whispering lullaby in my ears.

When my mother picked me up to carry me to bed with her, she was always smiling. "The figures dance so beautifully for me, my little love. The Afro-American community is contributing devotedly to the treasure of the mahal. The daughters saw her and blessed her, also the queens and the concubines." (Someone had once read the Bible to my mother; bits and pieces kept appearing in her talk.)

In the morning when I woke, she was gone—she had to be at work at seven. When I was very small, when I first remember things, like wet diapers and throwing up in bed, there was someone who stayed with me, an old old woman who sat in a rocker all day long and listened to the radio. Her name was Miss Beauty. I don't remember her ever feeding me, but I suppose she must have. She died one day, in her rocking chair. I thought she was asleep so I went on playing with my doll. My cat—we kept one to kill the mice that played all over the old house—jumped on Miss Beauty's lap, then jumped down again quickly, coming to sit next to me in the window. "You heard her snore," I whispered to the cat, very severely. "Don't wake her, she won't like that at all." At the usual time I heard my mother's key in the lock and the funny little nine-note tune she whistled every evening just inside the door. (It was from *Lucia di Lammermoor*, I discovered years later in a college music-appreciation class, and I rose in my seat with the impact of memory.) I put my finger to my lips and pointed silently to Miss Beauty. My mother hesitated, eyes flicking between us, nose wrinkling like an animal. Without moving, she bent forward toward Miss Beauty. Then quickly, so quickly, with a clatter of feet across the linoleum floor, she snatched me up and ran outside.

After Miss Beauty's death, there was no one. I stayed by myself. We moved to a nicer neighborhood, a street with trees and double cottages behind small front gardens. (The landlord had paved over our garden with pale green cement.) I never felt afraid. If I got lonely, I could sit in the big front window and watch the neighborhood children play in the street. Of course I never joined them.

Only once during these years did my mother have a visitor. He was short and wore a plaid coat and a wide-brimmed hat, and the ring on his left hand flashed colored lights. He was waiting for my mother when she came home after work. They talked briefly, standing at the curb next to his big white car, then the two of them came into the house. He smiled at me, saying, "Well, well, now, is that your little girl? Hello there, little girl." My mother went straight to the red sofa, reached inside the top cushion. When she turned around, there was a gun in her hand. She just stood there, her long fingers wrapped around that small dull-blue gun, both hands holding it firm and steady. The man stopped smiling and backed out the door. He never said another word. Nor did my mother.

The very next day we moved away from the house with the front yard of green-tinted cement. My mother rented a truck, and she hired two men to load it for us. Our beds, the red velvet sofa, the two folding bridge chairs, the refrigerator and the gas stove, the enamel-topped kitchen table, the armoire with the cracked mirrored doors—they fitted neatly into the truck, along with the boxes of clothes and dishes and my mother's sewing machine, which was the only new thing we owned.

"Hurry," my mother said, carrying some of the smaller things herself, "we haven't got all day. I am paying you to be quick."

Grumbling and complaining, the men finished the loading and took their money and stood on the sidewalk to watch us leave.

"Get in," my mother said to me, a quick sharp command. "Be quick."

We drove down highways lined with withered brown palm trees, past endless intersections where traffic lights stabbed out their signals like lighthouses. We waited, part of an impatient horn-blowing crowd, while canal bridges opened to let gravel-filled barges glide past through oily water.

And my mother said nothing at all. When I could wait no longer, when the silence between us seemed more dangerous and frightening than any nightmare, I asked, "Why are we running away?"

"To be safe," she said.

"Is it far?"

"It is far enough to be safe," she said.

When we finally reached the place where we would live,

she hired two more neighborhood men to take our things up the stairs. She had moved without leaving a trace behind.

I guessed it had something to do with her visitor, but I did not worry. In all the stories my mother had told me, there were always threats and pursuits and enemies to be avoided. It was the way a princess lived. And my mother was always there, to bring me to safety at last.

When we sat in our new home, in the clutter of boxes and furniture, when we were safely inside, the door locked behind us, my mother smiled at me, a great slow smile that showed square strong teeth in the smooth darkness of her face. "My hidden princess," she said, "my lotus flower . . ."

The accustomed endearments tumbled from her lips, the expected exotic songs of love and praise. I, young as I was, noted the change. For the past two days, and on that long drive across town, she had spoken rarely, and then only in the crisp blunt language of everyday.

Now, by the smooth soft flow of her words, I knew that we were indeed safe. We had passed through a series of lodgings—I think I remember them all, including the one where I was born, the one with a chinaberry tree outside the window—but we had finally gained our castle, the one we had been searching for. There was even a turret, to command the approaches and to defend against enemies.

The house stood on a corner. Its old clapboard walls rose directly from the sidewalk through two stories of flaking gray paint to a roof decorated with fancy wooden scallops. In the dark spaces under the eaves generations of pigeons nested and fluttered. At the second-floor corner, jutting over the sidewalk, was a small turret or tower, capped with a high-pointed roof like a clown's hat.

Inside the tower was a hinged seat of varnished wood entirely covered by scratch drawings: flowers and initials and hearts, dancing stick figures and even a face or two. Here we stored odd bits of things: old shoes, an umbrella with two broken ribs, a doll in a pink-and-blue gingham dress, an Easter bunny of purple and yellow plush, a black patent purse. Roaches lived there too; they ate the stuffing from the doll and the feather from her hat, and they ate spots of fur from the Easter bunny so that it looked burned. I thought they had also nibbled the edge of the patent leather purse, but my mother said no, it was just use-worn.

Day after day, I sat on top that jumble of things, above the secret workings of insects, and I watched through the windows, three panes of glass on the three sides of my tower, which my mother washed every month so that I might see clearly.

Most of the floor below us was occupied by a drugstore, a small dark place that smelled of disinfectant and sugar candy, of brown paper and cough medicine. On two of the other corners were small houses, one-room-wide, perched off the ground on low brick foundations and edged by foot-wide runners of grass. On the third corner, directly across from my window, was Providence Manor, a home for the old. A tall iron fence enclosed an entire block of grass and trees and even occasional blooming flowers, a wilderness that stretched out of my sight. Just inside the fence was a gravel path where, on good days, the old people walked, some slowly on canes, some with arms flexing rapidly in a military march, some in chairs wheeled by nuns in black habits and white headdresses. They rotated past the spear points of the fence, every good day taking their quota of sun and exhaust-laden air. After dark, on rainy nights, the flashing sign in the drugstore window beat against those railings, broke, and ran off down the shiny black street.

Downstairs, directly below, in our small slice of the old house, were the two rooms that were my mother's workshop and showroom. On our front door—up two wooden steps from the uneven brick sidewalk—was a small neat sign: MO-DISTE. My mother had lettered that herself; she had always been very clever with her hands. It was her first real shop, this one. It was her first real success. The first of many.

I spent my days either at my window or in my mother's workrooms. The rest of the house, the other two rooms, I scarcely remember. I was either a princess in my tower or a mannequin in my mother's clothes.

Not until years later did I realize that all the faces I saw were black. (To me they had no color, no color at all.) The people walking on the street, the old on their therapeutic rounds, the Sisters of the Holy Family, the drivers impa-tiently threading their way through the heavy street traffic, my mother and her customers—they all wore black skin.

As did the children in school.

Eventually I had to go to school. My mother did not send me when I was six, as the law said she must. For one extra year I dreamed and flaunted my beautiful dresses. I doubt that the authorities would have noticed had I not gone to school at all. I think it was my mother's new friend who fi-nally persuaded her. For my mother at last had a friend, a good friend, whose visits were regular and predictable. For him my mother bathed and did her hair and cooked spe-cially and smiled when the doorbell rang.

My mother's friend was a tall, heavy man who came to church with us every Sunday and afterwards held my hand as I walked along the top of the low wall that bordered the churchyard. He owned a small cab company—he drove one himself—whose insignia was a lightning bolt across a bright blue circle. His name was David Clark, and he took me to school and picked me up every day of my first year.

I went to parochial school. Navy skirts and white blouses

and black-and-white saddle oxfords, all of us. All of us rows of little black raisins, waiting to be taught to read and to count and to love Lord Jesus.

Ah, yes, but I was the only one picked up by taxi every day at three o'clock. The children stared at me as I rode away, the Indian princess in her palanquin, the treasure of the mahal above Leconte's Drugstore.

On the first day of school my mother went with me. I remember very little about that day—I was nauseated with excitement, griped by fear—but I remember the clothes she wore: brown and beige linen, a long-sleeved blouse, and an eight-gore skirt. I saw the nuns' eyes flick over us in brief appraisal: we passed with honors. (I took it as my due. I wonder now how my mother felt.)

The school smelled of peanuts and garlic bologna. The floor of my classroom was spotted with puddles of slimy liquid. Oddly enough, the other children's panic quieted me. In the reek of their nervousness, my own stomach settled, and when the harried janitor arrived with a bucket of sawdust to sprinkle on the vomit, I helped him by pushing aside the desks.

That first day was the longest I have ever known. And the hottest. It was early September, and the afternoon sun burned through the window shades to polish our faces with sweat—all except the teaching sister. Her face remained dry and dull as if coated with a film of dust.

I never grew used to the noise and rush of children leaving class. When the bell sounded, I always waited while the room emptied. Then, in a pause disturbed only by the soft sounds of the teacher gathering her papers, I walked slowly through the door, last and alone.

For first grade, I had two skirts, made by my mother according to the uniform dress code of the parochial school system, and two blouses. Every second day, when I came home, I was expected to wash my blouse carefully, using the kitchen sink and a small scrubbing board that my mother kept underneath, propped against the pipes. I then hung it on the back porch inside the screen, where no bird could soil it. Every so often my mother was dissatisfied with its whiteness, and she would wash it again in bleach. The next time I wore that blouse I was certain to have a rash across my neck and shoulders where the fabric rubbed my skin.

Later on, when my growing required new blouses (the skirts had deep hems to let down), my mother made them slightly different. She added small tucks down the front, two tiny rows on each side of the buttons. I noticed the nuns looking at me—they were very strict about uniforms in those days—and they must have talked to my mother. My next blouses were perfectly plain. What the nuns couldn't know about were my slips. My mother made my slips too, and they had all the elaborate decorations that my blouses lacked. They were tucked, with drawn lace and wide banks of crochet at the shoulders, and a deep flounce of lace at the hem. Only one nun ever saw them, and she wasn't really a nun. She was a novice: very young, shorter even than I was. She was cleaning the bathrooms, and I, not noticing her, was fanning myself with my skirt against the heat. She stopped and fingered my slip. "What lovely work, what exquisite work." Then she looked shocked and ashamed—perhaps she had made a vow of silence—and she went hastily back to her pail and mop.

After my first year at school, I took the city bus home. The stop was at our corner. All I had to do was cross the street and open the door. Once inside, I rushed to bathe, to brush my hair, to put on the dresses that my mother would sell. Wearing her clothes and her dreams, I would move carefully among her customers, gracefully, as only a princess can.

The lotus blossom. The treasure of the mahal. In the women's faces I saw greed and covetousness. My mother's order books rustled busily. I myself drew spirit and sustenance from the flickering eyes and the fingers stretched out to touch. The small crowded room became my castle and my kingdom.

This then is the story of my mother. And of me.

The Middle Kingdom

～～～～～

H O W shall I tell you about our years together, my mother and I. Teacher and pupil. Wizard and apprentice. Without ever once saying so, she taught me the mysteries of the world and the people who walked its surface. She taught me disguises to let me move safely through the ranks of my enemies. She taught me the greatest enchantment of all: how to walk like a princess in kingdoms of our own making.

We built two kingdoms, she and I. One of walled gardens where roses bloomed all year and gold carp swam in marble lily pools, where she was queen and I was princess, where our castle gates were guarded by the flaming swords of cherubim. Through all our ordinary days my mother and I carried this gleaming private world with us, hermit crabs, walking ponderously, castles on our backs, secure.

Our second kingdom, a kind of distant shadow of the first, was strong and firm and enduring in the human world, rooted in reality, based on money and property and the logic of commerce. Its treasures were measured by bank accounts and corporate statements.

In this world I was a dutiful daughter, a serious industrious student, member of an emerging underclass. In this world my mother was a businesswoman, an embryo capitalist. A woman of flickering eyes, setting traps for dollars. A sorceress of spells and illusions of beauty whose customers followed her devotedly.

Even as I did.

In my fifteenth year, as I prepared to enter the eighth grade, the horizons of my world expanded abruptly, explosively. My good grades, my impeccable behavior, my mixed racial background, and my mother's tireless importunities—they had all combined to get me a scholarship to St. Catherine's, a boarding school run by the Ursuline nuns.

In those days we were still living in the apartment over Leconte's Drugstore, the one with the tower window seat. I stared at the familiar four corners below and wondered if I would miss these crowded streets. I had seen pictures of St. Catherine's: a cluster of Gothic buildings in the midst of green pastures that sloped away to misty blue hills. I had even charted the exact distance on a road map (eight hundred thirty-two miles) and the direction (almost straight north).

The school sent a list of required clothes—and an offer of financial assistance in providing them. We refused. I knitted my own sweaters—one navy, one white—a scarf, mittens, and a cap in the school colors of blue and gold. My mother made my clothes, all of them: the uniform skirts and blouses and blazers, the nightgowns and slips and panties, one casual dress for Saturdays, a dressy one for Sundays, and a heavy coat, heavily lined.

David Clark, my mother's friend, bought two pale blue Samsonite suitcases for me. "A young lady needs to look good," he said, "when she starts a new life out in the world."

I opened the suitcases carefully, slowly. They were the first I had ever owned. When my mother and I moved, we used cardboard boxes from the grocery.

"Well, now"—David Clark settled in his big chair, sighing with tiredness—"look at all those winter clothes. You'll need them, that's for sure." My mother brought him coffee and began massaging his shoulders and neck. Driving a cab all day stiffened and cramped his muscles. "I saw enough winter when I was in the army, enough snow and ice and cold to last a lifetime."

With a remembering chuckle he began the story of his wartime service, one we'd heard a hundred times before. Still, my mother and I listened attentively because the telling gave him such pleasure.

He'd been a waiter in an officers' club, first in England, then France, then Germany.

"The English women, now," he said, "they were real fond of us GIs with the black faces. They couldn't wait to find out if we was black all over or just spotted like a dog. Pure curiosity, that's what it was." He shook his head slowly. "Only fight I ever had was on account of a woman. I didn't want to, never did enjoy it none, but the guy looked like he'd kill me for sure. The funny thing was, he didn't rightly know how to fight, so I just tapped him upside the head. And that was all. I used to wonder, did he go back later and knock that woman around."

He'd done a bit of black-marketing too, he said, smiling at the memory, and when he came home he had enough money to buy two cabs and start his company. He always ended his story the same way. "That war was the making of me," he said.

My mother went on packing my suitcases, neatly, competently preparing me for my new life.

The two of them drove me to the airport. David handed me ten one-dollar bills, folded in half. I put them carefully in my new wallet in my new purse.

My mother kissed my cheek, and I walked on the plane.

That was all. Never once had my mother said: You are very lucky to have a scholarship to such a fine school. Or: You must work very hard to repay the trust the nuns have placed in you. Or: Take care to be grateful.

You see, my mother was never grateful. She accepted this scholarship for me the way she accepted everything, as if it were her due. All her life she'd depended on the kindness and generosity of strangers, and she had come to expect it.

I had never been on a plane before; indeed I had not been anywhere farther than a Sunday afternoon drive. But I could pretend to be an experienced traveller. There was a thin old woman sitting across the aisle from me—the plane was quite empty—and I copied her every move. The stewardess smiled when she came to check my seat belt, and I smiled back politely.

I changed planes in Atlanta. Because we were late, the airline sent a car for me, a car with a flashing light on top. I was escorted down special stairs, through a locked door, across the hot tarmac. I sat in the backseat by myself. The driver whistled a quiet tune as we drove between lines of parked planes, passing caterers' vans and baggage carts and men in overalls and earmuffs dragging hoses from fuel trucks. The closed van windows shut off the sound almost completely, reduced it to a kind of mutter or moan, a hollow echo.

This, I thought, is what it's like to be a real princess, protected and isolated and secure.

Another locked door, another stair, another plane. I took down a pillow from the overhead bin. I smoothed my skirt carefully—I was wearing a dark plaid suit—put my purse in my lap, and folded my hands.

A short flight this time. The stewardess leaned over me. "Someone's meeting you?"

"Yes, thank you," I said formally.

She looked at me curiously. "You're not American, are you, my dear?"

"No," I said calmly. "I'm not American."

And at that moment, it was true. At that moment I was from a faraway place, a strange and different country. Another identity to wrap around my bones, like clothes.

In the morning I woke in a small room, alone. I'd slept through the morning bells. I was getting my school uniform out of my suitcase—rummaging through my mother's careful packing—when one of the nuns came to find me.

"I am Sister Mary Elizabeth. I'm in charge of this dormitory wing."

I didn't look at her; I was trying to dress; the buttons were unfamiliar and I fumbled with them.

"I was here last night when you arrived, but I expect you don't remember me. It was so late and you were tired."

"Yes, ma'am," I said.

"I knew you would oversleep. Remember now, the first bell you hear is the rising bell; the second is the breakfast bell. I'll show you where the bathroom is."

Soon we were rushing down unfamiliar halls to breakfast. I could hear the clattering of dishes long before I saw the double glass doors that opened into the dining hall. Just inside the door, Sister Mary Elizabeth stopped. "Here we all are."

And I had a chance to view my new schoolmates, my companions of the term.

Before me was a wall of white.

I felt I was falling; my stomach lurched and came to rest in my throat.

A whited sepulchre, that was the phrase that flashed in my mind. We had read that in religion class just before school closed in June. Last June. Black June. Far away now.

White blouses, cotton, short sleeved, round collared. Like mine. White faces. Not like mine.

They filled the room. Millions of them, as far as the eye could see. Endless, gleaming. Their hair was of various colors, brown, yellow, red, but under their school uniforms were bodies of matching white.

Sister Mary Elizabeth put her hand on my shoulder, urging me forward. A few of the nearest faces stopped eating, turned to stare at me. Pale eyes, like daylight seen through the bottom of a Coca-Cola bottle.

The nun led me to a table near a window. A table for eight. One vacant place. On a tray my breakfast: orange juice, milk, and oatmeal. "You must be hungry"—she made a quick nervous gesture toward the food—"but hurry, child, it's almost class time. Don't worry about where to go. All new girls have an old girl to show them around. Here's Jennifer. She'll help you."

I drank the milk quickly, tasted the oatmeal. The bell rang. I took a few more spoons of oatmeal. Jennifer shook my chair impatiently. As soon as I looked up, she turned away, moving quickly through the emptying dining room.

She did not glance over her shoulder. She did not speak to me. She walked through a maze of corridors and doors and courtyards. I followed. She stopped at a classroom and pointed me inside.

Most of the girls were there already, talking, giggling, rustling through new textbooks. The smell of chalk and new erasers hung in the air like fog. I took a seat just as the teacher entered, a nun with a flushed face and red pimples across her chin. "This," she announced, "is our homeroom. You girls who are returning already know what I am about to say, but I must explain to the new students. This is where we start every school morning. I will read you the day's announcements; we will discuss special projects and excursions and social events. We will work together and we will all become friends."

I looked at her blistered chin and thought: That is Indian Fire. A girl at school last year had it, and they sent her home. I wonder if this nun is contagious. I wonder if we will all catch it.

Another bell, a short peremptory squawk—and homeroom time was over. The girls scrambled from the room. As their fluttering skirts passed me, I sniffed the disturbed air. An unfamiliar smell. Not perfume, that was not allowed. Ivory soap—yes. And something else. Quite strong, a little vinegary. The arriving class poured through the door as I collected my books. The smell grew stronger: vinegar and orange peel.

It was the smell of white skin. I stood still, sniffing carefully. Yes, of course, that was it. Soap and skin, both white.

My guide, Jennifer, was not waiting for me. No matter. I had my class card; I knew what came next. In the corridor the crowd thinned; classes were about to start. I should be in American history. Where was it? Was it even on this floor? We had, I remembered, come up a flight of steps.

"Excuse me," I said to a passing student, "do you know where the American-history class is?" She hurried past, as if I had not spoken, as if I were not standing in the middle of the hall, as if I were invisible.

I must find it myself then. Each door, I noticed, bore the name of its current class. The first said ALGEBRA I; the second, FRENCH IV. On the right another corridor, two doors on each side and large double doors at the end. I hesitated, undecided: should I turn or go straight ahead?

"Can I help?" Her rubber-soled oxfords squeaked on the polished floors as she hurried toward me; her uniform skirt flapped like a sail. "You're new, aren't you?" She was thin and tall; her skin was freckled to the color of a red Indian; her hair was the color of a carrot, long and straight and pulled into a ponytail. Her eyes were the yellow-green of a cat's. "Where do you need to be?" She pulled the schedule card from my hand without asking, glanced at it quickly. "Okay, you're almost there. Wasn't Jennifer supposed to stay with you today?"

I shrugged. "I'll find my way."

"Oh come on," she said, "all new girls need somebody to get them around this big barn of a place. I'll speak to Jennifer at lunch and see what went wrong. Until then, I'll take you from class to class. I won't forget."

I nodded my thanks. Looking into those yellow-green eyes, into that freckled kind face, my insides shook with fury. I hate you, I thought simply, I hate you to eternity.

American history had a lay teacher, a gray-haired portly woman who was writing on the board when I entered. She heard the door and said without turning, "Well, miss, you are late."

Twenty white faces swivelled toward me. I could feel the

light of their pale eyes bounce like arrows against my impenetrable armor.

"I was lost." My voice was deep and rich, not a girl's voice at all. I spoke now as I did to the customers at the fashion viewings, slowly, precisely. "I am sorry, but I'm new here. And Jennifer," I tattled, "forgot to meet me."

"Oh really." The teacher turned, slapped her chalk on the desk. "How can she be so irresponsible. I will speak to her. Sit down, my dear, and we will get back to our work."

Now two people were annoyed at Jennifer. Perhaps I could make it three.

At the end of that class, my friend with the carrot hair was waiting. I smiled at her, a professional model's smile.

"Okay, kid," she said with cheery heartiness. "This time we'll make sure you're on time. Did Miss Fowler jump all over you?"

"No," I said. "I told her I was new and lost."

"She'll lecture you about promptness sometime soon, I bet. It's her favorite subject. She hates people to be late and upset the opening of her class. There, that's where you want to be." She pointed to a door where a steady stream of navy-and-white uniforms entered. Like a stream of ants, I thought.

"My name's Sandra Robinson," she said with a smile. "I'm in the same dormitory with you, but not in the same wing. They put all you eighth graders together. Who's your roomie?"

"I don't have one."

The slightest hint of a pause. Then, "You're lucky. I still don't have a private room."

At lunch I discovered a change in seating arrangements. I had been moved to a table with Sandra Robinson and six of the older girls, all juniors and seniors. "You'll eat with us from now on," Sandra said. "We can do a better job of showing you around. Until you learn, that is."

Right then and there I began to be afraid. I recognized the feeling—that chill in my chest, from those long-ago days when my mother and I fled from place to place, moving and hiding and moving again. Pursued by something I did not understand, could not change.

And the difference was this. In those past days, I knew that my mother would triumph, that we would find our way at last to a shining lovely safe place of our own. Now I was alone. I needed to run, to hide, but I did not know where to go. I did not know this country.

That evening, I emptied my suitcase. A pleated skirt needed pressing. I took it to the utility room—washer and dryer, iron and ironing board. Two girls leaned on the washer, laughing. They looked up when I entered, did not answer my hello. I pressed the skirt carefully, then went back to my room.

I unpacked the rest of my clothes, refolding them to fit the new shelves and drawers, reluctantly changing the familiar shape of home, saying goodbye with each piece, fingertips across the cloth.

(In the months ahead, I would often touch these things, whose needlework was at once a testament and a promise from my mother to me. I drew strength from her strength, and patience from her patience. And I found something else here, something not from my mother, who was too distant, too complete, too indifferent for such emotions. In these bits of lovingly worked cloth I found the twin powers of hatred and anger. My keys to survival.)

I stood for a long time at the window of my single room. Below was a courtyard—brick walks and a fountain in the middle—with a rose garden, all pink and red. The bushes looked leggy and untended; the ground was covered with bright fallen petals.

Across the courtyard was the main classroom building. Through uncurtained windows I saw blackboards and neatly lined desks. Cleaning women moved through methodically. Behind them, room after room went dark, as if they packed light into their heavy trash bags and hauled it away forever. As if the last of days were ending and there would not be a sunrise tomorrow.

Beyond the building, I saw grassy fields stretching to a line of trees in the distance. It seemed a long way off.

Tomorrow, I thought, I would find out what was beyond the trees.

I settled myself on the windowsill, knees bent. This would be my world then, this courtyard, path, building, empty slope, and wood. I would see it every night before I slept.

Already the September air was chill. Winter would be real here, grass and flowers would die, trees would turn into skeletons. I wondered what snow was like. All I knew of it were the balls sold by street vendors in summer, mounds of shaved ice flavored with syrup. In my father's India—I had looked it up in the *Children's Encyclopedia*—there was deep snow all year long in the mountains. Kings and emperors craved it for their feasts; fast couriers brought it to their summer palaces where clever cooks flavored it with rose water and fruit. In the snowballs from the streets of my childhood, I had tasted the delight of princes.

That first night at school, after the bell had rung for lights out, I lay in bed and tried to remember my mother's songs. Eventually the sound of her voice did come to me, but it was thin and fine, delicate and useless.

The days passed, one after the other. I went to class; I

studied after class. Most of the students ignored me, looked through me, as those girls in the utility room had done that very first day. In the dining room I sat with Sandra Robinson and the six upperclassmen. They spoke to me politely, gravely, asking me about my classes, reading my papers, explaining math problems. Once a month, on Saturday, they'd insist I go shopping with them. I had no money to spend, but I sketched the clothes in the windows, and I drew caricatures of the shoppers. The girls found them very funny. They did not seem to recognize themselves, did not seem to know the joke was on them.

Except perhaps Sandra Robinson. Occasionally in the halls I'd feel her eyes on me. I'd look up, smile graciously, and incline my head.

Once Sister Paula, the principal, called me to her office. I sat properly, ankles crossed, hands folded in my lap.

"Your teachers say you are doing well in all subjects." Sister Paula sounded surprised. Had she then expected me to fail?

"It takes work to keep up," I said politely. "But I am sure I can manage."

"You are not bored?" Again the note of surprise.

"No, Sister, I am too busy to be bored."

"Your room is comfortable? And our food, does our food agree with you?"

Did she think I ate beetles and grubs? Why wouldn't school food agree with me? What difference was there? Except, perhaps, that these servings were larger, and meals arrived with clockwork regularity three times a day. Often, when my mother was busy, we would go without eating for an entire day. Sometimes too (though not lately), there'd be nothing in the house and we would have to wait for her paycheck on Friday afternoon.

"My room is very comfortable, Sister, and the food is very good."

"You're not lonely?"

"No, Sister."

She did not ask if I were ever afraid. Had she done so, I would have lied, of course.

After a month or so my classes seemed to become easier. I began to have free time. Sandra Robinson, attentive as ever, noticed the change. "There's an after-class instrumental-music program that's pretty good. Do you like that sort of thing?"

I shrugged. At home there'd been no sound except the hum of a sewing machine and the rustle of tissue-paper patterns and my mother's own murmured chanting singsong. We had not owned a radio or a TV.

"Why not try it?"

I did. The school had only one extra instrument, a violin, so I studied that. It made no difference to me. I soon discovered that I did not like music.

Why then did I work so hard? I think now that it was a form of aggression, of warfare. I attacked the school, my enemy, to plunder the only valuable thing it possessed: knowledge. Knowledge that I could carry away with me, safely hidden inside my head.

Thanksgiving week all students went home. Except me. The airfare was too expensive, so I stayed. Me alone, princess in my echoing castle. With the nuns as my retainers.

I kept busy. I relined my drawers with white tissue paper. I tightened loose buttons and repaired snagged hems. I explored the fields and woods beyond my window and discovered a six-lane interstate on the other side. I watched the passing traffic for hours, my teeth chattering with cold. I got a history of music from the library and studied it carefully,

using a dictionary for the unfamiliar words. I practiced my
violin exercises, hour after hour, until the new soft calluses
on the tips of my fingers bled and stained the gut strings.

That week it snowed, the first I had ever seen. I opened
my window and stuck my bloody fingertips into the soft ac-
cumulation on the sill. (It was not so cold as the vendor's
flavored snowballs.) Then came a hard freeze. The marks of
my fingers, like bruises, stayed on the sill.

I did not go home for Christmas either. Again I was alone
with the nuns, and for a longer time. One day as I was passing the music room—in the empty quiet building—I heard
Sister Lucy singing, tentatively, striking a few piano chords.
I went in.

"Child, I'd forgotten you were here." She still wore the
traditional habit, and inside its coif and wimple her small
face was red and wrinkled as an old apple.

"I should like to learn to sing," I said.

She blinked at my directness.

"I want to join the choir."

"It would be a good way for you to make friends," she
said thoughtfully. (I neither need nor want them, I answered
her silently.) "Come, let's see what sort of ear you have."

Twice a day she worked with me. I grew confident and
my voice grew steady and true. I could follow the piano
scale. I could read simple scores, turning the silent marks
into sound. I practiced dutifully, triumph filling my veins
like brandy.

Soon I was singing in the choir. (How happy the director
was to see me—there were only three contraltos.) I stood in
the midst of the group and sang with them, me like a speck
of dirt in all that whiteness.

At the reception after our recital on Easter Sunday Sister
Lucy sought me out, and found me where I usually was,
standing against a wall, in a corner, alone, watching.

"My dear," she said and her small brown eyes beamed from their wrinkled hollows, "I am so proud of you."

I nodded, eyes properly, demurely, downcast.

O little old lady, smiling at me, you don't know that I have stolen a part of you. When you appear in heaven, that heaven you believe in, the Recording Angel will say, O Sister Dear, your soul looks as if it has been nibbled by mice. There is a piece missing. Your wisdom is depleted, your value reduced. Who was this thief? The black daughter of a black prostitute? Or the daughter of an Indian king?

Often during that first year, I thought of myself as a secret presence. (After all, did not the students already look through me as if I were invisible?) I was the mouse in the pantry, the moth in the woolens, the worm in the ground, moving silently through the heart and halls of the school.

I imagined one scene over and over: at high school graduation, I emerge from my concealment. Draped in honors and ribbons, I step into brilliant sunlight, to a curving path like the yellow brick road in *The Wizard of Oz*. I float along, strewing flowers from my long slender fingers. Behind me this cluster of buildings, school and church and gymnasium, crumbles. Walls collapse, even the bricks crumble into dust like termite-riddled pieces of wood. . . . I have, like a spider, sucked the vital juices from this place. I have amassed its knowledge; I have learned its prayers; I have absorbed its attitudes, its good and its bad. I have transformed them all into me, leaving nothing behind. This citadel of whiteness has been looted by a single black thief, whom they declared invisible. Their magic has become mine, and I will now carry it away to my mother in her secret fastness far to the south. . . .

So I dreamed for the future.

For the present I smiled politely at Sister Lucy and imag-

ined her turning to dust, her habit, black wool and white
linen, sinking slowly to the floor, into a heap of old unwanted clothes.

Because the school required it, I wrote to my mother each
week. Not letters, which I knew she would not bother to
read. But sketches: of dresses and coats, skirts and blouses,
handbags and jewelry. My own designs, my dreams.

My mother did not write; I telephoned home. There was
a pay phone in the dormitory hall; we signed up to use it at
ten-minute intervals. Sunday was the most popular time, but
I chose Wednesday, every second Wednesday, at nine-thirty.
David Clark always answered. He told me his news—the
weather (rainy weeks were busy and profitable for a cab-
driver), a horse he had won fifty dollars on, the sandwich
shop he had opened in a downtown office building. Then it
was my mother's turn. She described her latest ideas in careful detail, telling me exactly how she had integrated my designs into them. Business was good, she said, she had hired
two women to do piecework for her. She told me who they
were and what sort of families they had. Even so, she said,
she had to work until midnight to keep up. She was thinking of leaving her job at Lambert Brothers Department
Store, but they'd just given her a raise and she liked the regular paycheck every week. She wanted to move her shop to
a nicer location; she was looking but she hadn't yet found a
place she could afford.

I listened but said nothing at all. They seemed to want it
that way. The call never lasted the allowed ten minutes.

In the new term, at midyear, another black face appeared
in the dormitories: Adele Abbott, a junior. She was short
and square, with a wide face, a flat nose, and kinky hair she
straightened and held in place with a thick gel. She lived

nearby and went home every weekend. Her father was an accountant, her mother taught school, she told me, and home was a steel town. She herself had worked in the mill last summer, right at the furnaces, where the heat was so intense she wore long underwear for extra protection under the regular protective gear. "You've seen that big Rockport plant, you know what I'm talking about." When I said I hadn't seen it, nor even known of its existence, she looked surprised and then annoyed. "Where have you been? In a cornfield?" She played the piano very well and knew endless songs by heart. Her favorite seemed to be "Star Dust," and its old-fashioned sounds floated through the halls in the free period just before bedtime, mixing with the rock from a dozen different radios (light rock, of course, the only kind permitted).

She lived in the junior-senior dormitory, a separate wing, but we were often together. She sat at my table in the dining hall, us two little black peas close together in our pod. She wrote a piano-violin version of "Danny Boy," simplifying it for me. We practiced it carefully and played it everywhere, for school assemblies, visiting parents, school benefactors. We even provided background music for an alumnae fund-raising luncheon. (Adele did most of the work, of course. The only song I played well was "Danny Boy.") Once, passing me in the hall, a girl said, "That sounded nice. I guess you people are born musical."

I stopped, open-mouthed and startled, not by the words, which didn't even anger me, but by the fact that someone had actually spoken to me.

Adele had a steady boyfriend, his name was Stephen; he was twenty-four, had played basketball in college, and now worked in his father's insurance business. His photo was hidden under the sweaters in her drawer.

In April, the night of her birthday, Adele broke the one

single inviolable law of the school: she slipped out of the dormitory. Using a bit of wire, she disconnected the burglar alarm on a window in the science classroom. She climbed out, dropped the few feet to the ground. On such chilly nights the watchman never left the warmth of his guardhouse. Nothing moved, not even a bird, as she crossed the playing fields and climbed the low rail fence at the Lexington Road. Stephen was waiting in his car.

She had trouble climbing back; the window was higher than she'd thought; she got brush burns and scratches on her knees and elbows. In the morning she went to the infirmary, saying she'd fallen on some concrete steps. The nurse shrugged with disbelief but picked out the largest pieces of grit, scrubbed the wounds clean, and said nothing at all.

Next evening Adele came to my room and closed the door after her. "I want to show you something." She was almost shivering with excitement. "Can you keep a secret? Swear you can."

"Of course I can."

"Look." She unbuttoned her blouse, unhooked a safety pin from her bra. "Stephen gave me this last night. For my birthday." An engagement ring, a round diamond set in gold. She slipped it on her finger and turned her hand back and forth in the light.

She didn't notice my silence. "I have to wear it under my bra during the day, but I sleep with it on every night." She held her hand under my desk light. "Just look at it."

In the small room, windows shut tight against the spring night chill, I was overwhelmed by a dislike of her, a physical dislike. Her short square body, her stiff shiny black hair, the rasping sound of her excited breath, her perfume...

"Aren't you worried about the nuns finding out?"

She shook her head, not taking her eyes off the ring.

"You're not even supposed to be wearing perfume."

Her eyes glittered in the desk light, black eyes with points of sparkle in their depths, and she smiled a happy wide smile. "I only wear perfume when I go to bed. By morning it's worn off." Her smile brightened. "Once, though, Sister Bernice, you know her—in the food service department—once she asked me if I was wearing perfume, and I said, 'Oh no, Sister, that's against the rules. You must be smelling the vetiver sachets I put in my drawers to keep away the moths and the roaches.' She was so stupid she believed it."

The bedtime bell rang. Adele withdrew her hand from the circle of light. "I'm not telling anyone else. Just you."

"Whatever," I said.

A week or so later, I walked across the quadrangle on my way back from choir practice—we practiced in the chapel these days, preparing for our ambitious Graduation Week Concert. I was alone as usual; the other girls had gone off in groups, laughing and gossiping.

"Wait!" Sandra Robinson caught up with me. "That sounded pretty good, don't you think?"

I looked into her smiling face, freckled to the color of a paper bag, and I thought: You are a fool to think you can make me feel at home with kindness. I will never feel at home here.

We walked in silence for a few steps. Dogwood edged the quadrangle like thin smoke. The air was heavy with the smell of new-broken ground. Gardeners had been preparing the flower beds.

"They'll plant hundreds of pansies," Sandra Robinson said, sniffing the telltale air.

"I don't really like pansies," I said. All those little faces looking at me, all those wide surprised eyes.

"You will when you see these," Sandra Robinson said, "you'll love them. It must be something in the ground or the light here. They are just absolutely gorgeous."

Must you convince me of even that? I thought. Must I agree with everything? Is appreciation of the beauty of pansies part of my education ...? I think, perhaps, I hate all flowers.

Ahead of us the dormitory door opened. Light flooded out, flowing toward us like water on a beach.

I stopped. "I'll tell you a secret, a really serious secret. Adele's engaged. She slipped out the other night, and Stephen gave her a diamond ring."

I felt a shiver of pleasure as I broke that confidence. "But you mustn't tell anyone," I said. "Not anyone."

But of course she did.

And of course the nuns soon heard the talk, as they always did. The Sister Superior called Adele's parents for a conference. And questioned her friends, including me.

"Did you know she left the dormitory?"

"Yes, Sister, I knew. She told me when she showed me the ring."

Frank. Open. Direct. A minority child like me must be forgiven her sins. The jungle is still close to her. She requires understanding. Her moral code is not fully developed.

"She brought the ring to my room for me to see."

Sister Lea, called Sister Lesbos among the girls, tapped her fingers on the desk. "You know that what she did was against the rules, do you not? Why did you not come to me? Or to any of the sisters?"

But this was too much. My ever-present imp of the perverse rose up in me with a lion-like roar. I felt a surge of protective feeling for Adele, for those bones wrapped in a skin of my color.

"No, Sister. I could not do that. Not ever."

"We cannot have you girls running all over the country-side at night."

"She would be the only one, I think." I spoke clearly, deferentially stating my opinion. "No one else has the courage. Or perhaps no one else is that much in love."

She looked at me strangely, curiously, as if I were some exotic zoo specimen she had not seen before. "Yes. Very well," she said.

Sandra Robinson said, "Why did you tell me about Adele's ring when you knew it was a secret?"

I looked at the freckled face, earnest and sincere. "I told you not to tell. Why did you?"

She looked upset, and hurt.

"Why did you even listen to me?" I insisted. "Why do you care what us two black folks do?"

She spun away.

In the days that followed, Adele and I behaved with perfect politeness toward each other, though the talk at our table in the dining room was strained and stiff—about the choir or the play (I was helping with the scenery) or the softball team or the new French teacher, Mrs. Delatte, hired after Sister Winifred's heart attack. And all the while the nuns debated Adele's punishment.

Finally they were agreed; the school rules were too important; they must not be flaunted or ignored. Adele was expelled.

She came looking for me, of course, and found me at my locker between classes.

"Black nigger bastard," she shouted down the length of the crowded hall. "I hope you burn in hell."

I was a little surprised. I had not known she was so religious.

I absorbed her hate like nectar from a flower. I smiled into the shocked faces of the students around me. I smiled at the teachers who came running. I expanded, until I myself filled my universe.

I was no longer invisible. The whole school had looked at me, had seen me, and had to admit that I existed. The students seemed more frightened and bewildered than angry. Around me the dining table was silent. I walked completely alone—to class, to choir practice, to the theater workshop. I was excluded from the Saturday shopping trip. No matter. I ignored them. I pretended that they, in their turn, were invisible.

It did not last long. Soon Sandra Robinson was back at my side, her face indicating understanding and sympathy, kindness and condescension. (I was sixteen years old and I despised it.) Others joined us. I became part of a group; we studied together, six or eight of us, learned tennis, memorized poetry, practiced our beginner's French. We imagined we were friends; we said so out loud.

Such was my first year at boarding school, an eighth grader, almost two years older than my peers, and light-years apart.

By mid-June I was home. My mother left her job at the department store to work full-time at her own shop. "She finally did it," David Clark said with a wide proud smile. "I finally talked her into it." He had gone to the bank with her; he had cosigned the loan.

By mid-July we had moved from our apartment over Leconte's Drugstore to a house on Maple Street, a double house, one side for us to live in, one side for the workrooms and the showrooms. We took the old sign with us to hang beside the different door: MODISTE.

There were changes, too. My mother still made children's clothes—there were at least a dozen new designs displayed in her sketchbooks, and her two hired seamstresses worked busily on the steadily increasing orders. But now she also made elaborate clothes for newborns, long christening dresses of lace and silk, bonnets covered with embroidery, buntings of fine transparent wool.

(I held one of the finished caps in my hand, admiring its intricate swirling design of seed pearls. "This could be for a bride."

"Yes," my mother said. "I will get to that. In good time.")

During the year I had been away, she had designed new dresses for me to model, dresses for a sophisticated young woman. (She looked at my hands, picked them up, and turned them over, examining the quick-short nails and the calluses made by the violin strings, then showed me how to bend my fingers—just slightly—to conceal them.) I had always looked older than I was. The sleek understated dresses suited my appearance perfectly. And they sold very well. My mother hired another seamstress.

"Have you noticed?" David Clark said to me. "She is really happy, she has planned this for so very long."

Yes, I had noticed. In the months I'd been gone, my mother had changed. She was far more at ease now; she moved with the careless grace of a shadow; she spoke easily with her customers, thoughtful, concerned, charming. Before, when I displayed her dresses, I had been the princess and she the invisible presence. Now she'd emerged to stand beside me, as the dowager queen.

She no longer worked on Sunday. (She no longer went to

church either.) In the morning—early, she always woke with the first light—she worked in her garden, a two-foot-wide brick-outlined strip along the four sides of the house. She planted impatiens across the front, a crowded mass of pink and white. Along the sides she put a jumble of petunias and daylilies and a few rosebushes and half a dozen violets. In the back, under the kitchen window, was a bed with four cabbages, an edging of parsley, two staked tomato plants, and seven stalks of corn.

She spent all Sunday morning weeding and fertilizing, only stopping now and then to sniff the smell of chicken roasting in the oven: that was how she knew when it was done. At ten minutes to twelve David Clark parked his cab in the driveway. He brought a bottle of bourbon and a bag of ice, and he and my mother had a quick drink before dinner. And it was always the same dinner: roast chicken and stuffing, sweet potatoes with marshmallow topping. After, if the weather was good, we went to the Botanical Gardens in the City Park. In the midsummer afternoon, the flowers seemed diminished, wilted and cringing in the heat. We opened our umbrellas against the sun and walked on, listening to the chattering drip of large fountains whose waters smelled strongly of chlorine. We bought a bag of taffy kisses and another of popcorn as we strolled along the seawall, where there always seemed to be a small breeze, and watched sailboats moving ponderously across a lake of blinding glare. On rainy Sundays we went to the movies. In the dark my mother fell asleep instantly, head held straight, and woke only when David touched her arm. On those rainy days we bought a dozen doughnuts and went home to make a fresh pot of coffee. That was our supper. At seven o'clock my mother began yawning, and David went home to his wife. No matter how much time he spent with us, he always went home at night.

He'd half explained his life to me once. "I got married just before I went overseas in forty-three. I didn't have any family except my brother, and he was in the army too. I wanted to have somebody to get my allotment check and maybe my insurance. I sure was worth more dead than alive."

And my mother said, "She is crippled. A disease of the nerves."

Which was as close as my mother ever got to explaining anything.

In September I returned for my freshman year of high school. My mother packed my clothes as carefully as before, now including the one party dress the school required of all high school students. Mine was peach silk with a wide lace collar and a flowing eight-gore skirt.

The school buildings were the same, as were the playing fields and the gardens and the chapel and the classrooms and the endless echoing halls. Sister Winifred had died of her heart condition, and Mrs. Delatte still taught French. The history department had another teacher, a young woman from town, just out of college, her name was MacIntyre. We called her Miss Mack.

My guardian angel Sandra Robinson was there, once again appearing at my elbow or watching me carefully from a distance. This year she was president of the senior class and editor of the school newspaper, and her talk was about colleges and entrance exams, full scholarships and tuition waivers.

And there were three new black students. We were all freshmen and we shared two double rooms next to each other. In the dining hall, on opening day, Sandra Robinson gathered her four black lambs and settled them at her table.

The other chairs filled up with politely smiling girls, filled up so smoothly that I knew the Sister Superior had issued orders.

No matter. I was used to it. I had adjusted. Indeed I had. I could walk these halls and paths and fields with a feeling of assurance, if not of belonging. I did all that the school expected of me. I made friends when I would have preferred to be alone. I sang in the choir; I had an occasional small solo part. I practiced my violin; my callused fingers moved with something like facility across the strings. I learned to play tennis and badminton. During my years at parochial school I had learned basketball; now I played forward on the varsity team. I taught myself to type on one of the unused machines in the Upper School Office. I kept an A average and was on the honors list every quarter; for that I wore a small blue-and-gold bow on the collar of my uniform blouse. I joined the drama club again and worked on the scenery for all the productions. On Saturday mornings—just as we had the previous year—a group of us rode the school van to the Riverdale Shopping Mall. We drank Orange Julius and tested all the counter perfumes and tried on long dangling earrings until the salesclerks grew weary and told us to leave. We ate hamburgers with onions and chili and wiped our greasy mouths delicately, remembering our manners.

I could afford such treats now. I had money in my pocket, mine to spend. With the school's help, I'd found a job—I produced special invitations for special occasions: bridal showers, birth announcements, luncheons, anniversary parties. Whatever the occasion or the theme, I illustrated it in watercolors and lettered it carefully in script copied from a library book on calligraphy.

Oh yes, I had adjusted. But not everybody had. I lived with an intimate view of misery.

My roommate, whose name was Connie, cried in bed every night. I soon trained my ears to shut out the sound of her sniffles, and I slept peacefully until the morning bell.

Because we were now considered to be young ladies, we were required to learn social grace and polish. On the first Sunday of every month, the high school held afternoon tea. The parlors were decorated with flowers and shiny-leafed bay branches. Linen and silver emerged from the housekeeper's locked closets. We girls put on our party dresses and our high heels and added light touches of makeup. (Perfume was still not allowed.) All sorts of people were invited; the rooms were always crowded. Benefactors of the school. Alumnae and their husbands. Businesspeople from town. Local priests. Missionaries on their soul-saving way somewhere else. Teaching brothers from St. Dominic's College just across the valley. Visiting parents. Journalists. Writers. Professors from the state university. Politicians discreetly campaigning for reelection. And always, each time, boys from one of the neighboring schools. Sometimes they wore gray military uniforms (imitations of West Point), sometimes the embossed blazers of a Catholic school, sometimes the tweed jackets of a nonsectarian one.

There was hot tea, and fruit punch made with iced tea, and cookies and little sandwiches with vegetable fillings. There was music too; Miss Ellison from the music department played piano medleys of all the Broadway shows. We circled the rooms, chatting politely for two hours, while the senior girls checked our manners and poise.

I never understood why the boys came. Perhaps they were required to appear.

I know that I enjoyed those afternoons. In my lovely dress, with my hair brushed straight down my back, I moved with a model's slow deliberation. ("You look like you're sleepwalking," a girl whispered to me.)

The older people talked to me seriously, the professors especially. I had learned to ask questions to cover my ignorance. One kind man, with a bald head and fuzzy eyebrows, introduced me to topological algebra between bites of watercress sandwich. Another explained to me the value of computer modelling in economics. Sandra Robinson, always at my elbow, urged, "Talk to the boys. Just go up to any of them and start a conversation. Try it."

When I finished my turn at the punch bowl, fifteen minutes of ladling pinkish liquid into imitation cut-glass cups, I singled out a tall thin brown-haired boy. "Is this your first visit to St. Catherine's?"

"I came once last year." He was wearing a tweed jacket and a navy tie. The shirt collar was too small for him, I noticed; he had left the top button open.

"I wasn't in high school last year," I said, "so I couldn't come."

"Does that make you a baby?" He smiled; he had good strong teeth, the sort you see in toothpaste ads.

I walked over to an open window. He followed. We leaned against the sill and talked. He was a sophomore at Milton Academy, he said. He played the clarinet and had spent the summer at music camp in Michigan. "What did you do last summer?"

"I'm a model," I said quietly. And liked the way it sounded.

"Yeah?" He seemed impressed. "How long have you been doing that?"

"All my life."

"How about that. You like school here?"

"I have to go to school someplace."

He laughed, a short hard snort. "You're so right."

Miss Ellison was playing "Some Enchanted Evening." On

the piano a bouquet of flowers shivered; a dahlia dropped to the polished wood. The copper-colored petals looked like red hair. Like the head of a very small Anne Boleyn, I thought, and was pleased by my allusion. I must use it in an English paper sometime soon.

"You going to the game Friday?"

"What game?"

"You don't know? You sure you really are in high school? Baldwin, that's last year's state AAA champion, is going to play St. Aloysius. And the thing about it is that St. Aloysius this year has the coach who was at Baldwin last year. Now do you see?"

What game are they playing? I wondered, but I didn't ask. I just nodded.

"So are you going?"

"I might. Maybe."

"There'll be plenty of car pools from here—but you're only a freshman, so I guess you didn't know that."

I sat back on the windowsill. Across the room Sandra Robinson's eyes watched me. "I suppose I will go."

"I'll look for you. Buy you a Coke at halftime."

"Yes," I said.

So. I had arrived. As soon as possible I would tell my friends. They would be jealous, I thought.

I participated. And I smiled. But I said very little.

"Don't you ever talk?" someone asked me.

I shrugged. A girls' school is a constant babble of voices, laughing, simpering, whining, complaining voices. Even silent prayers in chapel were a shrieking gabbling demanding din to ruffle the ears of the Almighty.

"She has a philosophical mind," Sandra Robinson answered for me. She had appeared, as she always did, from nowhere. "She considers things carefully. . . . Look now, little one, why don't you join us after dinner tonight? There's a group of us'd be glad to see you."

It was a great compliment, an invitation to join the intellectual elite of the school. I smiled my thanks, and truly meant it; I so enjoyed being praised for my intelligence. It is a weakness of mine, then as now. I am quite aware of it, though I make no attempt to correct it.

The evening discussion group was Sandra Robinson's idea, begun three years before. After dinner, when the kitchen staff had cleared the tables, ten or fifteen girls, mostly seniors, gathered in one corner, feet propped on chairs, elbows planted firmly on tabletops—attitudes strictly forbidden during meals. For an hour or so, between the departure of the kitchen staff and the arrival of the night janitors with their heavy cleaning equipment, the dining room was ours to lounge and talk. The upperclassmen. And me.

"Well now," Mrs. Delatte, the French teacher, said. She was dinner chaperone that evening; the teachers took turns, a week at a time. "Such a serious gathering. This must be a meeting of the Académie!"

So that's what we called ourselves. For a while we tried to speak only French, but that didn't work. No one was really at home in the language, except one girl from Quebec. We went back to English but kept the seriousness. There were no jokes, no pictures of boyfriends, no gossip. We talked about the future of the world, how to live a meaningful life, the duties of one human being to another. We were, I suppose, reinventing the Ten Commandments . . . until the sound of rattling polishers and floor machines scattered us back to our dorms.

Sandra Robinson's favorite subject was self-knowledge. She was then reading Freud on the unconscious. (She kept her copy, a small book with a red cover, hidden in her room.) Night after night she talked on and on, arguing, questioning, presenting her own thoughts in a long monologue. The other girls, bored by the subject, drifted away. She went on lecturing to me alone. "It's all a matter of self-knowledge. If you know what you are, you can accept what you are. But how do you know yourself? That's the real problem."

"Not for me," I said truthfully. "I never thought about it."

She took a deep breath. "Okay then, if you don't want to look at yourself, you can start with your family."

"Freud says that?"

"I'm saying that. You can look at your family and you see yourself."

"I can? Well, my mother's a retired prostitute who's got a dressmaking business now. I've got a more or less resident stepfather who's a cab driver. Now, how does that say anything about me?"

"I didn't mean details." Sandra Robinson looked very embarrassed. "I didn't ask you about that."

"Of course you did," I said cheerfully.

"No." She got up and began to pace around the table. "You're just not listening." She sounded more confident now; her classroom lecturer voice had returned. "What I'm saying is that you should make some effort to know yourself, all the secret thoughts and feelings you aren't aware of."

"I'm not interested."

"You should be, that's the point. The unexamined life is not worth living—who said that?"

"Freud?"

"No. And don't be silly."

"Any kind of life is worth living. Better alive than dead, that's what I say."

"You can be very annoying." Sandra Robinson tapped me on the shoulder.

"Everybody tells me that. . . . But they love me just the same."

She took a deep shuddering breath. "Oh come on now. Stop being so vain."

There was a rule at St. Catherine's that all freshmen must be able to swim the length of the pool four times. The thought of the warm chlorine-reeking water made my skin crawl, but I put on a suit and went to the pool.

"You can't swim at all?" The swimming coach, whose name was Nydia Carter, looked at me with horror. "You have never even tried? Not ever? Just think what would happen if a boat sank or you fell overboard."

"Yes, ma'am," I said politely, "but I've never been in a boat. And where I live I am more likely to get hit by a car than drowned in a flood."

"Oh dear," she said, "oh dear. Well, you'll just have to learn now."

"I could teach her, Miss Carter, if you're busy." Sandra Robinson emerged from the pool, sleek and dripping.

My guardian angel, my alter ego, my own personal policeman.

"If you would, my dear." Miss Carter looked relieved.

"Okay, kid," Sandra Robinson said cheerfully. "Let's start right now. You really mean it, you've never even gone wading?"

"Of course I mean it."

"It's easy."

"Okay," I said, "okay, start teaching me."

She pushed me in.

Water was hard, I realized as I broke the surface. I curled myself into a ball, arms around knees, and sank. I felt tiles under my feet; I opened my eyes and saw wavy lines of grout. I held my breath, my head puffed like a balloon. The water was heavy on me, heavy as earth, and I was buried. In a panic I thrashed out, felt something, grabbed it. It was the splash rail on the side of the pool. I hung on, looked around, saw an expanse of empty pool, looked up, and saw Sandra Robinson grinning at me.

I shook the water from my eyes, gingerly released one hand, and stretched it out to her. She shook her head. Panicked, I returned the hand to the splash rail.

She sat down at the side of the pool, legs crossed Indian fashion, laughing.

"You tried to drown me."

"Straighten out your legs, girl. They're all curled up, straighten them out and stand up."

Warily, I did. One touched bottom, then the other. The water was only waist deep.

"You sank like a stone," Sandra Robinson said cheerfully, "curled right up on the bottom in three and a half feet of water."

"It's not funny. I could have drowned."

"You came up, didn't you? I told you swimming was easy. Let's get on with the lesson."

Later, tired, furious, half sick with embarrassment, I sat on a locker room bench, dressing.

"Don't be mad," Sandra Robinson said. "It's just a way to start. It's the way my father taught me."

"Then your family are cretin idiots."

"Oh come on." She stood behind me, bent, kissed the left side of my neck, then dragged her lips across my shoulders.

I dressed quickly and left, running across the quadrangle in the cold air.

I did not understand what had happened. Not for a few hours. Then, drowsing through evening prayers in the chapel, I jerked alert with the shock of understanding. I was not horrified or sickened by the fact of aberrant sexuality. (I was, if anything, quite curious about it.) But I was very annoyed at myself. I had been foolish. I had relaxed, grown careless, and been caught unaware. I did not care for such surprises.

After months of lessons, I managed to pass the swimming test, barely. (I hated the water.) Sandra Robinson remained the archetypical older sister, kind, thoughtful, considerate, protective. But now her level glance sparkled with mockery and laughter and secret knowledge.

I went back to the violin, cut my nails short and built up the proud calluses on the tips of my fingers. They did not hurt so much this year. They did not bleed so much. I played with the school orchestra now, sheltered securely in the midst of the second violins, working through endless dull scores.

I joined the track team and spent my free afternoon hours training on the cinder oval beyond the tennis courts. I liked distance running; I liked the feeling that the world drew back to let me pass. At first I heard everything, my feet on the cinders, car horns in the distance, birds in the nearest trees, voices from the tennis courts. Then those sounds faded into perfect silence. My arms, my legs, flexed and relaxed without will or effort. I moved through not earth, not air, but an entirely separate space all my own. . . . Around and around the track until sensations came back: the thud of my feet, the ache in my back, the harsh scratch of my breathing. Sweat poured down my arms, down my fingers. When I rested, hands on knees, body bowed with cramp, sweat fell from my forehead, salt rain on the grass.

Late in the year, in November—the missals we held at Mass said Advent and were counting the Sundays to Christmas—my roommate, Connie, refused to answer the rising bell. I showered, dressed, returned for my books, and found her still in bed, crying. (Had she cried all night, I wondered, and how could anyone do that?) I pulled back the blankets that covered her head. "Come on. It's morning."

People look ridiculous when they cry, blotched and bumpy, like a stone or a lump of earth thawing in the sun. I tossed the covers back over her.

"You'll be late for class," I said. "Come on"—I hesitated, trying to remember her name—"Connie, you can't have any tears left. It's a wonder that bed hasn't floated away on its own river."

No answer. I left.

At the end of the second class period, the two other black girls stopped me. "Is Connie sick?"

Two black raisins, I thought, squat and ugly. "You should know. She's your friend." I changed books from my locker. "You three are always together."

"She didn't come to class, not the first or the second."

"You even take classes together! Such good friends. Well, she was in bed when I left."

"Shit," they said softly to me. And hurried off.

When I returned to my room that afternoon, Connie was gone. The bed was made neatly and tightly; the things on her desk and dresser were arranged in orderly rows. A few days later, all her things were gone; her closets and drawers were empty. I had a room to myself again, a large room, quite comfortable.

I was called to Sister Lea's office. For an instant I wondered if I had done something very wrong. But my grades were good, and I had broken no rules, because I had no reason to break them.

"Connie has gone home," Sister Lea said.

I held myself deferentially, waiting.

"A complete breakdown. A total collapse." Sister Lea twirled a pen on her desk blotter. She had large heavy-knuckled hands, like a man's. "We need to know what happened, precisely what went wrong, so it will not happen again."

"Yes, Sister," I said obediently.

"Did she ever talk to you about problems?"

"She hardly spoke to me at all, Sister."

Sister Lea sighed. "But you've been roommates for three months."

"We had different schedules, Sister. I suppose that was it. Or perhaps she just didn't like me."

"Did she seem unhappy?"

"Yes, Sister."

"Explain then."

"She cried in her bed every night."

"Every night?"

"Yes, Sister."

"And you didn't tell anyone."

"No, Sister."

"Why was she unhappy? Her class work was good, she had friends, two especially."

"Yes, Sister, the other two black girls."

"They went to her room, found her still in bed, and informed the sister in charge."

"I told her to get up, Sister. I told her she would be late to class."

"Yes," she said slowly. The fingers of one hand played with the knuckles of the other. "It is hard to believe, child, that you could see someone so miserable and not try to do something about it."

I opened my eyes wide, to let the gleam of her desk lamp reflect from the black irises. "What could I do, Sister?"

"You might have told someone. You might have told me."

"I didn't think you'd be interested, Sister. You've got this whole school to run. And she must have liked crying or she wouldn't have done so much of it."

As I left her office, I heard—clearly, distinctly—the sound of cracking knuckles.

The other two black girls did not return after the Christmas holiday. I lived on, a single in my double room, next to their empty one.

(The following year there were eight black girls enrolled. As fast as they left, I thought with a smile, the good sisters found replacements, exponentially. I was proud of that word. I had just learned it.)

My high school freshman year passed into the spring. The mails began bringing seniors the answers to their college admission applications. Sandra Robinson was accepted by all three of the schools she had chosen. We, the members of the Académie, had a party for her in the dining room after dinner: fruit punch faintly flavored with wine, and a large cake decorated in the school colors, yellow frosting and blue roses. For the correct shade of deep navy blue the bakery had used far too much dye, and the blue roses were bitter to the tongue.

Much later that night, when only small dim lights burned in the halls and the building shifted and creaked and muttered to itself, Sandra Robinson slipped into my room and my bed. And to tell the truth, sex with her was not unpleasant.

The term ended. School closed. I returned to my mother's house and its familiar routine. The business was doing well. A few white faces appeared at the shop door, not many, two or three at a time, but they were enthusiastic and ordered lavishly from the sketches and the swatches my mother showed them.

"Do they come to your regular showings?" I asked.

"Of course not," my mother said. "I even have a separate design book for them."

That struck me as very funny, but I didn't dare laugh.

That was the summer I visited the Sister Servants of Mary Home for Children, where my mother had spent so many years.

I asked her to go with me.

"Why?" she said.

"I don't know. I just want to. Wouldn't you like to see it again?"

"I have seen it. I pass it now and then when I am in that part of town."

"And those men, the ones you remembered in your prayers...wouldn't you like to find out where Clark County is?"

"No," my mother said.

I went without her.

To amuse myself, I turned a streetcar ride into an adventure. I became Orion, the mighty hunter. I saw myself dressed in skins, carrying a club, wearing a beard and a gold crown, following my mother's spoor, stalking through the urban wilderness.

It was a brick building: three stories, lines of small windows on each of its floors. Steep stairs led to a narrow front door so squeezed and squinched by heavy walls it looked like a guppy's mouth. In front was a statue of the Virgin wearing a crown of stars and a flowing blue dress. Across the street was a small park, scrubby grass and a small lagoon where pink concrete flamingos stood fishing in green-scummed water.

The community was at meditation. I waited in a small square hall, with two staircases at the far end and another statue of the Virgin Mary in the center. I sat in one of the wooden chairs that stood against the wall, a tall straight chair with a back carved into the face of a lion. A trickle of moving air passed me, carrying smells of laundry soap and furniture polish and something like mildew. Boards creaked and groaned softly as the building shifted on its foundations, a sound very like a sigh. Behind one wall something stirred, light and rustling; it could have been a mouse.

Eventually a nun appeared. You could see that she had once been fat, but the flesh had fallen away, and the contours of her face melted into her neck in folds, for all the world like a turkey. She might have been imposing in coif and wimple, but she wore the modern habit—a gray-and-white kerchief on her head, gray-and-white dress, a small rosary dangling like a watch fob from her belt. She was, she said, Sister Celeste.

We went into her office, a jumble of papers and ledgers and binders, where she listened to me with the professional patience of a religious, nodding gently like a car's dashboard ornament. When I had finished, she paused for half a minute, organizing her thoughts.

"Yes, I would have been here in those days. But the home was much larger then; it is hard to remember just one of the hundreds."

I wanted to say, to shout at her: My mother was different. She was a princess lost in the thorny forest of the night, an enchantress, herself under a spell. . . .

Instead I waited silently.

After a few minutes Sister Celeste said, "Sister Agnes, who was in charge then, kept wonderful records." Her toe tapped steadily on the floor: one, two, three, pause, tap, tap,

tap, pause. "But they were destroyed in a wiring fire in the small storeroom."

So it was gone, the name Mary Woods written in a firm precise nun's handwriting; certificates of baptism and confirmation; perhaps even a picture of a first communion group, an image of Mary Woods fixed on paper.

Sister Celeste rubbed her finger along the wattles of her neck. "I do seem to remember, it has been so many years ago . . ."

"Was her name Mary?"

Sister Celeste was annoyed by the question. "The foundlings were often named Mary. To put them under the protection of the Blessed Mother."

My mother had never looked for protection to the Christian gods. She had her own, along with her spells and sorceries. . . .

Sister Celeste went on, "I can see her face quite clearly."

But her inner vision was not a photograph for me to view. Was this truly my mother, the one among all those Marys?

I shifted in my uncomfortable chair. "What was she like, this child?"

"She only wanted to draw and paint and sew. She was so very clever with her fingers, she made beautiful altar cloths. She was left-handed, I remember that. We made her go to school, but it wasn't any use, she could not seem to learn."

My mother loved to draw, all those dresses with their elaborate details, their rich colors. My mother was left-handed. My mother could not read well. She had learned very little in school.

"Sister, what did she draw?"

Sister Celeste's eyes moved slowly back to me, focused. "Everything and nothing. There was just no way to stop her. Finally Sister Agnes let her cover one whole fence with pictures. A tall board fence at the back of the play yard, she worked on it for months—trees and flowers and two-headed animals, and people. The people, I remember, always had green faces."

My mother. Large, teeming, carrying millions of years of Africa with her. A stranger drawing strength and fertility from the foreign earth into her bones and blood. Disguised as a child ...

"I saw Sister Celeste," I told my mother that evening.

She was sorting out fabric orders, the kitchen table was covered with papers. "And how is she?"

"You're not listening. Sister Celeste from the Home. I went there."

"Did you?" She arranged the orders into two piles, secured them with clothespins.

"I thought it was interesting that she was still there."

She shrugged. "Where else would a nun be?"

Then David arrived, hungry for supper. And we never spoke of it again.

Unlike me, my mother did not look back.

A G A I N school. Nine months. Like a pregnancy, I thought. Nine months to incubate knowledge and give birth to a bit of paper that said I could advance one level. Well, no matter. By now I was a skilled survivor.

Our personal and social development progressed rapidly these days. We were encouraged to turn our attention outside the classroom, into the big world. With other private schools in the area, we went to Audubon Society meetings, Sierra Club gatherings, State Historical Society lectures, to planetariums and art museums. We took a long bus ride to view the treasures of ancient Egypt, small bits of gold we barely saw as we hurried past. We hiked to special meadows to study wildflowers and identify edible weeds (each of us with a copy of Euell Gibbons in her backpack). We took overnight trips to battlefields, and national monuments, and cemeteries, and the childhood homes of presidents. We camped in mosquito-ridden national parks with strange slippery rock formations and deep river gorges.

And sports, all kinds of sports. There were whole weekends of competition followed by awards banquets. I was voted the Regional Most Promising Athlete and wore a small silver charm around my neck. The silver had been badly cast, so that the running figure seemed to be fleeing in screaming terror.

There were picnics and hayrides and bonfires, all carefully chaperoned. There were homecoming dances and holiday dances, spring dances decorated by flowers, and autumn dance floors lined with piled pumpkins and silver-beige stalks of dried corn. On Sundays, after church and midday dinner, we went to promenade concerts in the park pavilion; with crowds of other young people we strolled about, sipping our Coca-Colas, wearing our best clothes, watching each other.

I cultivated my silence and my detachment carefully— rare flowers in a cold climate—as I watched girls chatter and giggle, faces contorted with vivacity, bodies vibrating with eagerness, while boys stalked stiff-legged like roosters, mint-flavored breath panting into the air.

O children, little children, the things I could teach you, the ways and skills my mother gave to me. . . . I myself, in my virginity, I am weary of sex. I know it for the business it is.

I was asked to the fall dance at St. Michael's School by a boy named Thomas Dorsey. A tall, thin boy, whose father

taught history at the state university, whose mother gave
piano lessons in the afternoons. He pointed them out; they
were both chaperones at the dance. His father was stocky
and balding and red-faced; his mother, taller than her husband, was wearing a long dark cape. "That's lovely," I said
to Thomas Dorsey as we ate the sticky cakes and drank the
cherry-flavored punch.

"What is?"

"Your mother's cape."

He glanced up briefly, uninterested. "She makes them."

"How do you mean, makes them?"

"I mean she *makes* them. She's a weaver. The back room
in our house is all full of her looms and stuff."

"Would she show me?"

"Tell her you're interested and you'll never get rid of her.
She loves to talk."

Mrs. Dorsey invited me to her workshop. She picked me
up at school the following week. (The nuns positively
beamed with pleasure: I was integrating socially.) We spent
almost three hours in her studio (so she called it); and she
showed me how she made cloth, step by step. It was all
there, the raw wool heaped in baskets, the carding combs,
the spinning wheel, the looms, and the separate outside dyeing shed. "It really smells," she said, "that's why it's back
here."

It was one of the happiest afternoons I have ever spent. I
told her so.

"I see that." She grew even taller in her pride. "Your eyes
are positively glittering."

Well, yes, I suppose so. I had never seen Appalachian
crafts before—the weaving, the quilting, even the basket-
making, danced like jewels before my eyes.

"In Slocum County, where I grew up," Mrs. Dorsey said, "these are things all girls learn, and don't think anything about it."

"Would you teach me? If I came back?" It was one of the few times in my life I have asked a direct question. I do not usually risk being told no.

"Will you have time? I hear the nuns keep you girls very busy."

"I have every afternoon," I said. "I could come then. The nuns will arrange a ride for me," I said confidently.

And they did. Three or four times a week a senior town girl dropped me off after class, and the wife of the maintenance engineer stopped for me on her way to school to pick up her husband shortly after seven. Sometimes I was late for dinner, but the nuns did not object.

I spent hours watching Mrs. Dorsey at her looms. The work was tiresome and dull—though not half so bad as the spinning, she told me. We soon ran out of talk, so she began to sing the songs she'd learned as a girl, hill songs, monotonous and repetitious and hypnotic. I brought my violin from school and we sang together, her reeds against my strings.

Sometimes Mr. Dorsey came home early and played the living room piano and sang with his wife, voices raised loud against the clacking loom. And sometimes Tom was there and brought out his guitar, and all of us played together. For a bit, in the midst of those songs, we were a family, really, truly, a solid southern mountain family, father, mother, son, and daughter, three white and one black.

Later, when my enthusiasm ended, as my enthusiasms always do, I wondered what had fascinated me so. Perhaps I fancied I was becoming a part of her life. The daughter she'd never had. These skills and sounds and melodies came from her family to me so that I became a part of her traditional America, my native land, where I was a stranger. I intended to slip into her world, to hide there until I belonged to my country as much as she did.

Or perhaps that wasn't it at all. Perhaps my happiness was nothing more than a feeling of freedom—of being away from the echoing halls and bare formal rooms of the convent school.

I spent Christmas Day with the Dorseys, their brothers and sisters and cousins, grandmothers and babies. Dozens and dozens of them. A tribe, uncounted. I was the speck in the uniform white flour.

It was also my first Christmas celebration. My mother and I did not celebrate any holidays, and at the convent Christmas was a religious occasion.

Some people, those from farthest away, came days early, filling all the beds, even the folding one in Mr. Dorsey's study. Two young men camped out in sleeping bags in Mrs. Dorsey's backyard dyeing shed. They had thick arctic sleeping bags and knitted caps and down-lined drawstring helmets. It was cold in that unheated building—snow fell in flurries and blew into drifts and the ground rang stiff and hard with frost.

Most people arrived very early on Christmas morning, bringing food: turkeys and hams (and the carving knives to go with them), fried chicken and a roast suckling pig, huge casseroles of sweet potatoes, red and green gelatin salads decorated with mayonnaise stars, pumpkin and pecan pies and half a dozen coconut layer cakes. They all brought liquor, too, wine and whiskey and brandy and rum. As fast as they arrived, Mrs. Dorsey set out the platters and plates and stands—there were five turkeys in a row on the dining room sideboard—until every table and counter was filled. The bar was on the glass-enclosed side porch, a long board trestle covered with red Christmas cloth. All the bottles went there, in neat straight rows. When the top filled, bottles lined the floor along the wall.

"Come help me." Tom Dorsey picked out two bottles, checked the labels carefully, and carried them into the kitchen. "You stand by the door and keep it closed for a minute. I don't want anybody to see me." He opened one bottle, sniffed, and carefully poured the contents down the drain. "Don't want to splash it," he explained with a grin. "The stuff is like paint remover."

A strange odor floated through the kitchen, sweet, musty, odd. "What was that?"

"Mrs. Frank Pope's dandelion wine. This other bottle is her rhubarb wine and it's even worse, so out it goes too."

"Wait," I said, "I want to taste it."

"You have lost your marbles." He handed me the bottle. "You'll be sorry."

It was a regular wine bottle. I lifted it to my lips and tasted. Very sweet and prickly on the tongue. I poured it out.

"I told you it was awful." Tom hid the empty bottles under the sink. "My mother doesn't want to hurt her feelings, but she doesn't want anybody drinking the stuff either. So she told me to get rid of it."

"It wasn't bad or nasty. It really didn't taste like anything."

"Drinking that stuff won't make a hillbilly out of you."

I stared at him. "I don't want to be a hillbilly."

"Sure you do. First comes weaving and dyeing. Now comes drinking homemade wines. Pretty soon you'll be drying apples on window screens in the attic and stringing bean pods from the rafters. Maybe you'll start making your own soap like Grandma Jenny."

"Who's Grandma Jenny?"

"Well"—he grinned—"she's not my grandma. I'm sure of that. I think she's some kind of relative of Pa's. She lives in Goshen, in Smith County. Up a narrow little valley, way back from the road, all rocks and trees and a spring coming down. She calls it a hollow. You want to be old-timey, that's where you got to live."

"I don't. I told you I don't."

"Anyway, we went to visit her once. She had an old quilt my mom wanted to copy. But first Grandma Jenny's got to show us around the place—the house and the new cistern, her garden, and her chickens, and the new cow and the way she pruned her apple trees. She was making ash water that day, fixing to make soap. And I can tell you, making soap stinks."

"Is she here now?"

"Comes every Christmas, one day early. Wouldn't miss it for anything. Tall old woman with a face like a horse and hands like a prizefighter's. You know, busted knuckles. Anyway, like I was telling you, my mother got the quilt pattern she wanted and everybody kissed everybody goodbye and we climbed down to where the car was parked. When we're driving away, my mother looks back up where we've been, and she tells me she was born in a place like that. Only she got out fast as she could."

So Mrs. Dorsey was a fugitive too. "Wherever she learned, your mom's weaving and quilting are beautiful."

"Sure. You want to hear more about Grandma Jenny? Her son now, he makes real high-class likker. Look there, those two bottles. That's from him. It's rum. It's as good as his ma's wine is bad. He makes it from hog molasses in a nice little still right behind the house."

"He does what?"

"He feeds some to the hogs and runs some through the still."

"I think you are being stupid. I'm going to see what everybody else is doing."

In the living room Mr. Dorsey was playing the piano. Under his thin yellow hair his scalp was red and shiny with sweat.

Somebody shouted, "Hey, bro, play 'Silent Night.' We need to do some singing."

Mr. Dorsey wiped the top of his head with his shirtsleeve. "Here we go, Cap."

They sang. I watched. They were all so very much alike, blond and red-haired. They looked tattered, I thought, mottled and lumpy like the rugs Mrs. Dorsey hooked.

The front door was open; wind blew through, cold and wet with the breath of snow on it. I stepped outside, pulling the door closed behind me. On the boards underfoot were half a dozen smashed kumquats, their shiny white and orange glazing in the cold. The entire porch was cluttered with overshoes and boots, umbrellas stuck upright to dry, two baskets of pinecones tied with red ribbon, and one basket of kindling with a sprig of holly on top. From porch to sidewalk was a line of red plastic poinsettias, stems stuck into the muddy snow-streaked ground. From the bare lower branches of a sugar-maple tree a paper Santa danced and dangled, for all the world like a jolly hanging man. Cars lined both sides of the street, as far as I could see, until the street disappeared over the lip of a hill and all there was beyond was a view of the interstate highway and the Goodyear factory.

There were other parties going on in the neighborhood. The corner house—two stories, green shingled—was so crowded that people gathered on the front lawn despite the cold. They hopped from foot to foot, shouting out toasts. In the house directly across the street bagpipes began playing. After a minute or so the piper himself emerged, a short square man, kilted and capped. The crowd at the corner, noticing, drifted toward him. He adjusted his cap and sporran, shifted his pipes, puffed his cheeks. Whistling and creaking, he searched for a tune, lost it, found it again, blared it out, triumphantly. People drew back, parted by the suddenly coalesced sound. The piper marched twice in a circle, drawing confidence from each step, then set off down the street, pipe tassels fluttering, a clear high melody streaming behind, a deeper rumble coming from the bag across his front, like a second stomach. Everyone fell in line behind him.

The Dorseys and their friends rushed out, cheering and clapping, carrying cups and glasses, and joined the parade. Two dogs followed. One, a kind of collie, stopped long enough to bark at me.

I turned back to the house, shivering in my light sweater. Tom was standing in the door. His eyes were very shiny and red-edged.

"I thought maybe you'd gone off with the big parade."

"Too cold for me," he said.

The pipes were fainter now; the melody changed; the crowd cheered approval. "Where are they going?"

"Them?" Tom shrugged. "Who knows. Last year they went all the way to that traffic circle on Cumberland Drive. Whatever Mr. Kidd feels like. He's the piper."

We went back inside. "This happens every Christmas?"

"What are you so all-fired curious for? You studying to be white? Yes, dear girl, every single Christmas long as I remember. Now what else do you want to know? Who's Mr. Kidd? That's his daughter's house there, he's visiting. Why does he play the bagpipes? I don't know. Okay?"

The house was quiet now, just a murmur of conversation from the old people in the living room.

One woman twisted her head to look around the sides of

the wing chair by the fireplace. "Would you get me a cup of coffee," she said to me.

"Yes, ma'am." I followed Tom into the kitchen.

"She thought you were help." He snickered.

"It's happened before."

"Now don't get huffy. You gonna bring her the coffee?"

"No."

He was still giggling. "Maybe you should be nice to her. Her brother makes the best corn whiskey around; even ages it, my father says."

"I can buy my own whiskey."

"Not like this, you can't. It is something special. I'll show you."

He handed me a half-gallon vinegar bottle filled with pale liquid. There was a label pasted on the side: FLOYD. "What's Floyd?"

"Her brother, you dummy. I told you he made it. Go ahead and taste."

I looked around for a glass.

"Don't be a nigger," he said, "nobody's looking, just have a swig."

"I am a nigger," I said firmly. "I do not have to try to be one." I unscrewed the top and took two quick swallows. My eyes started to water, then just as suddenly grew dry. A great soft aromatic sweetness flooded into my mouth, a taste like nothing I'd ever known.

"You see why people say he's the best? Let's have a proper drink now."

"Of this?"

"Sure. Nobody will notice, and if they do they won't care. It's Christmas."

We mixed the whiskey with ginger ale and decorated the glasses with orange slices and cherries stolen from the top of a coconut cake. We sat side by side on the kitchen counter, sang carols, and drank. We turned on the radio and danced. We had a second drink and listened to the far faint sound of the bagpipes returning. And sometime later I sneaked outside, to the very back of the yard, behind Mrs. Dorsey's dyeing shed, and vomited into a little shrunken patch of snow.

I stayed quite a while, waiting for the dizziness and the hissing in my ears to pass, waiting for the cold air to clear my head. As I walked back to the house, using the narrow side path along the fence, I heard voices in the dining room. The window was open an inch or two, so I heard clearly: a man and a woman.

"She's a student at St. Catherine's," the woman said. "Betsy told me."

Betsy was Mrs. Dorsey. I stood perfectly still in the frost-burned ivy.

The man said, "I didn't know they had Negro girls at St. Catherine's."

"She's the first. They say she's brilliant."

"Good of Betsy to ask her here for Christmas."

"You know Betsy, the soul of kindness," the woman said.

"Well," the man said, "I hope she has a good time."

"She's very polite," the woman said. "And it isn't her fault that she's colored."

"Colored?" The man laughed, and I could hear the ice rattle in his glass. "That's no high yellow. That is black, might even be Gullah."

"Hush," the woman said. And there was just a hint of a giggle hanging in the air.

And that was my first Christmas as a White Chile.

By the end of those Christmas holidays I had finished my sketches for clothes made with Mrs. Dorsey's materials. She herself wasn't enthusiastic. "Honey, these are homespun fabrics, country fabrics, you can't go and use them for fancy dresses like that."

But that was just exactly what I wanted to do. And I knew that my mother would agree.

My Christmas present had been one of Mrs. Dorsey's shawls, deep heavy uneven texture, rich earthy colors. I sent it to my mother, along with the sketches I had done. Yes, my mother said, if Mrs. Dorsey could supply enough material. After a flurry of phone calls, the orders were settled. Mrs. Dorsey's loom clicked steadily, hour after hour into the night—she got her sister to help her. Two more sisters travelled up and down the state, collecting pretty hill-country quilts. And the following season my mother introduced a special limited line of American clothes, all very expensive. (It was, I think, my mother's first venture into the truly upscale women's market.) Rough woolen coats, wide shouldered, flare skirted. Swirling capes lined with peau de soie. Quilted waistcoats over long satin skirts. Despite their price, the clothes were immensely popular. That season prosperous blacks walked about wrapped in the traditions of the Appalachian white. I wonder: Did their skins grow paler, did they feel the melanin leach away under the pale English aegis?

No matter. It was a successful partnership. With the profits the Dorseys got a new car and a kitchen stove, a new piano and long pale green silk curtains for the living room.

For two years I remained friends with the Dorsey family. I went to their house for every holiday. I went on a canoeing trip with them; the wind blew so hard that we gave up paddling, made camp on a sandbar, and waited to be picked up by the motor launch. I went to their university homecoming football game one November. I went to an Easter sunrise service way up in the hills, in a natural bald where the ground glittered with frost and the whole expanse of earth seemed to stretch away from my feet. If Christ had risen, I thought, it would have been from a place like this, not the rock and stone and twisted cedars of Palestine.

And one afternoon during my junior year, in his mother's dyeing shed where I was coloring endless yards of cheese-cloth for a school pageant, I seduced Tom Dorsey. I don't know why. I did not find him particularly attractive. Certainly my heart did not race at the thought of his body; I did not smile to myself at the memory of his face. I think it was simple curiosity; I had never had a man. My mother had taught me about sex, its refinements, its amusements, its delights, but the trouble seemed scarcely worth it, until that afternoon when I decided to experiment and Tom Dorsey happened to be there. He'd been bragging about the women he'd had. Some, he hinted, were friends of his parents. "All right," I said, stepping close to him, "show me." He looked frightened, but because he was a man, however young, he had to agree. Within a few minutes I had demonstrated that I knew far more than he.

His parents found out. I suspect it was Tom himself who told them, either in contrition or an excess of machismo. The invitations stopped; I never entered their house again. Tom and I continued to meet, stubbornly determined. What had once seemed an adventure became a kind of duty, a chore. Winter cold ended our meetings. I think Tom was relieved. I know I was.

Some years ago, in St. Catherine's *Alumnae News* (which comes regularly twice a year), I read that Thomas Dorsey married Alicia Parker. I remembered her: two years younger than I, a short fat giggling girl with fuzzy blond hair.

Because I was home only in the summer months, my impressions of my mother come in separate flashes, like photographs. They tell a story, to be sure, but without continuity.

Run through the projector of my memory, the images move jerkily, imperfectly, like an old movie. Even so I could see a change in my mother's world. Black and white were reversing themselves. . . .

My mother's business grew. As the black community prospered, so did she. At her original shop, Mary Woods Modiste, the showings were crowded with eager buyers. Here she dressed the black debutantes, their mothers and grandmothers. Here she planned the big expensive black weddings. She insisted on doing the entire thing herself, bride and bridesmaids, flower girls and ring bearer, the mother of the bride, the mother of the groom. It must all go together for the right effect, she said. She even designed the bouquets and the flowers for the church. (David owned the florist shop.) Her veils were particularly elaborate, with half a dozen different kinds of lace and seed pearls and masses of fresh flowers to be sewn on at the last minute.

Now, the summer of my last year of high school, my mother opened a new shop, the most ambitious one of all. It was on LaFreniere Square, one of those historical districts which are remodeled ever so carefully according to nineteenth-century blueprints and plans. There was an iron-fenced park in the center: very green grass and pink crepe-myrtle trees and a bronze general holding out his arm to the pigeons. Around the park was a tight circle of expensive town houses and stores: interior decorators, jewelers, architects, a couple of law offices, a haberdasher, two tailors, and a half-dozen dress shops. And my mother. Her door was marked by a polished-brass sign with a single word in flowing Spencerian script: *Mary*. Nothing else. It was very low key, very discreet, until you got inside. Then it was all art deco, glass brick and steel and shining chrome. My mother had copied the rooms from a thirties magazine.

The customers who came through that handsome doorway in a steady stream were exclusively white.

At this shop I worked as a saleswoman, silent, effi-
cient, helpful. Two college students were the models. One in
particular appealed to my mother. Her name was Melissa.
She was tall as I, as thin as I, with short blond hair and
huge blue eyes naturally shadowed in black. Thanks to my
mother's magic, the women who bought the clothes saw
themselves as Melissa every time they looked in their
mirrors.

My mother patrolled her small kingdom carefully, according to a rigid unvarying schedule. Early each morning the
ready-to-wear workrooms, which turned out a line of expensive children's clothes for the hotel boutiques downtown. I'd
designed this label, three trees, thin brown stems and green
crowns as puffy as a cumulus cloud. No name. No other
identification. . . . Next the made-to-order workrooms. These
woman were Spanish speaking—my mother had learned
their language (when had she done that?) and always spent
an extra few minutes gossiping with them about love affairs
and children. The rest of the day she divided between her
two shops. By ten o'clock she was displaying her clothes to
the customers at Mary Woods Modiste. She understood
these women; she knew how to make them accept her ideas
as their own. She knew how to manipulate their dreams and
flatter their egos, all so subtly, so gently. By three o'clock she
reached her new shop, the one of gleaming art deco behind
a nineteenth-century facade.

Here she changed clothes, growing even taller with high
heels and fitted dresses that emphasized the thin angles of
her body. Like a presiding goddess in her temple, her presence filled the structure. I walked in her shadow, watching,
learning. Her successor, yes, but not her model, no longer

the bones and flesh on which her dream images were hung. My black skin was unsuitable for her increasingly white audience.

Like any princess I valued my position. I watched for signs of palace coups; I searched for evidence of power shifts. When my mother fitted her thoughts to Melissa's white body, I watched for signs of betrayal. I looked distrustfully at the suppliers, the white women who sold my mother hand-dyed silks and taffetas, the special seamstresses who made the fine trousseau lingerie. How exquisite the work was, I touched it with the very tips of my fingers, carefully.... And I remained alert in this new world.

My mother had conquered the black kingdom. She had triumphed in her own land; now she was entering neighboring territory. And she was—I remembered Melissa's pale blondness—using enemy troops, mercenaries, to invade it.

Or so I thought during that last summer of high school. That long image-ridden legend-filled summer when my mother led us into new and dangerous territory on voyages of conquest and discovery.

Every evening after work a group of Melissa's friends met her at the door. College students like herself, laughing and hugging, so healthy and slender with well-tanned faces and dentist-perfect teeth, they seemed to have stepped from the pages of a fashion magazine. My mother and I bade them good evening and watched them go. Then we finished the last of the day's details, smiling at each other with satisfaction, until David came to pick us up. Over the years he had changed into a handsome man, tall, portly, brown skin, and silver hair. The three of us were a striking group, silver and black, very theatrical. We too were figures from a slick magazine. Our caption: *Modern black family enjoys new prosperity.*

Well fed and clothed and groomed, each evening we

progressed in triumphant splendor along the walks of the nineteenth-century square to David's new Cadillac. Like my mother, David was prospering. His downtown lunch restaurants were successful; his cab company had expanded to sight-seeing buses.

One day Melissa invited me to join her friends for a drink. "We go to a place called Jacob's. Just about everybody is there."

"Fine." I had never been to a bar. "Fine."

Jacob's was at the end of a row of brick buildings, on the corner. In front was a small patio with tables and umbrellas. Inside was a single large room, with red plush curtains hanging from brass rods and a mirrored brass-trimmed bar across the far wall. It was crowded, inside and out, the music almost lost under the roar of voices.

"It's the place to be right now." Melissa showed me around with a proprietary air. "Ladies' room's over there. We always sit on the patio."

So I became part of that jolly laughing group at last. We drank beer and frozen daiquiris and inhaled each other's perfumes and aftershaves mixed with dust and gasoline fumes from the passing traffic. It was indeed just like one big party. After an initial surprised pause—how often in my life have I seen that—people were eager to talk to me, to ask where I was from, and where I worked, and what school I went to. They wanted, I think, to see if I was really truly black, and not just a painted-up joke. Of course I told them that I was Indian, and I hinted gently that I was also a princess. They looked impressed, even if only for a moment. I was content with that. After all, their attention never stayed long on any one thing. A change of breeze, a passing car horn, a different song battering our ears—and they forgot what they were saying or thinking.

I began to enjoy myself as I had never done before. Senses

dimmed by alcohol, I forgot their color and they forgot mine. We were people drinking together after a day's work, flirting, seeking partners for the later evening, wrapped by the music and our own noisy chatter, young bodies in a summer night.

Later, as I waited in line in the ladies' room, I preened myself in the mirror, running my fingers lightly through my long straight hair, dabbing at my mascara, adding more lipstick.

A single sharp crashing bang on the door, and a shout: "Police on the way. Everybody under twenty-one get out right now. Use the fire doors behind the bar."

Immediately the small room began to boil all around me. Girls swirled in tight circles, snatching up purses and lipsticks and spray perfume bottles. Then I was quite alone.

Were they all underage, I thought. Was that possible? Or were they running because they had been startled, because a man's voice had shouted alarm? Did they scatter because it was pleasant and satisfying to panic?

I was nineteen—the law said I should not be here. But I wasn't about to go scrabbling off through that exit behind the bar, my full bladder aching at every step. I went into a stall, locked the door after me, and urinated slowly, unhurriedly. The floor shook with running feet; there were shrieks and shouts; a man laughed. I adjusted my panty hose carefully, washed my hands, massaged them with scented lotion from a small bottle in my purse. I settled my dress at shoulders and hips, snapped closed my purse. And opened the door.

The air reeked of perfume and sweat and tingled with the dust lifted by running feet. The velvet curtain behind the bar had been pulled half aside, but the fire door was properly closed. Some of the tables had been knocked over; a white-coated waiter was lazily picking them up. Music was still playing; couples still sat at their tables; a second waiter was taking orders. Uniformed police moved through the room, politely checking identification.

I walked out the front door. Three prowl cars, blue lights flashing, were partially blocking traffic. A policeman appeared directly in front of me. He was, I noticed, as dark as I. He looked at me deliberately and carefully, then stepped aside, without a word, to let me pass. As he did, he winked. One of his large puffy eyes hooded itself for a second and slowly opened again.

There was no sign of Melissa. I walked a block, then caught a cab home.

The following day I met Melissa in my mother's office. (My mother ignored us both. She sat at her desk, a large rectangle of dark wood, a banker's desk from a 1940 movie, sketching, drumming her fingers and tapping her pencil between strokes.)

Melissa said, "Your mother just got a wedding order. First one from this shop."

Well, I thought, a white bride. That would pose a problem for my mother. She would no longer have the advantage of contrast, of skin darker than fabric.

The bride's sketch was pinned to the wall. It was a dress from a fairy tale, a dress for a princess in an enchanted castle, all lace and seed pearls. At the neck was a single large pearl pin, carefully sketched in full detail.

Melissa sighed. "That's the bride's grandmother's brooch. I wish I had a grandmother like that."

I shrugged.

"You know, it used to be that the groom gave his bride a piece of jewelry, and the best man delivered it for him on the morning of the wedding."

"Melissa," I said, "you've been reading too many novels."

"No." She turned her large pale blue eyes on me. "That's the honest-to-God truth. That's what he was expected to do. Just like he was expected to pay her a formal visit after the birth of a child and give her another piece of jewelry, each and every time."

"Okay," I said. "I believe you. Now tell me what happened to you last night."

She giggled at the memory. "The police raid Jacob's all the time. There's always a couple of minutes' warning, and everybody illegal rushes out those doors behind the bar. And goes somewhere else, of course."

"I walked out the front door."

"Nobody stopped you, nobody carded you?"

"No," I said.

She sat on the edge of my mother's desk, gracefully, long legs displayed. "Nobody even looked at you?"

"One policeman walked right past me."

"Just like that? When they were checking all the IDs?"

"He winked. And I just kept walking."

Melissa was silent for a moment. "Maybe you look older, maybe . . ." A different note slipped into her light high voice. "Was it a black cop?"

"Yes," I said cautiously. "Yes, it was."

"Well, there you are." Melissa rubbed one carefully manicured hand down a long smooth arm. "There you are."

That summer ended and I went back to St. Catherine's. As always there were changes. Mrs. Alvin, who taught biology, was now principal of the Upper School. There were new lay teachers for math and American government and European history. What had happened to the nuns who used to teach those subjects? I couldn't remember their names.

The day before classes started, Mrs. Alvin called me to

her office. She was a short woman, square-bodied and sharp-faced, like some undiscovered and unclassified burrowing rodent.

She did not waste time in pleasantries. "My dear, this year we have fourteen black students in the Middle and Upper schools. I do not worry about their academic success—their test scores were very good. I do want to make their social adjustments as smooth as possible. And that is where I need your help. You have been through it. You know the problems they will have. I want you to try and anticipate those problems and solve them before they happen."

"You're asking for a miracle, Mrs. Alvin."

She bared her teeth in an animal smile. "Perhaps. But this is a convent, and miracles have been known to happen in convents."

"I can try."

"The Lord will bless you."

She was, I think, trying to be amusing.

Obediently I set out to find my fourteen little black lambs. I found the youngest first. She was in the infirmary. High fever and a flushed skin. The doctor had prescribed antibiotics, Sister Gertrude told me. (Nuns were still in charge of such things as the infirmary.)

"Sister Gertrude," I said, "how do you tell a flush on black skin?"

She stared at me for a long few seconds, then turned on her heel. "You are enough to try the patience of a saint."

I found others in their rooms. Again they shared with their own color. One, Mimi Desmond, was already packing to go home. She did not look up when I entered the room, and she would not talk to me. Her roommate, Beth, sat cross-legged on the other bed and spoke for her.

"She's had enough," Beth said.

"After two days?"

Mimi went on packing methodically. She wrapped a china figure of the Virgin in a sweater and put it in the corner of a suitcase.

"The nuns will want to talk to you first."

Mimi turned, looked at her roommate, then resumed her packing.

"She says this isn't jail and she can leave whenever she wants to."

Why on earth was Beth translating Mimi's thoughts, as if from a foreign language?

"Suit yourself," I said.

Again Mimi glanced at Beth, who obligingly translated for me. "She says she hates it here and she doesn't want to pretend she is white anymore."

I shrugged. What could I do? I reported to Mrs. Alvin.

"Oh, dear," she said. "One must expect this, I suppose."

After Mimi Desmond left, Beth stayed in the half-empty room, refusing to move. She wouldn't go to class; she wouldn't go to the dining room. (For two days I brought her meals. I do not think I was very gracious about it; I did not like being a serving maid.) Finally, her parents came for her. Her father, who was in army uniform, looked embarrassed. Her mother held a handkerchief squashed up against her face.

Mrs. Alvin said, "They had great hopes for Beth, the sergeant especially."

"Mrs. Alvin, have you noticed what is happening to my group? A disease called black flight is decimating them."

She pursed her lips. "You do like to aggravate people, my dear. You'll just have to take especially good care of your survivors, won't you?"

"Yes, ma'am, indeed."

.   .   .

That senior year was very quiet. I think that I was happy. Yes, I am quite sure I was. I'd created a desert and called it peace—whichever old Roman said that, he seemed to be speaking directly to me from my textbook. My desert was peaceful. My battles were all over. If I hadn't won, I had at least achieved a truce. Some of my classmates now invited me to their homes for parties, for holiday dinners, for special occasions.

I took college entrance exams; I talked to college representatives (the nuns insisted on that); I still sang in the choir, solo parts now. I learned to do petit point. I smiled nicely when the other seniors got their class rings. I had not ordered one, saying I couldn't afford to. Actually, I thought they were hideously ugly. If ever I had jewelry, it would be fine and old, like the brooch on the wedding dress.

I still was on the track team. I still trained methodically, faithfully, diligently, specializing in middle-distance runs. I won twice at district and once statewide.

And I had a season-long affair with the track coach from Riverside School in College Station, a slender brown-eyed man with the black hair and long thin nose of the Stuart kings in my history books.

At one of the fall meets—I had just come off the track, sweating and gasping and doubled up with cramp—I felt eyes reach me, touch me, tangibly, demanding. I straightened up and followed the glance backward—like following a string to its end, or a fence to its gate. At the end I found him.

He was standing a hundred or so feet away, in a group of trainers and coaches and spectators. I studied him carefully as I relaxed, flexing and bending, rubbing my thighs and calves. (St. Catherine's did not have a trainer.) As my eyes travelled along his steady glance, my breathing quieted and the knots in my legs loosened, leaving only the tight excited feeling in my stomach that I always have at the beginning and the end of a race.

I walked toward him; he turned away and stared across the field. As I passed, I touched his arm, not furtively but delicately and briefly. I walked on toward the stands, through the concrete passage marked PLAYERS' DRESSING ROOMS. Out of sight in the shadowy space, I began climbing an access ramp, searching. Old and badly maintained stadiums have a lot of forgotten corners, weedy, littered, sheltered spots. I found one on the second level. It had been a refreshment stand; behind the counter was an alcove storage room. When I turned around, he was there; he had been following very closely. For such a tall man, he walked quietly.

We made love in a shell of damp crumbling concrete. Overhead were spiderwebs fluffy as summer clouds. Underfoot were newspapers shredded by time and the wind, curled brown leaves blown from some distant tree, the shells of long-dead roaches, and crunching gravelly rat droppings.

He slipped away first, going directly down to the field. I continued my climb to the top of the stadium, where I walked across the parapet behind the top row of seats, watching the competitions below me.

"What on earth were you doing up there?" Florence Smith, the St. Catherine's coach, asked me. "I saw you, we all saw you. That could be dangerous."

Ah yes, but . . . while you were watching me, you didn't see another figure rejoin the small crowd. You saw only an eccentric black girl, silhouetted against the sky.

I did not yet know his name. There were no introductions before our coupling. In fact we had not spoken a single word.

Eventually he told me all there was to know. He taught civics and history and coached basketball and track. He'd wanted to play professional ball. He was thirty with a two-year-old child and a wife who was also the school secretary. I found no relief in his lovemaking, but I found satisfaction enough in the way he looked at me, the intent almost cross-eyed stare of his brown eyes. Anger, desire, disgust, it was all there. I found the emotions exciting, if not the man.

My interest in athletics increased dramatically. I badgered Miss Smith to enter me in more and more events. I trained hard, fighting through the pain of knees and ankles. Perhaps she was puzzled by my sudden change, but she said nothing. Perhaps she flattered herself that she had truly interested and inspired a student. Whatever. No matter. I competed in meet after meet, small ones and large. He was not at all of them of course. But I knew immediately when he was. I could feel his eyes find me, fix on me. I could feel the connection, our distant union. Even without looking for him, I knew he was there.

Sometimes I would slip away to him. Never hurriedly, no. Sometimes I delayed for hours, sometimes all day. Before I announced that I was going for a jog.

"I must get rid of some of my tenseness," I said. "I must relax."

Off I went, in my warm-up suit with the school name and colors on the jacket. He followed. Sometimes we made love in his car, sometimes behind vacant buildings whose windows said GOING OUT OF BUSINESS. Once my jogging led to a park, and we huddled under a low curved bridge, while flocks of ducks watched us.

And sometimes I would reject his signals and, ignoring him, go about my business like any serious high school athlete. Then he would find an excuse to come to our area to talk to Miss Smith, an excuse to stand near us, the demure group of girls, so sweaty and tired after competition, gathering our towels and bags, preparing for the trip back.

He began writing to me. I, who never got mail at school,

received a letter from my elderly uncle Ira, who lived in College Station. He'd heard I was doing well in school, he wrote, and he was happy about that. He hoped to see me soon.

The letters came almost every week. At times a postcard, at times a short note filled with pious hope for my future.

"I am tired of the game. I am tired of the letters," I told him.

"I like writing them," he said. And continued.

The track-and-field season ended. There were no more cinder courses for eyes to reach across. The bond between us snapped. The letters from Uncle Ira stopped.

One of the nuns noticed the change. "My dear, how is your uncle Ira? You haven't heard from him lately."

"He died. He was very old and he died."

"I'm so sorry. Were you close to him?"

"No," I said, "no, I wasn't."

Graduation practice began for us seniors. The choir met every afternoon at five, the orchestra at seven-thirty. The school's silver appeared, polished and gleaming in glass cases in parlors and halls. My white dress arrived, made by my mother to the precise pattern dictated by the school, reminding me of the blouses she made for me in grade school, the ones with two tiny illegal rows of tucks.

My mother and David planned to come to commencement. "That's right, kiddo," he told me during our regular phone call. "Your mother has a new dress and I've got a new suit and we are coming north to see the place where you have spent all these years."

Not so many, I thought, and then added honestly: too many.

I would go back with them, to the city where I had been born, the place I called home because there was no other lo-

cation that fitted the word. I would go because my mother
was there, and with her I shared a kingdom.

There, too, in the fall, I would enter the state university.
The nuns were very disappointed. You have been accepted
at some good schools, they all said, in one way or the other,
why won't you go to them....

But I had had enough schools, enough being away in a
strange land.

Late afternoon of Commencement Day I gathered with
the other graduating seniors in the school parlors, now filled
with flowers and trays of small sandwiches and tiny cakes
and bowls of fruit punch and decanters of sherry. We wore
our identical white dresses, while our bouquets of red roses
waited outside on the cool stones of the loggia. Parents and
grandparents and brothers and sisters arrived, tight-clustered
family groups, moving with difficulty through the door, like
clots in a bloodstream, to find the honored receptacle of
their common genes, to greet her with kisses and small
muted shrieks of delight. I held myself tall and straight and
glided around the edge of the room and waited.

My mother wore yellow, a candle flame, long and thin
and gleaming. Half a step behind her was David Clark,
solid, portly, prosperous in a pale gray suit. My mother and
I nodded to each other, as we always did, she first, queen to
princess. David kissed me on the cheek, as he always did.

"I need to tell you first thing," he said, "your mother and
I got married yesterday."

"She died," I said without thinking. "She must have died."

"Yes," he said, "she died."

I had never seen her, but still I knew her, that woman the
young soldier had married, not for love, not for passion, but
to have somebody to send his allotment check to, some link
to an everyday world. That frail sick woman he would

never leave, an invalid for thirty years, dying, but never dead. I had thought her eternal like a character in a story. Until now.

A diamond wedding band glittered on my mother's long black finger.

Just at that moment, the hired photographer, who had been methodically circling the room, popping his flashbulbs like firecrackers of light, caught us on his film.

~~~~~~

THE
PROMISED
LAND

~~~~~~

A N D so I returned to the place where I had been born. But my skin no longer fitted over my bones. My feet no longer knew their way through the streets.

I felt sharp twinges of regret for the school I had left. For the smells of wax and disinfectant, for clanging bells and the steady burbling of girls' conversation, for the rubber tread of nuns' heels on hard floors, for the squeak of chalk on blackboards, for the sweaty musky smell of shower rooms after a race, for the cocoon isolation of chapel, for the view from my window of a courtyard and a fountain and flower beds where a single gardener wearily planted pansies year after year.

I went to the house where I had lived the last of my childhood, the apartment over Leconte's Drugstore. The building was just as I remembered it; the walls had the same peeling paint; the roof slates were just as mottled; the ridge tiles gleamed dully under the sun. Across the street, behind the tall iron fence, the old people still walked their therapeutic rounds through the scraggly azaleas and the brown unwatered grass. The wheelchairs still creaked out their faintly cheerful sounds. The broken curb at the street corner was the same. The three cracked bricks on the sidewalk outside the front door were still rimmed with green moss. There was still a shadow where my mother's first sign had hung; and the door still bore the pale pink paint we had put there, she and I together.

These were our monuments, the physical signs of our passing, in the color of the door, in the screw holes and the edge marks of our sign. They held the shadow of us. Our ghosts lingered at this corner.

My mother and I had lived so many places, and in each one we left a part of ourselves. We were whittled away by now, thin and hurt, but veteran fighters for all of that, disciplined and able.

I looked again at the lights in the apartment over Leconte's Drugstore. I saw shapes moving behind the white curtains. Other people, not us. Then I left and did not come this way again.

That summer as I waited to begin college, I felt disparate and apart, a stranger in a strange land. This was not the world I had left months before. . . . That world was lost, irretrievably.

My mother—my foundation, my epicenter—had changed. Now that I lived at home, I felt it keenly. She was as kind and considerate as ever, perhaps even more, and our work association was as harmonious as ever, but still, things were different between us. (I do not think that she herself noticed the alteration. Only I. And David, perhaps.) Quite simply, she was no longer as interested in me as she once had been. Perhaps she saw me as a burden time had released her from. And perhaps she was right. Perhaps it was so.

How gradually, how gently we had slipped apart, like the surface plates of the earth, moving ever so slowly, but altering everything.

I saw my mother as a stranger from a distance. I saw that she was no longer restless, no longer driven from place to place. Comforted and strengthened by her wedding ring, she found roots and community.

She and David bought a house, a two-story brick, with a neat green lawn edged by boxwood, in a new suburb twenty miles outside the city. They added a Jacuzzi and a sauna— David had begun to have twinges of arthritis. Whether my mother suffered the pains of aging bone and muscle I never did know. She said nothing, seeming impervious or indifferent to things like weather and temperature. She could walk calmly through a thunderstorm; she could work in summer heat without showing the slightest sheen of perspiration on lip or forehead. She seemed to move inside a glass cage, visible, but untouched and isolated.

After my mother and David selected the house, their domestic instincts seemed exhausted. They asked me to furnish it.

Everything must be new, my mother told me.

"But what do you want?" I asked. "What do you want the new house to look like?"

"She hasn't time to think about it," David said soothingly. "She's worried about the delays in the fall deliveries."

"There are always delays in the fall deliveries. And I've got to know. I can't start until I know something."

In exasperation, my mother handed me two pages torn from magazines. "Like this," she said.

One was Monticello, the other Blenheim. I stopped asking questions and went ahead on my own.

I chose creams and blues and dark mahogany. I became the proper little homemaker, a disguise I had never assumed before. I ordered furniture and rugs and drew sketches of the finished rooms. It was like putting together a picture puzzle.

We did not bring with us a single piece of furniture, not a dish, not a pot or pan, only our clothes crammed into new brown packing boxes.

My mother, suddenly penny-pinching, would not pay for a moving service. We loaded our boxes into one of David's sight-seeing buses and drove to the new house.

Keep nothing, my mother had ordered. Disobeying her, I kept my treasure, child's treasure: a basket of toys. Two dolls with movable arms, carefully wrapped in pieces of hemmed flannel; a black-and-white china dog and a gray elephant with its trunk raised; a purple glass vase; a hand mirror with rosebuds painted on its pink plastic back; a set of jacks tied in blue cloth; a butterfly pin without a clasp; a handkerchief, lace cornered—they all fitted neatly in their wicker container; they seemed so harmonious, so correct, so much a settled organized part of me . . . that once again I picked up the basket carefully and carried it, as I had done so often before, to my new home.

The brick house with its green lawns and tall oak trees was only partially furnished. My mother was very strict about budgets, and I'd run out of money before I could do all the rooms.

"We'll finish next year," David promised.

One bedroom was completely empty, not even carpet on the floor. Each bath had a single set of towels, the only sheets were on our beds. There was no china or silver in the dining room breakfront, no table linens in the drawers. There were no trinkets or bibelots in the living room, no photographs on table or mantel. In the kitchen there was a single electric kettle and a coffeemaker.

My mother and David were not troubled by the fragmentariness of their world. They were content; they had what they wanted. From their windows they looked out on other well-kept houses with lawns and trees. On Sunday afternoons they smelled the smoke of cherry and mesquite from backyard barbeque pits.

I noticed something else. My mother's new kingdom was all one color. The owners of those pretty, neat houses, those Cadillac-filled garages, those velvety zoysia lawns, they all wore black skin.

We had not travelled so far after all. From the bleak neighborhoods of my childhood to this—a journey from concrete to zoysia, to be sure. But was it so very far?

My mother was particularly delighted by the front lawn and carefully inspected it daily for stray dandelions or chickory weed. (Did she remember the green cement lawn of that long-ago house?) David, with his bluff good humor, soon knew all the neighbors, and the sound of ice cubes echoed from our living room at cocktail time, and the smell of mesquite smoke rose from our brick barbeque on Sunday afternoons. There were people my age, too, home for summer vacation, laughing, friendly. We swam in all the neighborhood pools, played tennis, talked about clothes and jewelry and cars; some of us paired off; all of us flirted. Sex was heavy and demanding in the summer heat, as insistent and all present as the stifling smell of waxy gardenias at night.

The light that had illumined my fantasies, so lovely, so unreal, was gone. It had faded so slowly I hadn't noticed its going, only its absence. Now my days were lit by the sun's burning gases—simple astronomical fact, no more—my nights by a greenish reflecting planet. All because something else happened: a doppelganger rode with me, a second self, a sister under the skin, a betrayer. An ordinary woman, with ordinary needs, ordinary ambitions, who was me.

The university was about an hour's drive from my mother's green-treed suburb, a white ribbon of interstate under the wheels of my blue Mustang, David's gift to me. The campus—most of it—was very new. The red-clay ground looked torn and raw, even though landscaping crews had laid acres of St. Augustine sod and cast their rye and fescue far and wide.

Five days a week I parked in the east lot, an expanse of black asphalt, sectioned with white stripes like bones. From there I took a crowded shuttle bus to the center of campus. We all joked and gossiped cheerfully until the bus stopped; then we scattered like kittens scurrying for cover.

I was not, as I had been in high school, the only black. There were many dark faces in the halls, the classrooms, lounging under the trees. I vanished into the crowd.

My mother wanted me to take accounting; David told me to take a general business degree. I registered as a fine arts major.

Classes were no problem. All through that first year my grades rolled back to me, a steady stream of A's. St. Catherine's had prepared me well. Despite that, I spent every evening in the library, methodically preparing for the coming day. When I finished, I studied books of art history, of costume design, books of photographs. I sketched things that caught my fancy—all sorts of things, dresses, hats, jewelry—planning to use them in my own designs later.

At ten o'clock I took the last shuttle from the library to the parking lot. There were usually seven or eight passengers, all of us silent, sagging a bit in our seats, as we felt our day drag to its end in sleep: a middle-aged librarian from the circulation desk, another from the rare-book room, a graduate student from the math department, two under-graduate history majors, an ROTC instructor who had spent the evening reading newspapers in the periodicals room, a journalist who was researching a historical novel, an instructor from the art department.

I recognized the art instructor. I had seen the name card on his office door: Donald Poole. He was tall, red-haired, with a heart-shaped face and eyes the color of pecan shells. You could see the yellowish shine of those eyes in the dark bus. "Good night, Mr. Poole," I said to him each time at the empty parking lot.

During the day I saw him often in the halls of the fine arts building. Two large sections of freshman Introduction to Art History (a requirement for all prospective majors) were crowded into adjoining lecture halls. He taught one; I was in the other. Sometimes, when my lecturer paused for breath, I could hear his voice through the walls.

"Good morning, Mr. Poole," I said when we passed in the halls, his pink face looming above the crowds of students. "Lovely day, Mr. Poole." I'd read the schedule posted on his office door and I knew that he had three morning and two afternoon classes, including a photography lab; that Thursday afternoon was reserved for conferences with his advis-ees. I knew that each day, after art history, he had lunch in the faculty dining room. Half a dozen people from the art department walked over, like a group of gossiping old women, heads together, steps measured and slow.

I myself didn't eat lunch, not anymore. At the convent it had been bologna sandwiches on Monday, chicken salad on Tuesday, cheese on Wednesday, chopped ham on Thursday, tuna salad on Friday, and egg salad on Saturday.

Now I avoided even the odor of food, circling carefully

around the cafeteria with its surrounding embracing fumes of kitchen air, heavy with the tang of meat, of onions, of tomato sauce, all bound together by the sharpness of overheated frying oil. Instead, I went for a long walk, scarcely noticing the weight of my book pack. The campus was very large and still undeveloped. Some parts were flat and empty—old cane fields where you could still see shadows of the planted rows. Other areas, slight shell rises, were covered with oak and pecan trees, hackberry and cypress. I walked it all, taking long swift strides, feeling my runner's muscles stretch and then relax, learning all over again the pleasure of motion through space. Feeling how fine and soft and gentle the air was as it flowed across my skin.

Escaped from my drugstore tower, escaped from my convent school, free to wander the surface of the earth. . . . Well, only the walks and roads and paths of the campus, and only at lunchtime. A part-time freedom. But still free.

I had been away so long—five years at school—I was used to a different autumn, a northern autumn of leaf turn and leaf drop, where even warm days held the knife edge of coming winter and the predictable death of growing things: of flower beds turned to bare ground, of grass and fields gone pale with frost. I knew fall as a time of threatening and preparation, of woolen clothes and increasing dark.

I was surprised and amazed by this endless summer that stretched on toward Christmas, growing a little thinner perhaps, but keeping its light and its heat, its grasses and its flowers. Great tall hedges of white and pink bloomed in November. I asked their names: sasanquas. I looked them up— the rootstock for camellias, the encyclopedia said. I knew about camellias. There'd been a half-dozen bushes clustered at the front door of my grade school. Their flowers appeared just after Christmas holidays. Once a boy picked one to give to the nun who was our teacher. She thanked him with a smile and fastened it to the very edge of her black veil, right at her shoulder. All day long I stared at that small bit of pink drifting back and forth on a sea of black.

My first college semester ended. I wrote term papers, studied for exams, took them, saw my name on the dean's list. My mother got a letter from the school announcing the good news. She read it, slowly as always, and smiled. David folded the letter into his wallet and showed it to everyone he knew.

Like a proud father, I thought, only he wasn't my father. But perhaps he'd forgotten that by now.

At Christmas that year, they gave me a small gold circle pin. It was the first time I had seen a blue-and-white Tiffany box. It was also the first Christmas present my mother had ever given me. We had our first tree that year, too, all peach and silver to complement the living room colors. And a Christmas party to fill the rooms and a New Year's breakfast to toast the coming year.

Second semester began, the final half of my freshman classes. Same classrooms, same buildings, same schedule.

Every noontime I jogged for an hour, crisscrossing the campus methodically, until I was familiar with every walk (gravel, asphalt, brick, flagstone), every road, every parking lot, every building (brick, stucco, clapboard, metal siding, glass, Georgian, Gothic, classic revival, modern, Quonset barracks), every lawn, every field, every piece of sculpture, every birdbath, stone bench, and sundial. I knew them all. And I had my favorite spot, the unused area between the computer science building (four stories of glass and steel) and the Campus Police Headquarters (wooden army barracks with a tall antenna waving over the roof). I called it the Garden of Proserpine—we had read Swinburne those last weeks of high school and the soft drifting images still lingered in my mind. Here where the world is quiet. Here where all . . .

The Garden of Proserpine was enclosed by a brick wall covered by wild fig vine. Within were flower beds gone to weeds and thistles, and wide brick walks, domed like a turtle's back, mottled by moss and mold. At the center where there should have been something—a fountain or a sundial or a statue—there wasn't anything, just a brick circle and two concrete benches, shaped like scallop shells, shallow seated and high backed, inscribed GIFT OF THE CLASS OF 1937. I always sat there for a moment or two, listening to the chameleons chase insects through the rustling weeds, letting Swinburne's soft hundred-year-old words flow through my memory. Then I squeezed through a narrow break in the brick wall and walked across the adjoining stubble field of carelessly mowed grass. (How well kept St. Catherine's had been. My eyes were unaccustomed to neglect.) On the far side of this field was another path leading to a drinking fountain, a cement column with water burbling into its leaf-clogged basin. I cleared the drain with my fingers; it made small sucking breathing sounds. The water tasted strange, metallic and faintly bubbly like stale club soda. The path itself was overgrown, broken, and uneven. Many of the bricks were missing. With a pencil I dug away the moss-crusted sand of an empty spot. There, an inch or so below the surface, I found the missing brick sunk into the unresisting earth.

As if the earth were quicksand, I thought, as if everything, buildings, benches, grass and trees, and people, were sinking. I replaced the gritty covering, packed it down, left it to subside.

The path led through an allée of live oak trees. They'd been planted much too close together years ago; now their

branches locked overhead, solid, impenetrable, dark and
bare beneath. Their acorns fell steadily, heavily, a rainy pattering uneven sound. A happy sound, like laughter. They
covered the walk, left greasy nut oil smears on the path.
Stepping very lightly, I could balance my weight on the
fragile shells and skate across the surface, acorns beneath me
rolling like wheels.

That is what I was doing when I saw him. He seemed
to pop out of nowhere, to rise from the ground. I suppose
he'd been leaning against a trunk, his own darkness hiding him.

"Having fun?" he said.

"Yes." I saw denim jeans, denim shirt, wide belt with a
big silver buckle. "I'm playing I'm six years old and you're
playing you're a cowboy." He was a black man, wide face,
wide-set eyes, wide shoulders. A square.

He stood away from the tree trunk. "I wondered why you
walked back here every day."

I scraped the squashed acorns off my shoes, carefully,
against the edge of the bricks. "I like it."

"I come this way because it's a shortcut to the parking
lot."

"There's a fence."

"And a hole in the fence."

We came out of the little grove into the full sunlight. I
checked my watch and began to walk faster. "I'm late for
class."

We trotted down the gravel walk past Physical Plant
Maintenance, ROTC, Health Services. At the Biological Sci-
ences building, I stopped to change shoes.

"What's that for?"

"Running shoes look awful." I stuffed the Reeboks in my
book bag. "I thought you were going to your car."

"I am."

"This is the wrong way."

"Sure is," he said. "My name's Mike and I'll see you to-morrow."

"You wish." I hurried to class.

He was there the next day, waiting outside the classroom door.

"How did you know which room?"

"It's my old police training."

"Your what?"

"I was a cop for three years."

I stood stock-still, I was that surprised.

"That sure got your attention."

"Yes," I said, shifting my books from one arm to the other.

"Then I got tired of chasing bad guys and came back to premed the way my father wanted me to do in the first place. Come on, you need a Coke."

With fingers linked through the straps of my book bag, not touching me, he directed me to the vending machine inside the building's entrance.

"What'll it be? I'm a big spender."

"Nothing."

"Well, I'm thirsty." The can rolled into his hand. "Okay, let's go."

"Where?"

"That bench there. It's a beautiful day, let's talk."

"About what?"

"How the hell do I know what you want to talk about."

"Look," I said, "I've got a class."

"No, you don't . . . I looked up your schedule in the dean's office."

"You don't even know my name."

"Nanda Woods. I saw it on your notebook yesterday."

I gave a little hiss of annoyance. "They're not supposed to give out any information."

"The secretaries know me. I worked on a case out here and they might just think I'm still with the gendarmes."

I sat down on the bench, not sure whether I should be angry or flattered.

"You want to hear about that case? Of course you do. You're dying to hear about my case. There was a lot of thieving in the parking lot, radios, tape decks, all in broad daylight. We worked for weeks and never even had a suspect."

"No?"

"Not one. After a while it just stopped by itself."

We sat and stared across the campus. Because it was Friday afternoon people moved more quickly than usual.

"Are you going to the library now, the way you always do?"

"You've been following me."

"Yep. When you finish studying, have a beer with me at the Rathskeller."

"I stay until ten."

Mr. Poole walked down the steps of the art building. He was carrying a bright orange bag in his hand.

"Bars are still open at ten."

"It's too late then. I go home."

"Okay. What about tomorrow?"

"I work Saturdays."

"Where?"

"You want to know too much." I laughed and felt better. I had been beginning to feel caught or cornered. Or something like that. Not a pleasant feeling at all.

Monday it was raining hard. He waited outside my chemistry class. "I guess you missed your walk."

"No, I didn't."

"In the rain?"

"I walked around the lake. To watch the snapping turtles."

"You can't watch snapping turtles."

"That's why I didn't see any."

"Great," he said. "Just great. Have a Coke."

We drank it in the crowded lounge, smoky and sweaty and too noisy to talk.

"See you."

He wasn't there the next day, nor the next. I found myself watching for him. Then he was back, grinning, asking: Found any good walks lately?

That was how it went all semester. Sometimes he was there and sometimes he was not. Either way, alone or with company, I kept to my schedule. There was a week of storms, of swirling winds and skies split and streaked with lightning. Wrapped in plastic, I splashed along, undeterred, invincible. Every day I passed Mr. Poole hurrying to lunch, hunched and curled over against the rain, umbrella close over his head, eyes on the wet ground, moving at a trot. He did not seem to hear my greeting, but each day I said, "Hello, Mr. Poole."

The rain ended. The azaleas started to bloom, and the camellias put out their stiff waxy flowers. The oak grove was silent now, the acorn fall ended, the nuts stripped away by the storms. Under the trees the soaked ground smelled of spices, of nutmeg and black pepper.

He waited outside my chemistry class. He wore a black knitted cap perched high on his head.

"That was some weather last week," he said, falling into step beside me. "You walk in all that?"

"Yes."

"Me, I hate rain. I'd have skipped classes except for my mother. She gets so upset when I stay home. . . . It just ain't worth the fight."

"I didn't know you lived at home."

"You don't know anything about me. You don't even know my last name."

That was true. I never thought of him as having or needing a name. He was just him.

"My name," he said dramatically, "is Michael Joseph Mitchell. How about that?"

"Michael Joseph Mitchell," I said, "that cap makes you look like a hijacker on the way to Cuba."

"If I wanted to go to Cuba, my old man would buy me a ticket." But he stuffed the cap in his back pocket. "I'll see you around."

All that warm flowery rain-streaked winter, I went to classes, went to the library, studied. Once my English teacher stopped me. "My dear Miss Woods"—she was one of the older teachers who addressed her students formally—"you have a definite flair for words."

"Thank you," I said politely.

Behind their glasses, her eyes were pale blue, rimmed with pale pink. "I'm curious to know what high school you attended."

"I didn't go to a public school," I said quietly. "I went away to boarding school. Matter of fact, I integrated it, which was not a very happy experience," I added, watching the blue eyes blink with embarrassment. "But it was a very good school."

She smiled a tiny thin smile. Nodded her understanding. And never spoke to me again.

And that's the way it was. People seemed to pull away from me. Except for Mike, who appeared and disappeared on his own schedule, I was alone.

There was a kind of quiet over my days, a tinny sound, like the silence after an ice storm. (But of course we had no

ice here, only rain, and wind.) Evenings at home in my
mother's house, I closed the door to my bedroom and played
Der Rosenkavalier over and over again. The silver-blue music
echoed my feelings. It was like looking into a mirror and
seeing your own face there. The face I saw was white.

And of course I worked with my mother. Her designs
grew steadily more popular; her shops thrived. In April
Newsweek did a small story, including a picture of the two
of us—we looked quite elegant and stylish. The title was "A
Modiste in the Grand Tradition," and it compared my
mother to Mainbocher. Who is that? my mother asked. I
looked up the name in the library.

A few days later Mr. Poole stopped me. "Fine picture," he
said, "I recognized you immediately. Would you like an extra copy? I've got one in my office."

"Why yes," I said, "yes, I would."

His office was long and narrow. At the top of its single
window an air-conditioning unit rattled and creaked and
dripped into a metal baking pan on the sill. There were
bookcases along each wall, unpainted boards supported by
bricks. Over the desk was a single black-and-white photograph of a metal sculpture, the head of a man in a top hat,
sharp nose and smooth-painted features with a shirtfront
and tie.

Mr. Poole rummaged through the papers on his desk, began opening drawers. "I'll find it in a minute. I put it aside
specially."

"There." I pointed to a wire basket on the floor next to
the desk. *Newsweek* was on the top of a heap of magazines.

"I knew I had it." He handed it to me solemnly. "Please
give your mother my best wishes for continued success."

How could a few words of print be all that important? A
cause for rejoicing. Like a wedding. Or a birth.

"Thank you," I said properly. Then, pointing to the framed photograph, "What is that?"

"Remarkable, isn't it? Don't you recognize it?"

"Me? I'm just a kid from the slums." And at once wished I hadn't said it.

"Yes, well." His yellow eyes twitched like water drops on silk. "That's *Man with a Top Hat*, by Elie Nadelman. Active during the twenties and thirties. The original is in the Modern Museum in New York. I have a book on him somewhere, if you'd like to see it."

"No thanks," I said. "It just caught my eye."

Rolled copy of *Newsweek* in my hand, I gathered my ghetto around me and removed it from his office.

That evening as the shuttle bus left us in the brilliant artificial daylight of the parking lot, I called politely, "Good night, Mr. Poole."

One Friday—another week finished—I sat with Mike on the scuffed grass of the quadrangle. Suddenly he began doing push-ups, counting loudly.

"Whatever are you doing?"

"Push-ups."

"I can see that. Why?"

"You were dreaming, a million miles away. I didn't think you'd miss me. And exercise is good for you, they say."

"You look ridiculous, bobbing up and down like that.... I was thinking about the weekend."

"Yeah?" He stopped, flipped himself upright, wrapped his arms around his knees.

I hadn't noticed before how long his arms were, unusual on such a short man. "My mother's having a showing. That's what I was thinking about."

"Big deal?"

"Very."

"Invite me and I'll come. I'll even wear my good suit."

I was suddenly tired and angry. "I don't want to invite you. Anyway you can't come. You're the wrong color. This is my mother's white shop."

He began doing push-ups again. "You're black and you're going."

"I'm help," I said. "I don't count."

He lost his rhythm, his hand slipped, and he collapsed flat on his face. He found that very funny—he squirmed and doubled with laughter.

Melissa was spectacular. She shimmered, all pale and blond-gold. Orders hummed briskly into my mother's computer, discreetly placed as far out of sight as possible, in the corner of the shipping room.

I must have worked especially hard that evening, because I was too tired to drive home. I rode with my mother and David and slept all the way. I had never gotten that tired before.

Then the school year was ending. Despite my good grades, I panicked with anxiety. I gave up my lunchtime walks. I no longer played music in my room at night. Hour after hour I crammed my memory with facts and figures and names and dates. The morning of my first exam my hands were shaking so badly I could scarcely write. At my last exam I was shivering and panting for air.

When it was finally over, when the last word was written on the last page, I went to the library and slept soundly for three hours, bolt upright at a table in the reference room. When I woke, my hands were steady, my breathing normal. I caught the shuttle bus to the parking lot. There, I sat in my car and patted out a rhythm on the steering wheel. Beyond the square of mercury-vapor lamps the soft June night filled the world.

Thoughts jingled in my head like money in an empty pocket. *I have come through.* Some general said that, in some war. *A windy boy and a bit. Rosemary for remembrance. The days of wine and roses. When lilacs last in the dooryard bloomed.*

Disconnected words and phrases roared through my head. I let them thunder past, until they faded into the distance, to a whisper, then to silence. Just the way jazz funerals had sounded as they passed my tower window, once, a long time ago. Now I buried my college year.

I started my car and drove away from the bright enclosure of the parking lot into the dark city streets. I felt strange and very restless; my fingers kept tapping out a pattern on the wheel; my upper lip was twitching; my eyes hurt. Streetlights seemed to have halos around them, and traffic lights danced on their cables as if a hurricane were blowing, though there was no wind at all.

I hadn't eaten, not really, since the beginning of the exam period almost two weeks ago. Now I was hungry, so hungry my stomach hurt. I bought a red-and-yellow-striped carton of fried chicken. Its steamy reek of grease and pepper filled my car. Next I went to a liquor store and bought a bottle of cold champagne (Mumm's, the clerk recommended) and looked up an address in the phone book.

Mr. Poole lived in the lower-front apartment of a small building not far from the campus. The names on the mailboxes were all faculty; I recognized them from parking slots: Robert Myers, English department. John and Lila Howland, something to do with languages. Edward and Marcie Webster, economics.

Inside, sound muffled by the building walls, someone was

practicing the violin. The exercises were familiar. My fingers twitched into their remembered positions. I had been a capable musician once, not so long ago, less than a year. I never thought about it now, never missed the feel of those complex vibrations running along my jaw. I hadn't even owned a violin; I used the one belonging to St. Catherine's. I left it and its music behind, like a shell I'd outgrown. I held out my hands. The tips of my fingers were callus-free, and my nails were long and manicured.

The bell at Mr. Poole's apartment door had a message taped over it: OUT OF ORDER, KNOCK. My hands were full, champagne in the right, food in the left, so I kicked, sharply, loudly. When he opened the door, I pushed past him, champagne bottle held swinging by the neck.

(Like a dead chicken, I thought suddenly, remembering. My mother and I had once lived near a sidewalk poultry market where men in bloody aprons held out headless but feathered birds to their customers. As I did now, extending a box of small pieces all neatly battered and fried.)

It was a large pleasant living room, bare floors, white walls covered with paintings. There was a fresh clean air to the place; my greasy chicken smells swirled out like thunderclouds.

"I've just finished my exams," I said, "and I wanted to celebrate. So I brought supper."

Astonishment and real fear showed on his face. "You did?"

"Us black folks are just plain crazy for fried chicken, and everybody's crazy for champagne."

His face shivered and twisted so that I thought he might cry. I put the chicken box down on the Formica-topped coffee table. "We'll need glasses."

"I don't have any champagne glasses," he said.

"Any glasses," I said firmly, "are better than passing the

bottle back and forth like a couple of good old boys on a Saturday night."

"Yes," he said. "Yes of course. Will these do?" In a moment he produced two wineglasses of thick green glass with short heavy stems.

I handed him the champagne. "Can you open this? I don't know how."

He disappeared again. I walked around the living room (which I now saw was a dining room too). The paintings on the walls all looked alike, even the colors seemed to be almost the same. "You paint these?" I shouted to him.

"No." There was a loud pop from the champagne. "Vincent Muller did those. He shares this apartment with me."

"I thought they looked familiar," I said. "I saw something of his a few months ago. At an art faculty show."

"You have a wonderful memory." He poured two glasses and put the bottle (with a plate for a coaster) on the book-littered table between us.

I sat on the couch. He perched on the edge of a canvas-and-wrought-iron chair.

"To your academic success," he toasted formally.

"That's the ugliest chair I have ever seen," I said.

"It's a butterfly chair." As if I should understand, which I did not.

I tasted my champagne, then drank it. "Here's to the end of my first year of college. I'm sorry I didn't get to take your class."

"Perhaps another time, another subject."

The champagne burned my mouth. "Do you have any sugar? This would be better if it was sweeter."

He popped up instantly—as if I'd yelled "Fire"—and brought a box of Domino cubes. I dropped one in my drink. The champagne frothed up and over the sides of the glass, like a tiny pot boiling, or a tiny volcano erupting.

Ridiculous. I leaned back in my chair and laughed. Hastily Mr. Poole wiped the table and dried the floor. I poured myself another glass and took out a piece of chicken. Then I curled up my legs and began to eat. "Have a piece," I said.

He did. At first he nibbled, then he took a bite. "This is very good," he said. "Unusually so."

"Us black folks know where to get the best chicken."

He looked so horrified, so frozen with a mouth full of half-chewed chicken, that I said, "That's a joke."

"Yes," he said, "of course."

I reached for a second piece. "If you're not a painter, what do you do, except teach, I mean."

"I'm a photographer."

"Yeah? Tell me something then. I read about a photographer named Bourke-White, so I went and got out the back files of *Life* and I looked at her pictures. And I'll tell you what, they weren't anything. Stiff and wooden, you know. I might just as well have been looking at those Brady pictures of the Civil War."

This interested him, I could see. He poured me another glass of champagne and took another piece of chicken for himself. "They do seem old-fashioned now, yes. Styles change, of course, and you have to remember the sort of camera she used."

I settled back, half listening while he talked on with a teacher's enthusiasm. There was a warm glow at the back of my throat. I licked my greasy fingers carefully.

He was still talking when the door opened and a couple walked into the room. Mr. Poole's mouth snapped shut and he stood up. "This is my roommate," he said. "I told you about him, Vincent Muller, and this is Cindy Petrie."

I waved a chicken bone. "I'm Nanda Woods."

Vincent Muller said, "We came back to get me a coat and tie for that opening at the Downtown Gallery."

Cindy Petrie said to me, "I saw the story about you in *Newsweek.* The shop looked fabulous. Is Donnie doing some photographs for you? He really is very good."

So his name was Donnie. Not Donald, but Donnie. I hadn't known that.

And another thing. They assumed that this was a business meeting. A business meeting with Donnie. They just couldn't imagine any other reason why I'd be here.

Cindy settled down in the butterfly chair, had a taste of champagne. A couple of rooms away we heard Vincent Muller slamming doors and drawers, and then the final soft purring of an electric razor.

I said: "You must come, all of you, to the shop on LaFreniere Square." The one for white faces, I almost said. "My mother and I are planning something different, you might enjoy it. One Sunday a month we'll open the shop. Rather like a gallery opening without the pictures. There'll be clothes, of course, but that's not the real purpose. It's really just an opportunity for people to talk together, people who might not meet otherwise. I'll send you an invitation."

They looked pleased, they preened themselves, and they smiled graciously.

"Have a piece of chicken." I took one myself. After two bites I tossed it back into the box. "I'll be off."

"It was nice meeting you," Cindy said.

"I'm so glad you came," Mr. Poole said.

I smiled my goodbyes, thinking how much he looked like one of those slender pale white-and-yellow bean sprouts they served at health food restaurants.

I drove back to the liquor store and bought two more bottles of champagne, using my mother's credit card this time. And made a phone call.

"Would you like a visitor?" I said. "I want to celebrate the end of my exams. And I don't want to go home."

Mike said, without the least surprise in his voice, "I'll give you directions."

The champagne made me slow-witted. I got lost twice and had to ask directions. I didn't know this part of town at all, wide streets and big magnolia trees blooming ghostly white in the streetlights. The air smelled of sweet olive and musty drains and the soft spiciness of old wooden houses. Mike was waiting at the curb. Behind him was an ornamental iron fence and a wide low house with columned porch, floor-length glass windows, and a center door with an oval glass insert.

"Where have you been? You could have driven to Chicago and back by this time."

"I got lost."

"Even with my directions?"

"I forgot them for a while. Or maybe I got them backwards. Here"—I handed him the champagne bottles—"I want to celebrate."

"So do I," he said. "I just finished my last semester. I graduated."

"Well, goody good for you. So what do you do next?"

"I told you. Medical school."

"You did tell me. Then what?"

"Practice with my father. I told you that too. I'm beginning to think you don't listen to me."

"You are very very organized."

"And you've been at the sauce. Come meet my parents before they leave. Friday is their night for cards."

"Card night." How odd, how funny. I began to giggle. "Every week." Did they enter it in a desk diary? Friday: cards. Monday: movie. Wednesday: well, maybe they went to church on Wednesday. Such neat little packets of time, like envelopes all sealed and ready.

Mike said, "How many drinks have you had? Come on inside."

His father was short and dark with wooly gray hair beginning to bald. His mother was tiny, slim, and graceful the way a bird is graceful; her skin was pale, almost yellow, so that she seemed to glow. They looked comfortable, settled, at home with themselves. Assured, the way people are who've never been hungry or really poor.

His father said, "What a fine idea."

His mother put out a bowl of nuts. "I love champagne."

"Do you have any champagne glasses?" I said.

"Yes," his mother said, "if Mike doesn't mind climbing for them. They're in the top cabinet, over the refrigerator."

"That's wonderful," I said. "I want to have my drink very properly."

"I read about your mother and her new shop." She perched on the edge of her chair. I almost expected to see her flick her tail for balance.

You are light enough to pass the door, I thought. You could walk right in and no one would notice. Well, almost no one. Aloud I said, "I've worked for my mother since I was a child, and I've loved every minute."

I stopped abruptly. Surprised. That was the truth, the exact truth.

Mike came back with hollow-stemmed champagne glasses on a small round tray. We toasted each other: Happy times and best of luck.

When the phone rang and his father rose to answer, his mother said to me, "He's on call tonight, unfortunately for our bridge game."

Yes, of course . . . Mike had told me his father was a doctor. "What is his specialty?" I asked politely.

"Orthopedics," Mike answered for his mother who was staring off toward the muffled telephone conversation.

She turned back to me. "I think our evening plans just changed." She smiled. "Lucky for me I don't get as annoyed as my mother. Do you know, when her plans were interrupted, when my father had to go on a call, she would stamp her foot and say she never got to go anywhere. Which wasn't true, of course. She was just spoiled."

So her father had been a doctor too. Theirs would have been a proper household, a father with a good job, a mother who kept house and cared for the children, a couple with friends to fill their evenings in a world that could afford to spoil its women.

I took two cashews, selecting them individually, carefully. And another sip from my glass. My hand, I noticed, was not quite steady.

Mike's father hung up the phone. "It makes you wonder." He picked up his champagne glass and studied the slow stream of bubbles rising single file to the surface. "Last year I patched up a kid who'd smashed his legs in a motorcycle accident. Wild kid, the only question he ever asked was when he could get back on his bike. We sweated over him, I can tell you, and the lucky son of a bitch came out fine, didn't even limp. Now he's done it again, only worse. Skidded into a truck, the police say, and he's a real mess." He was talking directly to Mike, who was listening intently.

"Drop me off on your way then," Mike's mother said, setting her glass on the tray. "I'll take a cab home."

They left. Mike and I sat side by side on the couch in a quiet empty house. I poured more champagne. "There's a second bottle."

"That is the second bottle."

"You did tell me your father was a doctor."

"I know I did."

"He wasn't in any hurry to get to the hospital."

"No reason to. It takes a while to do the workups and get everything ready. He'll be there in plenty of time."

"It must be awful to be a doctor. All guts and bones."

"I'm going to be a doctor."

"I forgot that."

"Of course I don't have much choice. My grandfather, my father, and now it's got to be me."

"I couldn't stand having my life planned like that."

"That's what your mother did. Exactly."

"She did not."

"Oh come on, now. Your mother's an organizer. Before she even had a shop, way back when you were a child modeling her clothes, she knew exactly what you were going to do."

"How did you know I modeled for her when I was little?"

"You told me. You told me lots of things."

Had I then indeed? I didn't remember. "Clothes are beautiful things. Not like people's insides."

"You're just trying to flatter me."

We sat together in front of the TV and watched an NBA semifinal game and the late news. By then I'd drunk far too much to drive home, so I spent the night in the spare bedroom which had been Mike's sister's before she married and moved to Albuquerque. I don't remember if we had sex.

The next morning, waking in that unfamiliar room, I felt calm and detached. I seemed to move completely within myself, like a Chinese mummer inside a dragon costume. No one was awake yet; last night's glasses were still in the living room. I made my bed neatly, convent-style, then slipped quietly out the front door to my car. It must have been very early, though I didn't think to look at my watch.

The streets were quiet and traffic on the expressway was light.

At my mother's house the garage was empty. Saturday was her busiest day; she and David always left shortly before six. By now she'd be prowling restlessly through her shops, seeing to the affairs of her kingdom. After leaving her, David would go to his cab company office, to check books and route sheets. One of the returning drivers would bring him coffee and doughnuts. (My mother never ate breakfast.) Then—early to avoid the crowds—he had a golf lesson with the pro at the municipal course. After that he played eighteen holes with a group of his friends. He'd be home in late afternoon, expansive and sweaty with beer and exertion, in time to shower and dress and pick up my mother.

He loves her, I thought wonderingly. The idea had never occurred to me before. I wonder if she loves him.

I parked in the empty garage, knocking down a rake and a neatly coiled garden hose. I did not pick them up.

The kitchen was yellow and white, cheerful and cool, clear and clean. The gently moving air carried the faint petroleum smell of new filters. No one ever cooked here. There were no pots in the sparkling cupboards, no groceries on the shelves, no neatly wrapped packages in the freezer. The refrigerator held bottles of mineral water, the apple juice I had bought last week, and a six-pack of David's favorite beer.

Once upon a time—when I was little—the food on our table (always in serving dishes, two cracked and crazed bowls of pale green) was precious, our portions were measured in hours of work. And my mother had been a good cook: Sunday dinners of chicken and mashed potatoes and cream gravy. (And David dozing contentedly in the big chair afterward.) She'd enjoyed cooking; she was proud of her skill. No more. Not now. Not for a long time past.

I don't think my mother ever thought about food anymore, or felt hunger. Now that she could afford it, now that the days of shortages were past, she seemed to have lost interest entirely. Alone, my mother might have starved in her affluence. But she wasn't alone. David kept a list of restaurants and menus. He ordered from them, using one of his cabs for delivery. He seemed to be especially fond of Chinese.

Over the sink a faucet dripped slowly, a solitary sound. I tightened it. Perfect silence now, except for the faint hum of the air-conditioning system.

I was starting to feel the effects of last night's alcohol. My teeth seemed coated with slime; there were sore spots on my tongue. My hands were puffed and stiff; my rings hurt my fingers. I sniffed the skin of my forearm, sour and metallic, champagne filtering through my pores like smoke. I took the bottle of apple juice from the refrigerator, drank it quickly, burped.

What was it I needed now? Aspirin and a hot bath. Or was it a cold bath? No matter. I kicked off my shoes; they thudded against the crisp white vinyl floor. I pulled off my stockings and dropped them by the shoes.

I went through the house methodically, as if I were looking for something. First the entrance hall, where I peered at the outside world through a peephole in the door. The street was empty except for a Siamese cat sitting on the curb, tail delicately wrapped around feet, unmoving. I walked through the dining room, then the living room. I considered them curiously, impartially, evaluating my work. The colors were soft and comforting; the carpets were thick; the dark furniture was good-quality English reproduction. Comfortable, discreet. And empty.

I thought of the crowded white walls and the book-cluttered tables in Mr. Poole's apartment. Here the walls were a soft empty blue expanse, the tabletops were bare. The smooth polished wood looked at me like dark smiling eyes, waiting expectantly.

A year ago none of this belonged to us, not the house, not the land, not the sparse contents of the cupboards, not sheets nor blankets nor towels. Bring nothing, my mother had said. Nothing at all.

Time started here.

She would hang pictures on the walls—as she could afford them—and trinkets and photos would fill these dark-wood surfaces. There'd be silver on display in the dining room. David was talking about enlarging the family room for the pool table he planned to buy.

She—and with her, David—had walked away from the past. Simply, easily, like pulling down a shade. Completely and finally, the way a cicada leaves its casing.

But I hadn't been able to do that. Almost, but not quite. Not yet.

Sounds came back to me, uninvited: the sharp snapping of termite-ridden beams, like shots almost; the rumble of heavy trucks and the soft jelly-like shiver of the ground at their passing; the high-pitched whine of my mother's sewing machine singing through the dark nights; police sirens; fire bells; the screams of mating cats.

From my bedroom closet, from the far corner where I had hidden it, I took out my basket filled with toys, the talismen of my childhood.

Against the pale peach silk bedcover, the basket seemed twisted and shrunken and tattered. From it came old remembered smells, long streamers unrolling in the cool filtered air of this bedroom. I could identify each and every one; they were as familiar to me as the shape of my hands: dust (pleasant and faintly sweet); mildew; damp from old boards; plaster from walls that were crumbling behind their paint; gasoline exhaust from the crowded streets; sweat from black bodies close together; a living pine smell from the tarred dead trees that were power poles; the smell of sun on concrete sidewalks (soft, like drying clothes); of asphalt bubbling from road joints in the summer heat; the scorching of my hair pressed into perfect straightness on my mother's ironing board.

All these floated from the basket. Old friends, surrounding me, wrapping me in their magic. Again I was an Indian princess manqué, nourished and protected by fantasies.

The bedside phone rang. I ignored it. I packed my treasures carefully and hid the basket in my closet on a shelf behind my dresses. Lovely dresses, a dozen of them, all designed specially for me, designed to show off my height and my swift fluid motion. These were not clothes for a princess but for a modern young woman, clothes to fit my mother's idea of me.

The phone had stopped ringing by the time I closed the closet door. I showered, slowly and dreamily, then took a nap. I woke at noon—the sun had just reached the brick barbeque grill on the patio outside my window—dreaming that the phone had rung again.

I took a long bubble bath, decided I disliked the scent, and took a shower. When I finally came back to the bedroom, I found Mike pacing up and down.

"Where have you been?" Annoyance, even anger, in his voice.

"How did you get in?"

"I picked the lock, how else?"

"I was afraid I'd left the door open."

"You didn't. And tell your mother she needs to get better locks. Any child can open these."

"They came with the house, I think."

"Where were you?"

"Where should I be?" He seemed such a long way off, the other side of the world.

"I called you. I've been calling you all morning."

"Well, yes, I suppose I did hear the phone ring once."

"More than once. A lot more than once."

"I thought it was a dream."

"It wasn't."

A pause. He still seemed so far away. Our words crackled like rumpling paper in the distance between us.

"Mike, I want to get married. Do you want to marry me?"

He stopped pacing to look at me closely. "When you left my house, you drove straight here? That was all?" Crisp, quick.

I shrugged my indifference.

"Did you have an accident? Are you all right?"

Again I didn't answer. Just waited.

"Why did you sneak out this morning?"

"I didn't sneak out. I walked out the front door."

"But why did you leave without saying anything? Didn't you know I'd worry?"

"I am a strange person."

"I know that and I know you've got a hell of a hangover, but there's got to be something else. Something wrong."

"No, I'm fine. I'm just like I always am. . . . I have to dress now and go to work. And you haven't answered my question."

"I was thinking about it."

"So?"

"Yes," he said. "Yes, I do."

We were married a month later at the city clerk's office. That was almost sixteen years ago.

I finished college; I even got a Phi Beta Kappa key; I had

it attached as a fob to a small antique watch on a long gold chain. I wear it sometimes across the vest of a tailored suit. The watch has never worked, but no matter. There are always plenty of clocks. Mike finished medical school and joined his father's practice. They are quite successful. Some years ago, with a small group of partners, they even started their own hospital and satellite clinics.

My mother and David are well, still living in the house with the brick barbeque pit. On a dare from his golfing friends, David ran for town alderman, was elected, and is now in his second term. He says that next he will try for district assessor or state representative; he hasn't made up his mind. He is thinking of selling his cab company—it takes up too much time, he says—but he intends to keep the chain of lunch restaurants, six of them, in the downtown business district. He now plays golf twice a week. Occasionally Mike, who has taken up the game, plays with him. Mike prefers tennis. He has joined a tennis and racquetball club, a shiny new facility with a magnificent view of the city twenty-five stories below. I meet him for lunch there every Wednesday: carrot juice and a salad, all organic. Mike is watching his weight.

"Just look at my father and you'll see what I mean."

I think of his father's steadily thickening waist and his shiny smiling face. "Your father likes being tubby."

"Well, I don't." And he does not even finish his glass of carrot juice.

I don't play tennis, not anymore. I left my athletics with my music back in convent school. Still, I do enjoy having lunch with him; he is very handsome in his dazzling whites, and I admire, in my mind's eye, our ever-so-proper appearance.

My mother no longer runs the daily business of the shops; she appears only once or twice a week for a few hours. She still designs, and her clients are as faithful as ever. But now I oversee the transit of her thoughts from paper sketch to showroom mannequin. Now the daily business routine grinds against my skin, and she is young and free again.

She has her garden, and she seems quite content to spend endless hours there. (Only the heaviest rains force her inside to shelter.) She does most of the work herself; she seems to love the feel of dirt. I've seen her rub light friable soil into dust between her palms and then toss it into the air, solemnly, like a priest dispensing incense. Five or six years ago she and David bought the sixty- by one-hundred-and-twenty-foot lot directly adjoining their house, enclosed it with a high wall of old pink brick, and turned it into a separate garden, entered through a locked iron gate. Inside the paths are so small and neat they look Japanese; dwarf crab apple and pear trees are espaliered along the side walls. The grass is zoysia, soft and fine and brilliant green, algae-like. There is a scuppernong arbor where my mother and David sometimes play cards. In the fall the heavy yellow grapes hang close around their heads, untouched. I don't like the wild taste, my mother says. So the fruit falls to the ground or is taken by birds or shrivels into raisins on the vine. There is a foot-wide stream twisting through the entire area; its gentle flow is propelled by a pump hidden under a mound of clematis. There are no azaleas or camellias, or sasanquas, none of the winter flowering plants you'd expect to find in a garden here. Instead, in cool weather, there are masses of sweet peas, a pastel jumble of colors, shoulder high. Underneath, between the stakes of the trellis, are lines of lettuce and the spikey green of onions. The heavy blossoms of a slender medlar tree shiver and vibrate under the probing of a hundred bees. By summer the sweet peas are dead, and cosmos take their place, flat-faced flowers with feathery foliage. In the damp ground by the stream there are pitcher plants, small and green and question-mark shaped. Bedded side by side are crinum lilies and butterfly lilies, paper plants, and marigolds and petunias. There are rows of garlic and carrots and corn waving its tassels in the sun. On either side of the entrance gate are tall clumps of sugarcane, never harvested.

There are other growing things I don't recognize, things without names probably, the strays and waifs of the botanical world. My mother and David collect wild plants and seeds. They spend almost every weekend hunting for specimens, travelling from vacant slum lots to country fields and pastures. Their discoveries are usually leggy, brushy, sprawling things, quite ugly. There have been two exceptions: a wild iris, small and compact with flowers of clear deep yellow, and a small tree, very slender, with clusters of white flowers like tiny magnolias. The two seem to enjoy each other's company; neither thrived or bloomed until my mother planted them together in the damp mud by her stream.

Across the back of the garden, there is a wooden fence within the brick one, post and crossboard, six feet high. On it my mother has begun to paint a flower mural, working slowly and carefully. Only flowers. All sorts of them: roses and sweet peas and begonias, daylilies dripping pollen, convoluted orchids of bright red, and seven-petalled tulips of sky blue. She has worked on it for four years now, and she has finished exactly eight and a half feet.

Mike and I have no children. By choice.

"I don't think I'd make a very good father," Mike said. "I like things the way they are now."

"I've been a child and that's enough."

Mike burst out laughing. "That settles it. We grow old together alone."

His parents were upset. ("I had to tell them, honey," Mike

said. "I can't have them staring at your belly every month and wondering.") But they got over it. I once heard his father describing us as the typical professional couple whose work comes first. Anyway, Mike's sister provided plenty of grandchildren, three boys and four girls.

Mike and I are happy in our marriage. More than lovers, we are companions and friends, unfailingly polite and always considerate, each careful never to disturb the other. We live in a rational orderly world, its edges padded by steadily increasing cushions of money.

We are very busy at work; our free time is crowded with activity. (Just the sort of compartmented life I thought so very strange with Mike's parents years ago.) We belong to a gourmet cooking group and meet four times a year to dazzle each other with our skills. Our drama group meets every other month; we read Shaw and Shakespeare, Molière and Albee. We are active members of the Little Theater; I do costume design for its six yearly productions. I am on the governing committee of the new City Museum of Art. We go to the opera and the symphony; Mike is on the board of trustees for both of them. We go to all tennis matches and golf tournaments. We have season tickets for professional football. Mike and his partners have a box. In the noisy echoing sports dome twenty-five of us sit in comfort high above the field, whiskey-and-sodas in hand. And yes, I have learned to drink, only single malt Scotch. I can distinguish the different brands; my preference is Laphroaig, with its strong smoky taste. I like to sit in the outermost row of seats and let the waves of sound roll over me—shouts, cheers, jeers, whistles, drums, the thudding of padded bodies on the playing field. To my right, in the crowd below, there are flickering points of light, tiny points of light like Tinkerbell in *Peter Pan,* as ten thousand watch crystals on ten thousand moving arms catch and reflect the brilliant television lights. It is quite pretty, especially after a few drinks.

We travel abroad twice a year—last spring to Rome and Athens, last fall London and Paris. Mike is a wonderful tourist, boyish in his enthusiasm, as if the whole world were created just for his amusement. Everything delights him. Everything.

One rainy night in London as we walked back to our hotel (we were crossing Piccadilly Circus, I think), groups of men surged out of the Underground, shouting and fighting their way along the shiny black streets between the lines of cars.

"What the hell is that all about?" Mike said. "Get in here, out of the way." We stepped into the shelter of an arcade. The smell of caramelized sugar was heavy in the wet air. I peered through the lace-curtained front door: a tea shop.

"Will you look at that." Mike was watching the street, chuckling. "That's got to be football fans."

I leaned against the shop door and pulled off one shoe. An expensive Ferragamo, now soaking wet and ruined. "They could be overthrowing the monarchy."

"That's a good old-fashioned brawl, my love. In its purest, most delightful form."

There was something in his voice, a mixture of elation and amusement. . . . "Mike, you're enjoying it."

"Of course I am. It's not my teeth getting smashed."

In a very few minutes, from nowhere, the police appeared, formed a sort of line, and advanced across the pavement.

Like a street sweeper, I thought. And laughed out loud.

"You see, it is funny." Mike nodded approval.

The air filled with singsong sirens and more police appeared. Their lines stretched, circled, and pushed the fighters back down the steps into the Underground, leaving behind a scattering of injured.

We opened our umbrella and walked on, arms linked tightly together. The rain fell harder on the silk curtain over our heads as we splashed and kicked through puddles, jumped up and down curbs, imitating Gene Kelly in *Singin' in the Rain*.

Out of breath, Mike gasped, "Old girl, let's us go back to the hotel and take a hot bath and get a bottle of champagne and have a celebration."

"And what, sir, would we be celebrating?" The street cobbles had bruised through the thin soles of my shoes. I rubbed one foot thoughtfully.

"How the hell would I know? Because we're here, because we've been married a long time, because we're growing old. We'll celebrate anything you like."

We folded our umbrella; the cold rain streamed down our necks as we ran down the slippery streets.

Next winter we will go to Australia and New Zealand. My choice, my selection. Years ago, when I was one of a row of navy-and-white raisins perched at a line of desks in the parish school, I turned through the pages of an atlas and found Christchurch. A faraway place with a strange name. I copied it on the back pages of my notebooks, Christchurch. I spelled it in fancy curling script in the margins of my textbooks. And thought, I will go there someday.

Now I hesitated. Now I wondered: Did I want to go. Did I want to change forever that magic spot on my childhood map. Did I want to convert it to indelible images of real houses and harbors and ships and ocean.

"Stop dithering about it," Mike said. "We go when we can, wherever we can. And we always have fun."

Yes, we do, my love.

But something else is happening. One by one my dreams

are coming true. My cloudy images, those longing visions of a child's mind, are being turned into reality.

I do not want reality. I am not at all sure I can live with it. Not at all sure.

As he had in college, Mike disappeared occasionally. Without a word, unpredictably, he would not come home. He was never gone long; after all, he had a large practice to take care of. In a day or so he would reappear, looking and acting just as he had before, as if no time had passed.

The absences involved other women. I knew that, had expected that, though I could not tell you why. Perhaps, as he often said, I just knew him very well. The existence of other women, their presence or absence, their comings and goings, made no difference. I was not interested in those other beds.

Mike was very discreet. Only once did his other life brush against mine.

She was the receptionist at one of the clinics. I had talked to her many times on the phone and recognized her voice. She was light brown–skinned, small and plump, and dressed, nurse-like, all in white. Standing there at my door—she would not come inside, refused my invitation with a firm shake of the head—she told me that she loved Mike and wanted to marry him.

Did she now? Well, I had no objections. None at all.

She looked shocked.

"Did you think I would scream or faint? How silly of you."

Now she looked disbelieving.

"I'll give him a divorce anytime he wants. You can tell him that for me."

And that was exactly what the foolish woman did: rushed

back to the clinic and waited breathlessly for Mike to finish his morning rounds.

I went about my usual duties at the workrooms and the shops. At noon two dozen pink roses came for me. No card.

"How beautiful." My mother flicked a finger at the soft petals. "That would be a good color in cotton."

"Yes," I said.

Mike brought me a present that evening, a heavy gold link bracelet in a blue-and-white Tiffany box. "How beautiful," I said, echoing my mother.

"I'm embarrassed." Mike shrugged his heavy shoulders. "I didn't ever mean for this to happen."

"Of course you didn't." I twirled the bracelet around my wrist. "Would you mind, no more presents? I'd rather save the money and spend it on one of our trips."

When I next called him at the clinic, a few days later, a different voice answered.

As for me, my affairs have been quiet, careful, gratifyingly calm. And always of short duration. You see, sex is not a demanding drive for this prostitute's daughter—the irony of that is not lost on me. Since my marriage I have had exactly five lovers, four men and a woman. I have no one now. The emotional silence is quite pleasant.

We are well suited, Mike and I, comfortable and secure in our understanding of each other. . . . And completely free. Until last month we did not even own a home. We lived in a series of rented houses and apartments. In a way it was rather like my childhood, though these places were infinitely nicer, even luxurious, with their pools and Jacuzzis and marble foyers and granite-topped kitchen counters.

"I want my own house," Mike said emphatically every year or so. "I want to scrape paint and put fertilizer on the lawn. I want to hang tools on the garage wall, lots of tools, so that it looks like an ad for Black and Decker. I want to fix leaky pipes and build new shelves."

"You don't know how to do any of that," I reminded him.

"I'll learn."

So I looked for a house. Indeed I did. Over the years I called dozens of real estate agents, saw hundreds of properties. Nothing. I could not even find a rental house I liked enough to live in for more than a few years.

For a long time Mike found my restlessness very amusing. He told our friends: "My wife loves to move. She changes houses the way other people change cars. We move so often that sometimes I have trouble remembering the way home."

But I didn't like to move. No. I hated the change, the confusion. It was just that after a short while I knew everything about a house. The shapes of the door handles, the folds of the curtains, the neat lines of dishes in the cupboards. I could imitate the sounds the dishwasher made as it went through its cycles. I had memorized the washing machine's hisses and whines. I had timed the dryer's thumps. I could predict the pattern of leaf shadows on the windows at night.

And so we moved.

Eventually Mike grew tired of such eccentricity. Without consulting me, he bought a house—found it, inspected it, bargained over the price, talked to the bankers, and handed me the keys on a large brass key ring.

"We now have a permanent abode, my love. We are no longer nomads. This is our home and our castle."

A low white-painted brick house.

"I hope you will be happy here," he said formally. "I want you to be happy."

Behind the house a lawn sloped sharply down to a small slow-moving creek.

"What's that?" There seemed to be something swimming, something moving the water.

"Where?" Mike was testing the lawn carefully with his finger. "Sod webworms, we need to spray," he said knowledgeably. "What's where?"

"There." As I pointed, a small round shape climbed into clear view on a muddy log. "Now I can see. It's a turtle."

"Yes. Of course. Turtles. Specially for you, my love. I trust you still like them. I mean, they aren't something you've outgrown, I hope?"

"Turtles?"

"Back in college you were always talking about watching snapping turtles in the campus lakes. . . . These aren't snappers, of course, just plain old red sliders, but they'll have to do."

"I didn't know you'd remember," I said uncertainly. "I didn't expect you to. It was a long time ago."

"I remember everything you said. Word for word, mostly."

We both hesitated, silent, embarrassed by this sudden unexpected acknowledgment of love.

There was, at that moment, something between us, something that hovered in the air between us. A thread, frail, thin, to be measured in millimeters, but there nonetheless. For that one instant, it seemed I could see it—fine as a spider's web, shimmering with all the colors of crystal.

Then it was gone. We smiled at each other cautiously, warily, as we walked back across the worm-infested lawn.

This time I did not bring with me my carefully preserved basket of toys. I unwrapped it gently, considered seriously, and threw it away. The faint childhood odors now reminded me of graves and cemeteries.

And so alone I came into my kingdom. My portion, neither more nor less.